JOSEPH SMITH

Finally My Ambulance

VINTAGE BOOKS
London

Published by Vintage 2014

2 4 6 8 10 9 7 5 3 1

Copyright © Joseph Smith 2013

Joseph Smith has asserted his right under the Copyright, Designs
and Patents Act 1988 to be identified as the author of this work

First published in Great Britain in 2013 by
Jonathan Cape

Vintage
Random House, 20 Vauxhall Bridge Road,
London SW1V 2SA

www.vintage-books.co.uk

Addresses for companies within The Random House Group Limited
can be found at: www.randomhouse.co.uk/offices.htm

The Random House Group Limited Reg. No. 954009

A CIP catalogue record for this book
is available from the British Library

ISBN 9780099575870

The Random House Group Limited supports the Forest Stewardship
Council® (FSC®), the leading international forest-certification
organisation. Our books carrying the FSC label are printed on FSC®-
certified paper. FSC is the only forest-certification scheme supported
by the leading environmental organisations, including Greenpeace.
Our paper procurement policy can be found at:
www.randomhouse.co.uk/environment

Printed and bound by Clays Ltd, St Ives Plc

CONTENTS

Part 1

The Consolation

Across the room, staring down at the table at which he sits, is my enemy.

There is a movement in my stomach, a flooding of something cold into my chest as my eyes rest upon him. I hope that their sight is wrong: that if I break my gaze and return it to this seated figure a new aspect will emerge, one to prove he is someone else and not the man, the vision of whom has already altered my breathing, has quickly malformed my quiet expectation of enjoyment into one of dread.

I turn my head to check for my companion, to see at what stage he is at in the buying of our drinks, for fear that he has turned away from the barmaid after ordering, is leaning against the high dark-coloured wood and looking my way, perhaps with the intent to share silent mirth in the rare achievement of us coming to the pub – only to catch instead the sudden oppression that has passed over me. But this friend has not turned, is still bending over the bar-top and talking to the pretty girl, and around the small spot of relief for this I feel an instant guilt, a shame that breeds an anger for the presence of the other man, who I must look towards again, searching across the room of darkened wood and candles shining on tables, through the heads and shoulders of people seating themselves for the busy early evening. We are at the stage of arrivals and greetings, before the pub becomes full and people will have to stand, and talk loudly to be heard.

If we had arrived later then perhaps I would not have seen him, sitting there now still looking down, a man with a large round head lit pink by the ornate light fixture sprouting from the wall above it, his jacket a light green, a flash of orange where its lining is visible near his throat. And there is a possibility it still might not be him, that I recognise only similarities: the choice of bomber jacket and the close-cropped, receding hair; the curve of bulk from shoulder down to elbow. But I do not invest anything in this hope, because I know that soon he will look up, and when he does I will see the same face that looked across at me formerly, more than a decade past, in a pub not dissimilar to this: a first glance as fleeting and meaningless as any other with a stranger.

So I do not wait for him to look. I am already certain it is him and though I look away, up and out towards the black shine of the window and its long chain of white street lights above the road, I can feel myself being drawn, by a mixture of resistance and compulsion, backwards into darkened, shameful memory.

My friend appears, a large shape of black in his winter coat before me, the two long glasses he holds deposited on the tabletop with a single clack. He is saying something and I am responding, simple questions and answers, the form of which is well known to us: this happening as I watch him sit down to block my view of the wall behind him. Then he begins relating details of his work, and as soon as I hear the gist of it I know that my mind is free to journey, that in the length of time before it is called on for a true, unscripted response I will be able to follow it as it leads me, back to memory, to the moment when years ago in a different pub, a more distant part of London, I had dropped my eyes from a stranger, only to be aware that he was still looking at me: a trace of instinct that something is scraping at you and that you try to ignore, while gamely carrying on the conversation with those nearest.

But, because I was younger, less able to brush off even the slightest whiff of insult, and could not bear any implication that I was not yet a man, I did not ignore this invisible scraping. I waited perhaps to the count of ten before I looked back at him, a secret hope that by now he had turned away, a slight jolt of shock to find him still looking: impassive, leaning forwards slightly, his hand gripping a nearly empty half-pint of black stout, the same light green and puffy cladding then, as now, covering his arms and chest. And so our eyes were meeting for a second time, his expression unchanged but I imagine that in mine I might have attempted a sternness: not a threat but an indication that, though I may be slight and merely teenage, I would not willingly be stared down.

An error of youth that my mind on sleepless nights delights in!

He had not looked away and I was forced to drop my eyes – a minor slide from challenge into loss that was insignificant until I saw him standing up, picking up the small and empty glass from his table, all of this still an insignificance until I realised that he was not headed for the bar but our table, that he was walking over, a big man and well built, an energy to his gait: an eagerness.

'Here we go,' I had said to those near me, not truly afraid, still prepared to be amused.

And it had begun harmlessly enough, him calling out a greeting to all of us, a voice clear and loud enough to turn the heads of the boys that could not see him, to stretch their necks and raise their eyebrows. There was a momentary silence as they grasped for recognition of whom they saw, while another friend next to me, who had heard what I said and seen the man coming uttered something playful under his breath – something for me only to hear and the humour of which I think, looking back, I may have clung to. Then all of us fell quiet, the murmur of other people's discourse diffusing into it, but the social abrasion of having someone stood near you, standing there with familiarity and an overt expectance of its return, who is unrecognised and who has punctured your own sphere of talk and bond – this awkwardness did not dissipate, but became plainer, even after one of us returned his greeting.

Then he said something like, 'Having a good night, lads?' And in chorus we replied that we were – yes thanks mate we were – our voices made enthusiastic by the relief of sudden recognition, not of him but for what was occurring: a bit of unsolicited friendliness from an older man, who perhaps sees himself in the boys before him. But I noticed that he was not sensitive to our replies: he had heard them, but was not listening.

'I tell you what,' he said. 'Waiting here for a mate owes

me twenty. That's why I'm on these,' and he raised the half-pint glass, 'till he comes.'

Perhaps we offered a few nods and some soft snorting: these as mild expressions of our understanding, because we were not rich ourselves – we did not work; we knew what it was like to have to count the coins in your pocket.

And so in this simple way he got one of us to buy him a drink, promising recompense of course, once he had his twenty. But he did not retreat back to his table over by the wall. Instead he reached around with a quick movement for one of the many red felt-topped stools littering the pub's floor like rooks or pawns, easing it under him to take a place at our table. He sat there, large and rounded, light green and orange and then the pink of his head, lifting a full pint of black stout, taking a large gulp but without any obvious enjoyment – no sighing or leaning back, no renewed profusions of gratitude to the boy that had just procured it for him.

'I've not seen you boys in here before,' he started.

'No?' we replied. 'That's strange,' and a 'ha,' for the irony, because we were present there nearly every weekend. It was a dim and grotty pub and the toilets were atrocious. But it was the only one in which we could all get served: even those of us who, like me, looked desperately underage.

'No I haven't. What are you, students, then?'

Here we had to be careful. In order to buy alcohol we all had our stories: some of us worked, others were at university. Our histories mostly depended on the forged and laminated cards we carried in our wallets. But these fictions would not remain cohesive under repeated questioning.

'Some of us,' I said, to answer him. I did not like him

sitting at our table, and hoped that my friends, with greater knowledge of my voice, would detect this. 'What about you?'

'I'm not a student! Bet you are.'

'Yeah,' I said.

'You look like one,' he said, smiling. His eyes were on mine and they were grey and joyless. It was the mildest of baits, and perhaps for him merely a method of humour – yet for me there was a distinct insult within the phrase, a renewed challenge after the stupid staring contest that I had lost. With him saying this I felt returned to the same contest, and again losing. But I still hoped that he did not insult me, that it was merely his manner which made him seem capable of such a direct unfriendliness. I felt a small relief when he turned from me, to a boy with a large head and protruding eyes – who when younger we ourselves had mercilessly baited for his ugliness – and the man said to him, 'I don't know what *you* look like.'

This boy laughed and nodded, a flush of shame turning his face red: an old familiar shame that had followed him, which he thought he had left behind now that he was no longer a boy in school uniform, instead a young man and drinking among true friends. This shame and its embarrassment suddenly thrown back up at him by the casual remark of a stranger, and I could feel all the horrible hot and coldness of it as it crossed his face so visibly – and felt a sympathy for him – but keener the high whistling relief that it was not me, that it was not I who had been slighted.

We were all complicit at this point, some of us laughing too, while others, like me, chose an impotent silence.

The man reached out to this boy and told him he didn't mean any offence. 'What's your name?'

'Martin.'

'You weren't offended,' the man said. Martin took a large mouthful of beer, enough to be difficult to swallow. He shook his head while doing this, a gesture that seemed to ably show he had recovered, that no offence had been taken. But we all knew he had suffered in those seconds.

'What's your name?' I asked the man.

'My name?' he said, straightening. 'Don't you worry about my name.' His smile had gone. 'I know your name, you don't need to know mine, son.'

'I haven't told you my name,' I said.

'Don't worry. I know it.'

He was silent for a moment, reflective, happy with whatever name he had given me. 'I know all your names, boys,' he said, turning to the table as a whole and smiling. 'I've seen you all before. Not you,' he said, gesturing to us as a group, 'as in *you*, but lads like you. I can tell what you are just by looking. Older, wiser than I look, you know?'

'And how old are you?'

'You've got a lot of questions, son, haven't you?'

And as he said this I felt the first signs of his capacity for anger, of something beyond merely an abrupt manner: he had squinted his eyes at me as if in bitterness, and the small nods of his head while he spoke seemed to offer a willingness for larger, more violent movements.

But still, at any moment I expected him to stand up, to take his pint back over to the table he had begun at, maybe parting with another small fragment of unpleasantness. The boy who subsidised him would not get his money back, and we would gently insult him for this, and shake our heads and laugh once the night was over and we had split into smaller groups to take different buses home and, depending on the quality of the evening, the next day's anecdotes would either revolve around the odd and slightly aggressive man that had descended on us, or he would be completely eclipsed by a greater adventure, only recalled in weeks or months when no trace of the strange and mild discomfort he had forced on us would still survive.

'What are you looking at?' my friend has just asked me gravely, and I am snapped to the present and the man in front of me. The way he sits, his dark coat adding to his width, I cannot see the man at the wall. I have been looking at my friend while he talks, but he obviously senses that I am not seeing him. I look at him properly now, not to atone for a stare focused elsewhere but to survey him: this man I know well, whom I have had as a friend for many years. Because it would add to the evening, to tell him that the figure sat behind him near the wall is my enemy. Yet while I like and trust this friend, I do not trust his full consideration of me, and fear that if he were garnered with the knowledge that once I was not as strong as I must seem now, this estimation might become ruinously altered. I am ashamed that in order to protect his idea of me, I must protect my past: a duplicity that already has weakened our bond, but the alternative of which would surely weaken it further.

I am only glad that the decision not to tell him about the man does not bother me, that I have the strength to make it easily.

And back then, was I that lacking in strength as compared to now? The man was at our table: him sat there holding a strange court to a group of teenage boys not only at the beginning of their evening, but at the start of their exploration of a new world, and while then my waist and even my wrists may have been thinner, and my experience yet to be armed with a better sense of things and people, could I have been so different to what I have become?

I am moved to look at my wrist, to feel it with my other hand, revolving it slowly so that I can feel the bones and the tension of the skin. Then I lean back and to the side, the wall and light fixture becoming visible over my friend's shoulder, and there he is: the man, still sat there looking down, so unmistakably him that it makes my heart pound again, an anger dripping slowly down my arm so that at the end of the wrist I grasp in one hand, a fist is formed in the other. I remain there watching, careful to remain casual enough not to alert the capable sensitivity of my friend, and only leaning forwards again to block the sight of my enemy when I feel my heart returning to a calmer pace.

Back then the man had not left our table as I had hoped.

When he lifted his glass one of us said something that was relevant only to us: it was the name of someone and their circumstance, the words plain and unrevealing: 'What about Mark and that letter he got,' or something similar, the nodding and slightly false sounds of acknowledgement made in response to this statement our first attempt at solidarity, to exclude our conversation from the bulking presence at the end of the table. It was a transparent ploy, but we latched on to it. Except that after the first murmurs of interest and a few short comments about Mark and his letter, a narrow silence occurred: an opening that was small, but which in our hesitance we could not close.

'That's a bit rude, lads, isn't it?'

There was the possibility that he was attempting to comment on what we were discussing, but it was very slight. It was plain he was displeased, but at the same time grateful for this displeasure.

'What's rude?'

'Well here I am sat with you – you start talking about something you know I don't know anything about. I'm trying to be friendly, and you've just shut the door in my face.' His eyes were a bright and grey, flickering as he looked round at us. 'Do you not want me sat here? Do you want me to go?'

It was necessary to placate him. He was playing a stupid game but at that age we did not have bluster to plough straight through and destroy it, to say, 'No, no, you sit there, friend. Be happy. Join us. Enjoy yourself,' and then carry on talking as if he didn't exist, to smother his presence that way.

Instead, one of us said: 'Well,' and already he sounded apologetic, 'this is a private gathering.'

'Oh really?' the man said quickly. 'A private gathering. A private gathering, eh? In a pub. Does that mean I should leave the pub, that everyone else here should leave so that you can sit here on your own and have your own little private gathering?'

'That's not what he meant,' I said.

'That *is* what he meant,' he spat out. He had turned to me. His voice had not risen, but he was speaking quickly. 'You'd probably prefer it that way, wouldn't you? Just you and your little mates all alone in the pub,' he smiled, 'not having to worry about people like me.' The smile went. 'How old are you?'

'Eighteen,' I said.

He grimaced and turned his head. 'Rubbish.' Then he was looking at me again. 'When were you born?'

'Tenth of June seventy-six.'

He snorted. 'Yeah, well done,' he said, 'well remembered.' He clapped twice, the movement of his hands up from the table quick and sudden, the claps themselves soft and mocking. 'I think none of you are eighteen. I could go up to the landlord – he knows me – and tell him you lot are gonna get him done. I could do that and you won't be able to do anything, will you?'

I think a couple of us protested, went to reach for wallets to produce proof. The man put his hand up and began waving, shaking his head and smiling. 'Leave them there, lads,' he said, his eyes closed. 'I'm only having a bit of fun. Ha ha. I won't tell.'

And this was a relief. Even though I knew that what he did was not for a humour we could all share in, but for a different and nastier streak of entertainment exclusive to him, I was still willing to believe that everything was fine, that this man surely now had had his fill of teen-baiting, and would up and leave.

Because we could not. To do so would have been the end of our evening. Not only would we have failed to find another pub that would accept all of us, but each refusal at the bar would be a shameful reminder that we had been moved on, from the pub that we had begun to consider as ours, that we were slowly making ours – and by a single man when there were far more of us! Perhaps it was the collective hope that we were not experiencing a true unpleasantness that failed to unite us: to simply tell the man to leave. He would slip back into friendliness just as our hackles rose, and we would be coerced into accepting this friendliness, denying that in fact he was truly hostile in order to hide the fact that we were all deeply uncomfortable and a little afraid – most afraid that we were out of our depth, that we were not yet old enough to pretend at being men – because we could not respond to the hostility of this one man when we were many.

Looking back, it is clear that he knew this, that he had not lied when he said he had 'seen' us: a vantage point allowing him to ride along the edge of our insecurity adeptly, and without fear of slipping into true risk for himself.

Now, away from memory, I am standing up, holding my friend's empty glass, walking with it past him towards the bar. I can feel the presence of the man, like a burning in periphery, hungry for my eyes to turn there, as if to a car accident: the same fusion of moral uncertainty and compulsion. But I do not look. Walking to the bar I am surprised how calm I am: there is no fear in me, only a feeling that I am distant to him, that even though I am the only person moving and by default must be the most exposed to any casual observer – and if he has any interest in what is going on around him, he will see me – even though I am aware of this, he is hardly there at all. Or I am absent myself through numbness.

When I order at the bar it is from the pretty barmaid. Because my thoughts are turned inwards I make no effort with her, merely ordering quickly and without preamble, and to this she responds, either glad at my lack of interest or challenged by it – and I am not so introspective that I am unaware of this, to be amused by it. A decade ago I would not have been sensitive to her reaction – another miniscule sign that I was not the same person, not the same man – and bolstered by this event with her I turn to survey the pub that I have come to, looking over the dark shapes of laughing heads and the different-coloured glints of glassware, moving unhurriedly over the familiar landscape until coming to the bright green of the man's jacket near the light, and seeing that he too is looking up, is performing a similar survey.

But in the movement of his head and neck I sense a weakness!

A slight tremble visible there of age or ill health or alcoholism. Or it might be any of the other afflictions that years ago I spent hours cursing him with, praying for his debilitation, the control of these addictive and repeated fantasies perhaps the first step I took towards a greater manhood: a fledging that was not complete until I had banned them completely from my mind. The man is still looking about weakly, and I know that he will see me: he will turn to me where I stand with my back to the bar and I wait for him, calmly and without emotion, his eyes eventually catching mine without losing their vagueness. Perhaps there is the merest of flickers, or a change in focus as we meet again, but then nothing, so that either he does not recognise me, or he is unwilling to show that he does.

He looks away. I feel relief and a small joy as if justified, because there was no sneer from him. It was this that I dreaded most: some gesture or signal that would have required an instant response. Instead I am able to pay, smile at the barmaid, pick up the heavy glasses and walk easily back to the table, almost as if in the glow of achievement. My friend is there and I see the back of his head, a sudden bright blue below it where he has removed his coat and revealed his shirt. I am placing the drinks on the table and am in the action of sitting down when he begins talking – but suddenly his voice is receding and no longer making sense, as if the seat I am on is being pulled back away from our table, the wafting unreality of my surroundings dreamlike as I am subject to a thought and caught in its instant suppression.

Because I think that if I am truly different to the boy of that time, if I have grown and become stronger and more powerful, then surely I should walk over to my enemy and assault him, viciously and without mercy: a revenge for many nights spent in a despairing and acute self-doubt, my body lying still but my mind flipped from the verge of sleep into a flickering wakefulness, which would always end in a passionate desire to meet the man again – to come across him, he unprepared for the scale of my preparedness in some dark corner of London, and then to damage him with savage fist and foot before parting.

Except that the thought of this now creates a pulsing fear in me, and it is this fear that makes my friend's words unintelligible, and gives the light-headed unreality to the room and its voices that surround us. I have overcome this fear before now; I know what it is to do something I have been afraid of, but already I know that the pieces are not in place for such a moment, where one's will within fights and beats another, and as immediate as this knowledge comes a shame, an embarrassment for myself, who cannot simply rise, take a few purposeful steps and smash the thick glass I grasp against a man's head. Am I a coward, that I do not want to do this? And fear of this makes me lean back again so that I can see him by the wall, to see whether he sparks a new fear in me – and when he does not I look for the anger I held for him, an anger that was either buried deeply or died of its own accord, that one day I realised I did not feel any more, and had not felt in recent memory.

I must scratch for it, hidden as it is now, but soon enough I think I have its bright corner glinting in the earth: a simple vision of the man, still sat at our table, leaning forwards, his face alternating between a private humour and bitter earnestness. I can remember staring at his head, watching him speak and the movements of his face, and feeling a powerful dislike for what I saw, this image the one that my mind would preserve, would nurture until it was framed purely by hate.

'You should stand up for yourselves,' the man had gone on to say.

'We do.'

'No you don't. I've been sat here giving you grief and you've done nothing but take it! What's wrong with you, are you soft or what? If I gave you a clip round the ear now you'd just sit there and take it, wouldn't you?' This he said to the boy next to him. Suddenly he had raised his hand and feinted with an open palm, a small quick movement that was playful, but made the boy flinch back sharply, to look comic and weak in the reaction – one that as his friends we were embarrassed by.

'Easy, mate,' I said.

'Don't you tell me what to do!' he barked. Then to the others: 'Did you see him? Did you see him jump? Ha ha.' He had been grinning and pointing at the boy next to him, then he performed a full impression, complete with facial expressions, of how the boy had been startled. We watched in silence – or perhaps some of us did laugh along – the boy who had flinched smiling through this mockery in an attempt to show that it did not touch him.

'You boys are well soft,' the man said, taking a drink.

A brief silence, while we digested this insult, and then one of us said: 'We're just trying to have a good night.' This sounded like a whine to me, and in a sudden spurt of anger I managed: 'How do you know what we are? Maybe you should watch your mouth.'

'I know what you are just by looking,' the man sneered to all of us. Then he turned to me. 'And you tell me what to do one more time, son, you just tell me. Please, tell me what to do again.' He was nodding. 'I'd like it if you did. Do you understand?'

His eyes were fixed on mine. I did not look away.

'You're a bunch of girls. I bet not one of you would go outside now,' he pointed at me with a chopping motion of his hand, 'except maybe him.'

Our eyes were still locked across the table. I can remember feeling anger, much of it, swilling around as a tension in my jaw and hands, and fear: a difficulty to keep my breathing even and unobvious, and the rabbit-warning pattering of heartbeats in my chest. And also there had been a streak of pride – the vein of which I can remember being very uncertain at that age, so that any recognition of manhood would be gladly accepted, and from an enemy cherished even more.

Somehow I was proud that this thug, this man whom we did not know, who had sat at our table and striven to insult us, had gifted me with the suspicion of courage. And I had thought that within this gift was a further promise of under-standing: a connection that had been made in his recognition of something in me – some manhood that perhaps the others lacked, displayed in my level gaze, my willingness to return a challenge – and so when he was finally walking out the door of the pub, there I was, thinking in fact he was a reasonable man that needed to talk about something, who was not so bad as he seemed: because he was even holding the door open for me as I followed him.

My friend is similarly holding the door for me now as we step out into the cold. We have finished our evening, are limited at this point by our cars. Outside by his car we say our goodbyes: I shake his hand and remain standing to watch him get in. He is wondering why I am not walking over to get into my own, and pauses in his movements.

'Are you staying for another?' he says, having sat but with the car door still ajar.

'No,' I say, pointing over the road. He nods and then I am engaged in a dummy run to the shop where I indicated, waving as my friend drives past, a flash of his lights before accelerating powerfully down the well-lit road. I go into the shop, buy a small packet of mints, then return back across the road and into the car park, the sports car low and sleek in the poor light, but still shining darkly: a welcome and familiar shape designed to bring anticipation, which on the simpler parts of me is always effective, but that now I step towards with hesitation.

And when I am sat in this vehicle, the door having clunked softly to enclose me in its dark and pleasant interior, I do not insert the keys or lift my hands to the wheel, but look to the windshield, through which I can watch the exit of the pub. My heart has not stopped thudding since I watched my friend finish his drink, sigh and place the empty glass down on the table. This was the signal that indecision must end: that either I would leave my enemy and have to drown any regret for an opportunity not taken – or instead wait for him to emerge, as I do now. There is a thudding in my ears, a cold nervousness around my chest as I watch the door, an expression of which are my hands rising to clutch the steering wheel, its thick rim solid and full of promise, attached as it is to the symbol, this car: the exhaust of my success, a high-end luxury that has come to me, that I have reeled in with my labours.

I sit here within this machine waiting to commit violence, on the basis of a promise sworn to myself years ago, and because I am afraid and unthinking, slightly stupefied by this base choice, I know that I will do it if triggered – I know that I do not sit here in self-deception but am primed enough to be blind to risk.

An hour spent waiting, and in this time I repeatedly imagine the man coming out, the movement I will make to climb out of my car, and the parts of his body I will go for. Each time the door opens – every time the line of light appears on the ground, a brightness that grows to box in the shadow of whoever is leaving – my watching heart kicks, and I reach for the door. But female voices are heard, or the sight of different men, who are not my enemy, to allow me both a relaxation and disappointment.

When the man does emerge, as soon as I see him I take my hand from the door handle: I place it in my lap. He is staggering along with shuffling steps, one arm held out against the wall: this his horizontal pillar that he leans on and then must throw forwards again to create a stuttering progress. It would be easier than I had ever imagined, to approach him now and clout him, to watch him stagger afresh by my fist. But he is too weak! I have sat here building up a desire to destroy something that has already crumbled.

And I am relieved, a true and very pure relief, as I find the key and put it in the ignition, the engine catching quickly and with resolution, the feeling of the car moving beneath me, to bring me next to the man who has now left the wall and is shuffling unsupported along the pavement – almost picturesque beneath the ornate white street lights – because now I can believe that what he returns to is the pit, is the hovel and unhappiness: these things his profile, old and lacking in any belligerence, seem to confirm empirically.

The short drive to my home, along the kempt streets of the neighbourhood in which my life has surfaced, passing no pedestrians and only a few other cars, a solitude that does not lessen as I turn onto my street, and slip between the tall houses on either side, coming to rest on the crunching gravel, leaving my car hunkered on it among the other forms of svelte metal. I am not shaken. I was not shaken and now only feel tired, finding the right key for the external door, walking silently up the bending and thickly carpeted stairs to stand before the door to my apartment, the numbers highly polished brass, as kempt as any other fixture of the building, as the building itself, as neat as the street, polished and gleaming like my car and even the neighbourhood beyond – save for those who are lost and wandering through it.

I pass through and into the living room, past electronic machinery black and dustless that I do not dust, a large window that is black also but has a view of greens and urban distance in the day, the occasional red sky: a spectacular sunset to watch nestled on the sofa with alcohol, one of the black machines turning the room into a concert hall, spouting music through the shell-shaped sculptures stood on the parts of the polished floor not covered by silken rug.

I pass these things and enter the bathroom, the slatted blinds at the window allowing bars of orange light to enter from the street, slashing across the tiling, the basin and its mirror. This orange light, coming from the old lamp posts that have not yet been replaced like the ones near the pub, the horrible orange light that you pass through, and it is like passing through danger, the same orange light that the man and I those many years ago had stood in as we left the pub, him walking a bit further and motioning me to follow, me obeying the gesture of his arm, wondering what he could want to tell me, walking straight and proud because my friends had wanted me to stay, had told me not to go. But I had reassured them, had told them there was nothing to fear: I was just going to talk to him, to be reasonable with him so that if we saw him again in our pub there would be no trouble, we could hold our heads high, without shame, without totally failing the challenge he had set for us.

So there I stood, suddenly my group's leader, their bravest, alone to talk with this man, and he had motioned me further so that we could stand close to one another. His head was bent and he was nodding, and I knew he was about to part with the crux of the matter, would reveal the meaning of our encounter, and eagerly I stepped forwards to join him, perhaps my head was even cocked in the faith that its ear would be well provided for with wisdom, and as I took the last step to enter into the maturity of our conference I saw his face turning to me, the eyes wide and the lips pursed, expecting him to speak but instead the green flash of his jacket as his elbow flew up, its point hammering once at my mouth, a jolt to stun me and send me staggering backwards, my eyes instantly filling with liquid, the shock of the blow both an unreality and the only possible reality there could ever have been. He did not say anything; he must have walked off to leave me crippled by the pain that had emerged in my lower face: spitting out the blood on my tongue that was trying to suddenly gush down my throat, its warmth and iron, its sheer volume forcing it to spill out of my lips and streak down my chin.

That had happened beneath orange street lights.

I reach around for the switch near the doorway, to banish the layered effect made by the blinds, to lift the silence where memory can thrive with the humming of a fan. I move to stand by the sink.

Then I lift out the bridgework at the top of my mouth, a familiar loosening between the canines: a sucking at the gum there before it comes free and I have it out and beneath the tap, rinsing the spit and other things from it, to then drop it clinking into the glass of solution that always sits on the sink nearest to where I sleep. This glass of blue-tinged liquid, like a jar with a small and toothy specimen that follows me around the world, through business hotels and friends' houses, to emerge eventually in the bright and polished bathrooms of lovers: its presence there a sign of something beyond the ordinary between us, and the truth of it my consolation.

I Am a Neat Boy

About to leave, but hesitating, Michael risks the glassy depths of the mirror. He is old and worn but has made the effort. His hair is combed and tidy. He is well shaven. His face is clean and shines in places, is red in others. I am a neat man, he thinks to himself.

He is old but for a moment does not feel it – cannot see it in his reflection. Usually he makes no effort, is content to emerge from his home without thought or care as to how he might look, whether he repels others who had not noticed him until his scent stabs sharply at their noses. His hair will be unkempt, wild in places, greasy and matted in others. Stubble will choke his red face, or worse only part of it, and somewhere there will be a large redder gash where he has cut himself and given up. But tonight he has collected himself, groomed and dressed as he might have done in youth, when he would often stand before the mirror, poised to enter the night, admiring the perfect width of collar, the alertness of his shirt and hair and he would say to himself: I am a neat boy.

Then it was women that prompted him to say these things – now it is a woman again. He has heard her at church: leading the singing with a voice high and pure, a simplicity to it that instantly attracts him, a change from the warbling of the previous incumbent, whose voice would disappear from his attention, hazy as it was with the bell-like intonations of the priest, the warmth and the smell of incense. She produced in him a difference, a salience within a tired duty, her singing rising into the high stone curve of ceiling to be trapped there in resonance and echo, a sound clear enough to awaken something in him – even if it was merely the raising of his eyes, him straining his neck to see past the amassed heads of others until there is a straight line between his eyes and her image, one that will stay with him: a face perhaps his own age, the earnestness of her performance seeming to open the possibility of a great kindness, or understanding – hopeful illusions like the flock of something landing in his mind, but that he does not care to scatter.

She sings professionally, and when he saw the notice of her concert he became aware that he would go, but slowly, as if it had to creep through the resistance of other thoughts.

Because he is an alcoholic. Retired, his only commitments in the week are Mass and the off-licence. He is known in the area and tolerated if noticed because all he does is emerge from his home and begin shuffling down the pavement, taking the same practised path, an appearance of suffering to those who look closer, but with the plain caveat that he is a drunkard merely staggering politely to make his purchase, an exchange that will be made with a strained civility towards the shopkeeper, whom he holds nothing against but is aware must harbour some contempt for him – he of the daily late-morning procurement – and which

Michael tries to normalise with idle enquiry, white lies of his intent, the effectiveness of what he is saying mattering to neither.

Today he has not drunk. Now he must leave the house and take the Underground. It is a device he has not boarded in years, and that he rides seated, his back straight, aware that he has not drunk since the previous evening, wanting those around him to sense this difference in him, to know the cost of his neatness.

He emerges into the street. It is cold and he must pass a pub on his way, its lights a terrible softening of the night. But he is resolved and can walk past it with only a glance, no lessening of his step.

And when he arrives and collects his ticket and makes his way upstairs, into the long thin gallery that flanks the rear and both sides of the hall, he is elated to find that he is in the front row of the sharply terraced seats, that he can lean over the wooden structure and look unobstructed down to the stage.

He waits for her, a mixture of leaning forwards and sitting straight. The hall quietens: voices lessening until there are only a few whispers and murmurs, an anticipation of the darkness that falls to leave only the stage bright – then the sudden applause as the performers appear, the women in long and coloured dresses, the men birds of an opposite climate in black and white. Michael is expectant, a small thrill in his stomach and a tingling in the hands that clap along with those around him. He is happy and still grips to this happiness as his gaze passes over each of the performers, their faces unfamiliar, their movements careful as they make their way to the spindly lecterns they will stand behind.

But he cannot find her. He cannot see her among them and suddenly accepts she is absent. One of the men steps forwards and speaks to the audience, telling them of an unfortunate illness, his gratitude for her replacement brought in at short notice. And then they begin.

The music passes over him. He is not beyond under-standing it, but without her he has no guide, no key to its complexity, and having not bought a programme he doesn't even know what it is.

It is a short concert and there is no interval. When it is over he claps with the rest of them, stays clapping until the end. Then he gets up and is caught in the slow-moving flow of bodies: pigeon steps and the smell of the person in front until the main hall is reached.

Outside, near the entrance, a man is watching him as he comes out.

'I know you,' the man says. 'From church.'

'Yes,' Michael replies, though he does not know this young man, cut cleanly in a long black coat.

'Did you enjoy it?' the man says. Michael realises that the man is smoking, watches as he drops the stub and then crushes it beneath his foot.

'I was hoping to see Florence,' Michael says. 'I'm sorry to hear she's unwell.'

'You know her,' the man declares.

'Me? Yes, yes,' Michael says. 'I know her. From church. Did you see the poster there – do you know her?'

'I am her son,' the man says, a slight smile at the end of his statement. 'I wasn't informed of her absence either.'

'Her son? Yes. Well. Will you tell her that I came, that Michael came?'

The man pauses. His chin is held higher than before. He looks at Michael, and Michael understands that he is being judged, that the man is weighing him in his mind. Perhaps he can see the thirst in him, the burning at the back of his mouth and in his throat that has suddenly risen to prominence, vengeful with its force — a condition given away by the twitch in his hands, his uncertain speech. Or he can imagine the disappointment that Michael felt as the music began: the weight in his chest becoming heavier to sink him as he realised fully that there was no mistake, no alternative to her absence. Perhaps the man has passed one of his scuffing ambles to the shop and back and seeing him now, in his neat but frayed apparel, knows what an effort he must have made, and can even imagine him stood before a mirror, remembering his youth.

'I'll be sure to tell her,' the man tells Michael, and they part.

Prelude

With a breath of preparation, but mostly affectation, Gerald seated himself at the piano.

The lid was closed and before he lifted it he
let his hands expand outwards on the bright polished wood,
feeling the smoothness, the age, the quality of the instrument, as if it were possible to know these things from its
red-brown shining skin alone. Then the lid was open and
the keys exposed. He pushed one of the lower Ds. It remained
depressed after he lifted his finger, popping back up of its
own accord. His hand moved upwards and found the F in
the high treble – he struck it hard and heard the note whine
slightly – a weakened, ailing edge to its tone. But that was
it; they were the only flaws of the instrument and he spread
his hands out in a chord and pounced on the keyboard,
filling the room with a rich, thick sound that sustained and
sustained and continued to do so, until it was Gerald that
broke away: it was he that yielded first, lifting his hands to
decapitate the sound he had made, which survived fleetingly
in the corners of the room.

He was happy, sitting there, feeling his old love for the
piano. It was old itself and had its two slightly duff notes,

but it stood in the room of his mother's house without compromise, like a submarine that had surfaced among the flotsam of rugs and old furniture, the German name gleaming in gilt letters from the wood like a threat. It was not forgiving; it was hard work to play. The keys were heavy, the tone still bright and aggressive, but once you knew it – as he had all his life – once you had mastered it you could use the power you felt beneath your fingers and push great sound out into the world. As a young man living in this house he had done that many times, felt moments of great exultation after opening the windows and heaving up the wooden lid to reveal the lungs and insides of the beast, then sitting down to play the pieces that were a part of him, filling the street with himself.

The room was at the end of the house and there was a window in the roof where the sun was entering. Gerald got up to adjust the blind. The sun had been shining directly onto the piano and he turned to look at the light, waiting for the dust motes to appear in the bars he was making as he twisted the handle. When the lighting was correct he sat back down on the stool and reached into his bag. He straightened and put the music on the holder. It was still a new book and he had to press at the pages to stop them closing; then it was open in front of him and he placed his hands on the keys, a cool and smooth solidity beneath his fingertips.

But the telephone was ringing: infernal device that he could not hear, but could feel vibrating in his shirt pocket. The choice was either to remain poised and ride it out, or to answer the thing, the terrible thing foisted upon him. He did not like its insect struggle against his breast, so he pulled it out and read the name on the screen: Anna, his wife, she who had foisted it upon him. 'Hello?' he said.

'Hi. How are you.' Her voice was flat and tinged with accent.

'Fine.'

'Where are you?'

'At my mother's.'

'Should I come by?' she asked him.

'I've just got here,' he answered. With his left hand he began to depress the piano's keys.

'Oh. Okay. Well I might go to the pub quickly then.' She pronounced the word pub oddly, as if it didn't really belong in her mouth and she was uncomfortable saying it. Sometimes he hated the way she said it. She was a foreigner, she was Hungarian, she had a limited right to use such words, they were guests in her mouth, especially with an accent. Sometimes he loved the way she said it but today was not one of those days (who did she think she was?); he found the accent on the simple, small word thick and almost affronting.

'Yes, the *pub*,' he said. 'Okay, fine.'

'I'll see you back at home. Is that okay with you?'

'Sure, sure. You go right ahead, dear. Enjoy your friends.'

'Okay. Bye,' she said, her voice uncertain.

'Okay. Love you. Bye.' He paused and listened to silence. It seemed she had hung up so he lowered the phone and just as he pressed the red button he cut off a little voice, also professing love. Miniature, somewhat perfunctory love, he thought, placing the device on top of the piano, its small, sleek black form appearing parasitic, like a barnacle or similar, on the red-brown wood of the piano.

His day off was nearly ended; her work day had ended

and now she was beginning to loom in his mind. He inhaled. Then he returned to the music. He had made crude pencil marks all over the first page of the prelude. Above one bar he had written the word 'rarefied', even though, in the context, he wasn't really sure what that meant. But there was a problem with the piece, a major difficulty he faced and that was why he was at his mother's, why he had adjusted the blind just so because he intended to sit for the next hour and work it through. And as the prospect of the work ahead faced him, Gerald had a moment of doubt.

Weeks ago when he had first been learning the piece, his mother had knocked on the door to his house. He had answered and ushered her in and she had stepped through the door frame, an aged but well-turned-out woman, a mixture of smart clothes with the dash of the eccentric to which she was liable – in this instance a bright orange scarf, carelessly thrown around her neck below her mass of grey hair. She had entered the house and immediately Gerald had felt that part of him had been barged out of the way, as if she had seen the schedule in his head, his plan for bringing order to the world, and swept it aside. She stopped in the corridor and turned as he closed the door behind her. Leaning forwards her lips became pouted and he moved to her, kissing her lightly and mostly on the cheek. The cheek was smooth but it felt old.

Then she was off – she wandered around the rooms of the house as if on inspection, saying nothing apart from praising everything and anything new: the additions, ornaments, clothes and trinkets of Anna's that she found. He offered tea and as he left for the kitchen he saw his mother sitting down at the piano.

Suddenly the prelude was attacking him in the kitchen. The piece that he was slaving over, that was taking him hours of accumulated snatched-at practice, was now alive in his house and at the behest of his mother. The kettle was boiling but she played so loudly that he could still hear it coming at him. Couldn't she see his pained markings on the music? Didn't she understand that he wanted to have the piece to himself, not have it dug up unripe, shown to him before he had a chance to show it to others? Then he heard that she was slurring the top notes in the right hand. He put down the spoon that he was holding and walked into the living room, and moving up behind her pointed at the music open on the holder.

'Where,' he shouted, 'does it say to slur the top notes?'

Her head sunk into her shoulders like a turtle, but she kept playing, instantly detaching the top notes. 'Sorry!' she said.

Gerald looked at the back of her head. It was a great mass of grey hair – grey hair thick and going everywhere and framed underneath by the wild orange scarf. It annoyed him, but suddenly he felt sorry for her, and he thought how the back of people's heads could make you both annoyed and feel sorry for them. He loved her but here she was, unwittingly angering him by playing his prelude. She couldn't help but interfere and oppress, and at the same time as he was fighting her off he could see her desperately and terribly alone, a blundering soul carried into trouble by her exuberance – thick-skinned enough to shrug his anger off at the time but what happened later? When she was alone would she remember the ferocity with which he had shouted at her? He could imagine her crying, tissue in hand, a shake of the head at her own silliness.

But since he had heard his mother play it that way he had practised the piece and slurred the top notes. That was the depth of her influence. Nowhere on the music did it say to slur the top notes, but after hearing her he had been compelled to play it her way. Gerald frowned recalling this, because now his hands were at the piano in the artful, dappled mote-filled light, his eyes earnestly on the music and he was playing, slowly going through the piece and detaching the top notes. Had he slurred them because he shouted at her, out of guilt for that and for all the angry upward crimes of a son?

Anna had told him the facts as she saw them, her eyes narrowing and sparkling, her mass of dark hair framing her face in seriousness. 'You play that piano to tell her you love her.'

'No!'

She became villainous and then beautiful as her eyes widened. 'It is how you bond with her.'

'No.'

This conversation had been incited by what occurred only minutes previous to it. The radio had been left on accidentally to intrude into the dinner conversation when a pianist, a Hungarian like his wife, who he much respected, was suddenly introduced to play the prelude and fugue. He had darted to the radio and turned it up, motioned to his wife to turn her down, and stood for the full four minutes to listen.

'Hungarian!'

He enjoyed the performance but something was wrong, something was terribly wrong because the Hungarian had detached all the top notes in the prelude! And Gerald had to admit that it sounded good the way the Hungarian played it – so very good – so much better than even his mother. He knew then that he had to detach the top notes and instantly felt sickness for all the work that would entail, of taking the piece that he had slowly put together apart and having to rebuild it from the beginning. He was only a slow amateur: it would take weeks, not days. His mother had been wrong – again! Damn her and her interference! He had been right to shout at her. Perhaps, he thought, his annoyance at the back of her head was actually his instinct telling him he was about to be railroaded.

And now, in her house, in the process of undoing that which she had wrought, he could hear her voice, floating towards him on its piercing timbre.

'Gerald! Gerald!'

'What!' he called back. The telephone trembled and buzzed against its wooden host, startling him. He picked it up and saw that it was Anna.

'Gerald!'

The dimly lit word Anna looked up at him and vibrated.

'Gerald!'

'Wait a minute, my mother's going crazy in the garden,' he told his wife. 'What do you want, I'm on the phone!' he shouted to his mother. He could feel anger causing heat in his shoulders and a prickling at the back of his head.

'Can you get the door? I'm in the garden,' his mother called. He hadn't heard the door.

'I've got to get the door,' he said to his wife.

'Yes,' she replied.

'Did you hear me? I've got to get the door.'

'I am at the door!'

He pushed the red button and went to the front of the house. He was breathing calmly, and thinking that he must try to continue to breathe calmly.

There was a clear, plain windowpane in his mother's door and through this he could see Anna's head, a dark shape with the bright of the street behind it. This head was innocent, it had done him little wrong and certainly none intentionally – but Gerald could feel it in him that he was going to make it roll. It was a beautiful head. He opened the door and his wife approached him, smiling. Her hair was long and dark but neatly shaped, her eyes wet little stones in her head while her clothes were conservative – mercifully conservative but she gave them a quality. The way she walked and stood made her seem expensive, like some sort of European thoroughbred.

She was close enough that he could smell her, see the glistening of a front tooth. She knew nothing yet, it seemed, and the smile ignited her face, and the thoughts in which he held it – the things he had seen that had made him marry her, love her. But he was aware of this trick and it angered him further: mechanical, emotional response at the back of the brain as it was. Or maybe chemical. Couldn't she tell that things were going badly?

Perhaps, he thought, she is not so innocent after all. She had said she was going to the 'pub' and now here she was, dropping in unexpectedly, what a surprise, what a pleasure – here she was a huge living breathing barrier between him and what he had to do. The prelude was in limbo, painful and itching, neither slurred nor detached and now that she was here it would be impossible to make progress on it. Even if she left quickly he was sure the chance was gone – his concentration broken by irrepressible annoyance.

He turned and led the way into the house leaving her kiss-less and having to close the door herself. His mother was waiting for him in the living room, standing with an aspect of jolliness, thick ungainly garden gloves making her look like a giant puppet. Instantly this appalled him. He felt Anna enter the room behind him.

'Hello,' Anna said. The two women came together, kissed with neck and chin extended. Gerald watched them with disgust, for they were colluding. They seemed to him like two large blunt instruments, two sets of hooves trampling his one expression of sensitivity. They lauded him, praised him, claimed to love him and yet they had the capacity to completely disregard the qualities that defined him. He knew they didn't know how much he had just wanted to sit at the piano but he expected them to at least have a suspicion, an inkling. Instead his wife had arrived to prevent him from fixing a mess his mother had been the architect of. And now they were carrying on a pointless conversation while he simmered in the corner.

'Come on, let's go,' he said.

They were walking home.

They had not said anything directly, they hadn't openly declared it but they both knew they were upset with each other. Gerald could not believe that his wife was upset – what did she have to be upset about?

'What's wrong with you?' she said finally.

To him it wasn't an enquiry, it was an accusation. The anger he had been nourishing boiled at the back of his head.

'What do you mean, what's wrong with me?'

'You've been cold to me since I turned up at your mother's.'

'You weren't supposed to turn up at my mother's!'

'That's not nice – to say that when I come to see you when I didn't have to.'

'You said you were going to the pub,' he said, turning to her.

'I only said I might. What's wrong with you?'

'Nothing.'

He felt like a child. The way she said it made it feel like any wrong he might be, or feel, was his fault. It was always like this. Arguing with a woman, a Hungarian at that, was like playing chess against a better player – they always had you under pressure, no matter how dastardly you thought your strategy was.

Or how much you said to yourself beforehand: I will think every move through carefully, I will not make any mistakes.

Suddenly she was leaving him – she had turned away and was walking towards the crossing.

'Where are you going?'

'For a drink!' she replied. The way she said 'drink' was like her saying 'pub' – it sounded wrong, affected, accented, as if she were not merely flirting with her status of belonging within the language, but asserting it.

He watched as she waited for the cars to stop, as she stepped out onto the black and white surface of the road. There was the back of her head. She receded and his anger grew, a horrible feeling, like hate that you can taste in your mouth and this made him feel like a child again, standing impotently with hands clenched at his sides, his mother having stopped him from doing something.

And her walking away from him was just the beginning. He knew that having upset her he was in for much punishment before resolution could be reached. At the moment that was fine with him – he was still angry and could feel his anger thrashing nastily in him – but even as he rejoiced in this anger and walked off back home alone, righteously, the victim of all the wrong today, at the back of his mind was the realisation that he would recover far quicker than her and find himself even more alone by wanting to be happy again with his wife. She, he knew, would want the fight to continue. That made him even angrier as he walked and for a moment he thought that this time – this time he would outlast her, he would show her just how long he could stay officially upset.

But this thought was followed by the knowledge that he would surrender first, as he always did.

So later, Gerald was in the hallway when she returned. He heard the key in the door and froze between kitchen and living room, watching as the light came in from outside and the elegant silhouette appeared in the opening. She stepped inside and he could tell instantly that they were still in conflict. Her movements were more composed, her eyes stayed down and averted, well away from his own. He had hoped that maybe the alcohol would cheer her up, make her see the injustice of it all, but it had not. If anything it had compounded her unhappiness.

And in the length of a breath he hated her. He looked at her and saw everything suddenly being stripped away: all the ideas, feelings and associations that together perhaps constituted his love. It was as if in a brace of seconds a fire had ravaged the area of his brain reserved for this paramount social function – a mysterious place that had surprised him with its first activity and passion, and had developed more concretely to become the most treasured artefact in his mind – suddenly destroyed to leave his wife before him a woman like any other, an ordinary woman unimportant to the entire universe save a person here and there. Whose cheek would be soft if you kissed it.

Objectively she was nothing, and for the length of that breath she was nothing even to him. This was frightening, and he retreated to the kitchen, where he made dinner, and it was over dinner that they reconciled. It was done simply – he apologised, she apologised, they kissed over their plates and that was it. But Gerald did not really feel better and he suspected that Anna was not truly assuaged. This was the problem, he thought. You dive in with the apology, you strive to make things better again and they hold back that last particle of forgiveness just to remind you. Anna had once told him that when she was a child she had put salt in her father's tea to stop him asking her to make it for him. She said that she started with a tiny amount, and then increasingly, she had soured the drink. Gerald never forgot this because often he felt he was facing the same tactics, the same psychology involved in the tea-salting: post-argument she would hold back a kernel of discord so that even though he had what he wanted he would be unsure – and unhappy.

'You all right?'

'Yes,' she replied, a single grain of a lie in her voice.

When they had moved to the living room he knew for sure that he was still being punished. It was their ritual to end the day watching the news together, Anna with her feet up on Gerald's lap. They both loved to do it because it seemed to make them foolish sweethearts all over again every night. But now they were sitting on the sofa, apart – Anna with her legs tucked up to the side. When Gerald looked over he could see the light of the television reflected in her left eye, which was locked on the news and never strayed to him with a friendly glance. Her heels touched her buttocks mockingly. Gerald's lap felt empty and cold.

He was a man, an adult, and he was in pain. For him it was the withdrawal of grace. He knew she loved him and that he was held within this love, but he was only ever really glad of it when he could feel himself being dropped out of it, when he had angered or upset, when the grace, the favour she reserved only for him was suddenly suspended. He was saddened that she did not understand what it was for him to be dropped like that. She had dropped him now – sat silently on the sofa he felt like he was falling.

So he reached out and put his hand on her leg. She didn't move. He repositioned himself so that he could move over her, his hand on her thigh, his lips approaching the side of her head and then dropping to the part of her neck that was exposed. He kissed her, his hand moving up her thigh and beginning to go under her dress. Her arm came up and her hand was on his, but instead of encouragement this was censorship – it pressed hard, and then feebly tried to pull his hand away. She did not have the strength but the intent was clear and that was enough to stop him.

'No,' she said.

'Why?'

'It makes me feel empty when we've been arguing.'

She kissed him, got up and left the room. He could hear her going up the stairs, knew she was going to bed.

He didn't mind her leaving. She was right, after all – it was not like it had been any more – when sex was a way of saying sorry, of making up and obliterating everything else with not only the moment of it but the aftermath, which was sweet and lasting. Intimacy and domesticity had somehow taken this power away from it. If he had succeeded with the wandering of his hand, Gerald knew that he would have felt empty afterwards too.

He switched off the news. He rose from the sofa and went over to his piano, which was hidden in the corner of the room, a small low-slung object with the word Yamaha stuck on its veneer. He pulled out the stool, sat down and put his hands on the lid, sliding it upwards and inwards to reveal the plastic keys – an easy action, the lid light and false with none of the heaviness and fear for fingers that he got from opening a real instrument. He found the pair of headphones and plugged them in, put them over his ears. Then he flicked the on switch, waited for the little red lights to appear on the display above the keys. The music was already open on the holder, his mad pencilling seeming more ridiculous than ever.

He thought about the Hungarian pianist, and all the detached top notes. Who would have thought the world's pre-eminent pianist would hail from Hungary!

Then he began to study the right hand of the prelude, slowly and carefully detaching the top notes.

This Is The Educated Classes Talking

When I see a black person on television I want to like them.

If they are being interviewed – if they are a guest trapped in a studio that has the capacity to become dangerous to them, prowled as it is by wits sharpened by a greater education and opportunity, I fear that they will be exposed. And I know that often the presenters feel the same, that they do as I do: are leaning forwards with an indistinct nervousness in their chest, hoping the dark face will say something intelligent or insightful, willing them to do this so that they do not appear merely the furniture of equality – and to affirm that they truly do sit outside the skin of a stereotype and are not in some way standing, their hands on a rope, swinging a fan in unseen rafters.

I cannot help this racism, as that is what it surely is, because it wells up in me and springs to my lips involuntarily: mutterings I make through clenched teeth, surrounded by the Polish incomprehension of bus queues, or towards unruly Somali children in a shop that they are near to vandalising.

Or worse the slight shiver of fear that is now felt watching the figure coming through the door: the almost black skin, the tied-back dreadlocks, the sportswear and the slightly rolling affectation of a walk. But in an instant the fear dissipates, perhaps due to a trace of kindness in his face, his lack of interest in me or the general area where I sit with my son.

He approaches the counter and surveys the menu above it. My son and I are in a café in North London. We are not from North London and have not yet reached our destination, but someone needed the toilet and there being few toilets on the Underground, here we are making the best of it and having lunch. We emerged from the station and I looked about with a small hand in my own and an unexpected sunshine above – we emerged like this squinting, the primary desire to find convenience, the first impression looking about at the tattered shops and boarded windows, at the sudden concentration of human flotsam drifting past in both directions, that this is the type of street where people become stabbed: they become faces pitied and then forgotten once they slip from the media, an indelible wound appearing, similarly unseen, in the body of humanity that surrounded them.

And even the entrance to the café, a mere lifting of a foot, had been made in trepidation. Nerves swam in parts of me as we walked along the road, looking for welcome, a sudden and frightening oddness to find a pub overflowing with men in blue and white football shirts, picking our way through the natural barricade of their number, past this early smell of beer and the sound of a breaking glass to find further down from the station a large glass frontage with neon-orange and yellow stars clustered around the open door: the promotion of fare ignored in favour of an understanding of the tables within, decked with irregular formations of red sauce and mustard – and more importantly who sat at these tables, what reflections were being made in the chrome cylinders of salt and sugar. And as I stood there in the doorway with my son I saw all this and was seen myself by the three white men hunched over their large bean-spread platters, whose conversation did not stop, whose eyes averted casually to allow us to enter, unthreatened, to find a seat among the otherwise empty tables, near the back and facing the doorway.

These men had finished their lunches and left together, their patronage of the café and their belonging to the small world surrounding it proved to me in their loud and cheerful goodbyes to the staff behind the counter, which made my son raise and turn his head from his sandwich curiously, his eyes widening at the sudden volume, the straw of his drink that he had reached for poking at his chin and cheek before blindly finding his mouth. These large men had left to create a vacuum, in which me and the boy were suddenly dominant, could make our conversation and joking louder, between the peaks of which I would look to the floors and the wall near the frontage and enjoy their grubbiness, reading the misspellings backwards through the neon card, or note with pride the cleanliness of the table itself and the cutlery, the clarity of the glass from which I drank.

And so it had just been a flicker of fear when the man had rolled in, a brief unknown, just the shift itself from ownership of the space to its sudden involuntary sharing to cause unease. I heard the girl behind the counter call out a hello, the same hello she had given us as we made our way to the table. She had swung out from behind the counter, young and pleasant, perhaps Italian or Greek: long dark hair tied back and dark skin but not Asian, definitely not Asian, as she gestured to the tables with an expression of sympathy for the bafflement that their availability might cause, more pleasantness and kindness as she smiled at my young son and somehow helped him get into his chair without touching him or the chair – a girl doing her job but doing it very well so that even half-bent on the way down to sitting I was becoming comfortable.

Now this demeanour was on the man she faced across the counter. This to our side almost out of view but I could imagine the angled head, the expectancy in her eyes as she looked to the man who would be reading the array above her. I am watching the boy take a careful bite of his sandwich when beyond him out front through the glass a black cab appears, stopping close to the pavement, the rear door opening slowly and emerging from it an old lady, stooping as she gets out and still stooping once disgorged, one arm rising to wave while the other feebly pushes the door closed. It is Sunday and it is instantly plain as the vehicle slides off behind her that she will turn and stagger through the open doorway, that she has come here as she does most, if not every Sunday. With an able gait she makes her way quickly to a table, the girl calling out to her from the counter: the same hello but followed by a dear that the lady acknowledges with the same half-wave she gave the driver. She sits down heavily with a controlled collapse of herself into the chair. She does not lift the menu, has not looked above the counter, and looking at the back of her head I know that it is in part filled with the knowledge that they will bring her what she wants, that she does not need to ask.

A pleasant lunch then for the boy and me, almost assured of its place in our history by the enforced departure from the Underground; its memorability sealed in the sentiments provoked by the old woman and her habit, a thing I am savouring when the three figures appear in the window: three men or boys for a moment tightly bunched together as if shoaling, obvious signs of hesitation as they turn and look in through the glass. Two are black and one is white, their age at the end of school or perhaps just after it, voices beginning to accompany their images through the open door as they slide towards it: aggressive and bantering, swearing, and finally a long hissing suck of the teeth.

I do not want them to come in, I have marked them and instantly I am afraid. I look across to the man, who is now sitting, waiting, and see that he isn't looking though he must hear them plainly, and I understand he is making a point of not looking, studying as he is the device he holds in his hands. When the first of them breaks from indecision and steps through the doorway something is felt dropping slightly in my chest, watching his exaggerated limping walk, his white face a scowl, the sportswear, the angled cap, even a pouting of the lips – these things reflected with more authenticity in the taller youth behind him, who not only wears a cap but a long red and white patterned cloth that comes down either side of his long dark face, as if he must blinker himself from left and right, can only look in these directions by turning his whole head which he does as he enters, fixing everything around him with a cast, a binding thread spun by a listless boredom, a dangerous neutrality in his eyes.

I do not see the third member closely because I look away, down to my son: an instinctive checking of his status, which is fine, his sandwich diminishing further. The third youth has entered and instantly their bantering starts to build: the swearing used as punctuation, this the first endurance, the first fork in the road of action or inaction – for what would happen if I straightened in my chair and turned to them, asking them politely not to swear in front of my son? 'Excuse me. Can you keep the swearing down please. Young ears,' I might say, pointing to the four-year-old opposite. But of course I do not do this, I could not do this because that might bring any focus of theirs onto him, as if right now they do not see him, they hardly see us at all, as if we are dappled and motionless in long grass.

Now they are clustered at the counter. 'Hello,' the girl says. But this greeting is different. I have heard the three previous to this and the inflection has become flatter, the word said more quickly, the lilting welcome absent. Though I cannot see it I imagine her face has changed. And I under-stand that both the girl and I are now being racist, that because of the things we see and hear in these boy-men we are predisposed to caution, prejudice of their character and intent tightening our throats, putting unease in our stom-achs. I want them to behave normally but know that they won't, because I suspect as the girl must that they have brought more into this establishment than a desire for food, that they want more from this encounter, all such encounters.

'Bacon roll,' the white one says.

'Yes,' says the girl. 'Large or small?'

'Large.'

'And you?' she asks quickly.

'Chicken burger.' This is the one with the cloth over his head. He turns away and walks slowly to the middle of the room, his shoulders rolling sufficiently that this movement causes the fabric hanging down from underneath his cap to sway against his face and then away from it. The girl says something, and then: 'Can you get him?'

'Oi,' says the white one, turning away from the counter. 'What?'

'She wants you.'

The youth with the cloth looks to the girl and grunts. She pauses, perhaps considering the meaning of this grunt. 'You want salad?'

'You say excuse me,' he says.

'I did say excuse me. Open your ears, innit.'

He steps back towards the counter, a movement that starts quickly, then slows as he nears it. 'You being rude to me? Why you being rude to me?' His voice is expectant, almost playful, but no one is fooled – not the old lady who looks steadfastly out the window, or the man on the other side looking up from his hands.

'I'm not being rude to you.' But she does not soften her voice.

'Did she say excuse me?'

'I did say excuse me,' she answers firmly. Then the sound changes as she must turn her head to the kitchen behind, the same voice audible but suddenly transformed as it wields different rhythms and harsher consonants: as if in English her speech is polite and businesslike, but in Arabic a dark door can be opened.

There is a sucking of teeth. 'What you say to her?' the youth demands.

'I was giving her your order.'

I had not looked to the kitchen on entrance, had presumed

when the girl came out from behind the counter that it would probably be her father behind it, who ruled the space among knives and hotplates with thick arms and practised movements: perhaps a bald head and a moustache, a Mediterranean increasing in proportion and kindness as the quality of the food became apparent, the friendliness of the girl evident. And I also thought that when the three came in he must have been absent, rummaging in freezers or similar out of view at the back, and his reappearance would temper their behaviour: because suddenly the male proprietor would be present, a man who worked with sharpness all day and had seen many youths, many black youths come into his café and try to cause trouble – white youths too but mostly black – this is what I imagine him saying to his friends: mostly black.

Yes they are mostly black, they come in here and ask for chips and I say why don't you take the one off your shoulder, heh heh heh.

But this man, this fantasy no longer exists and with this realisation I become truly afraid: not for the boy opposite me or myself, not for the man or the old lady or the staff, but a detached fear for the situation itself, which is now on the brink of imbalance, which I can feel start to slide towards real danger when the youth repeats 'What you say to her?' with more urgency, his friends silent and listening, interested in her answer and the outcome of this interrogation, their slight rising away and straightening from where they had leaned on the counter giving them space, a movement recognisable – that would be recognisable even to the old woman as the preparation for further movement.

'I was just giving her your order. She's making it now.'

'You're speaking Arab, innit,' he says flatly.

She does not answer.

He snorts. 'Dat one, she's Muslim and she's cooking pork.'

'She's not Muslim,' says the girl.

'You're speaking Arab though. You're Arab.'

'No, I am not Arab.'

He sucks his teeth and turns away, as if amused. 'So, what, you just learn Arab and speak it, then?'

'I am not Arab,' she says again, and I can hear the blood in her throat, the anger that she tries to suppress – and also the eagerness, the edge of retaliation in her voice that she must know she cannot allow to dominate. I am sitting here watching the oblivious face of my son, him still chewing, my ear burning, my stomach loose and fearful knowing that the girl must not push back and give the youth what he wants: that if she reaches out with threat or riposte it could be the excuse that he and his flankers need to suddenly vault over and burst around the counter, to enter the kitchen and smash at the till and the women, all that metal and heat available to them, that they might use grimly and with focus: the driving of a blade forwards, the repeated beating down of a female head from above.

They entered wanting more than food, but how much more? Will this small argument sate them, or is this the prelude to violence, abrupt yet unsurprising having watched it approach steadily – felt it approaching like a sickness rising and I wonder if the man opposite and the old lady feel it too inside them as I do, or alone I am a coward and a racist, the only one with muscles strangling my insides – perhaps the only one of them to have been mugged, to have been beaten, to have grown up in a town and studied in a different town where you always looked out for the same face: the black face – because the black face is the one that brings you trouble, is the one that mugs and beats and steals and will come looking for you because you are racist. He knows you are racist and the only error he makes in this is not to wonder why you are racist, not to ask why you keep being racist in the face of him mugging you and stabbing you and beating you in gangs.

And right now I do not care that I am racist. I look across at the black youth with the tablecloth or whatever it is draped about his equine face and I can see none of the greatness, none of the tortured history of his race, the suffering and slow emergence from great suffering that exposure to which, be it by book or exhibit, instantly checks all casual slurs, dams whatever racism tries to surge through in me by unfortunate experience, by the unfortunate demographic of crime. But this expression of his blackness I hate as I have always done: the odd clothing and yawing gait, the barely hidden aggression, the tinderbox attitude to everyone as if willing the insult and prejudice which rightly is suspected to exist just beneath the surface of any facade not like their own – because in me at least it has been put there, is being put there now by the fear that sits in my chest, the anger that causes shallow breathing and the clenching of an empty fist.

'So why you speak Arab then if you're not Arab?'

'Are you Arab?' she asks.

'Me?' he says loudly, loud enough that my son turns to look. 'No!'

'So why you wearing a keffiyeh over your head?' her tone is polite, enquiring.

'I'm Islam, innit. Like you should be.'

'You're Islam and you're ordering a bacon sandwich,' she says.

And hearing this lie I think that surely now this will be the trigger, this is the beginning of another London news story and I should just grab my son and leave, for his sake. But I cannot for my own, which means that I must stay — that any moment now I might have to say something to try and placate, or through educated reason ameliorate this youth. Barring this at least remain to be quickest and then clearest with Police Emergency — and certainly not a scuttling out the door having left paper money on the table, because they would love that: they would slap their thighs and bend forwards and back, I would hear their laughter ringing in my ears, a recurring horror with a fresh washing of shame each time and I know this because I have heard it before and still hear it every time I surface from memory, from a median past: my nose blooded and broken, wallet and keys taken, my back pressed against the angle of filthy wall and ground, my face inches from the liquids and stenches there, watching the different pairs of trainers pad away from me, the whiteness of these objects no longer flashing painfully at my head, the sound of their owner's mirth and elation carried away above them.

'I didn't order a bacon sandwich. He did. You know dat. You know I ordered chicken burger.'

Now the white one speaks to her: 'Why you say something like that?' The third adding something that sounds like: 'What you saying, what you saying?'

'Yeah what you saying?' the one with the cloth demands with a sudden jolting half-shout.

The girl does not raise her voice. 'I'm not saying anything.'

'Yes you are, you're saying—'

'I'm not saying anything. You know I'm not saying anything.'

'Why you saying that I would order a bacon sandwich?' he shouts.

'I got confused, innit. It's your mate that ordered the bacon.'

He sucks his teeth. 'Confused? Dat's right. You're confused. You must be if you speak Arab and say you're not Arab.'

'Yeah. Well.'

'And what did you say to her when you spoke Arab?'

'I was giving her your order.'

'Yeah that's what you said but you could have been saying anything. Maybe if I come round to where you are I'll find out what you said to her.'

'Don't come round here,' she says.

'Yeah, why not? What you going to do to stop me?'

There is a deep voice from the man sat opposite, a patience in its tone, as if he merely requests the status of his order:

'Bro', Bro'. Just sit down and wait for your food.'

I see my son still chewing, his eyes watching the figures at the counter, no fear in them but an awareness that something is askew, that there is a novelty or abnormality where he is looking. And though I feel a strangling at my throat, although I fear for the pitch of my voice, I know I must say something, because the three youths have wheeled around in formation to face the seated man, are assessing him, are weighing him in order to gauge their own response.

'Just wait for your food, Bro',' the man repeats.

This is the moment where I should support him, where I should say something like 'Yeah lads, just take it easy and wait for your food,' and then maybe the old lady will finally turn from the window with 'Behave yourselves!' and they will somehow see reason, these youths – and perhaps a streak of awareness will run through them and they will feel the same lick of shame for themselves that they try to put in others, that they are putting in me now: their disease of cowardice spreading to those around them, who do not raise a voice to stop them.

I am pushing my chair back, swallowing, my palms on the table to push me up when the man across says: 'No, don't do that, Bro'.'

I think he is speaking to me: I feel a strange relief at the authority of the order, as if within him there is confidence enough to master the situation singly, that he is telling me to sit down and stay put – but I look up to see that in fact he speaks to the leading youth, who has stepped away from the counter to face him.

'Do what?' the youth barks.

'Don't step towards me.'

There is a sucking of teeth and a shake of the head. 'Yeah, why not, eh? Why not?' But he does not take another step.

'Just don't.'

'You threatening me?' says the youth, the two at his sides stepping forwards so that they stand in an irregular trident, his taller and red-shrouded head above the others, directing the whole formation to point at the seated man.

'You should chill, Bro',' the man replies.

'Yeah why's dat? Uh? Why you think you can tell me what to do?'

The man points out of the window, a slow and calm gesture with a long elegant finger that seems to conduct all our gazes to look where he wishes, towards the sunlit street: shadows like large blocks of darkness reaching out onto the hot road where the traffic and passing buses are suddenly absent, replaced by a mass of men who begin to appear from one side of the window as they cross the road away from us, the traffic I realise not absent but stopped to allow their disordered flow, which has already split so that one stream continues to cross the road while another has doubled back and is heading towards the café, the blue and white of their shirts flashing in and out of the sunlight, the first audible sound of their approach coming through the open door as a volley of jeering and swearing that follows the brief impatient beeping of a car.

'Chill, Bro', the man repeats. 'Cos them lot are gonna come in here and I don't think they're gonna like you very much,' the man says.

The murmur from outside increases as the men near, a sudden clarity of bantering insult and expletive as the first reaches the doorway and is stepping in, a large white male less aware of what is before him than the target he has been joking with behind – until he senses there is something in his way and turns forwards to see the youth with the cloth over his head, a half-obstruction in the corridor running between the tables towards the counter.

'All right, mate?' he asks the youth, sticking his head forwards, close to the face of the other, his mouth seeming to grin but his eyes wide and blank, their bulging unfriendly, mocking.

The youth steps slowly back to let him through, his companions moving similarly so that now the trident is flattened into a line that the fans file past to get to the counter, a minor horde, streaming in to fill the room with noise and the scent of beer, a squeezing and jostling at the counter when they reach it and spread along its length like an expectant herd, domesticated but unruly, the friendly use of elbows marked by a single indignant complaint from one of them, quickly drowned out with more insult and laughter. Some of them have shaven heads and they are all white. Their accents are London but I recognised the flag they hung from the flower-baskets of the pub we passed and know they are not local.

Suddenly from beneath the noise I hear the girl trying to say something. She shouts again and the men quieten enough so that she can be heard. 'Chicken burger!'

There is no movement. Expectancy quietens the rabble further and some begin turning around to see who is going to step forwards and claim this meal, who is taking too long and stopping the process of others being fed.

'Chicken burger!' the girl says again. 'Chicken burger!'

The youth wearing the keffiyeh over his head starts forwards, swooping downwards with the first yawing step so that the cloth presses to the side of his face. Bravely he starts to roll towards the counter, to where with my body leaned forwards and my head turned I can see the fans watching him coming, their eyes travelling up and down his tall frame, some of their mouths opening in amusement, others with open hostility towards this cultural product to which they must feel opposite, the hush deepening to a near silence as the scale of the youth's blackness becomes evident to them: his walk, his clothing, the head leaning back so that the blank stare comes downward, the strangeness of the patterned cloth at the sides of his head.

The quiet hangs like an invitation, a space in which a remark would be effortless – and I find myself waiting for it, leaning forwards, not breathing and feeling a tightness at the back of my head and neck. But when a voice is heard it is just the girl.

'Do you want salad, then?'

'No.'

'They love their chicken,' says a fan, to a ripple of laughter.

And I am shocked to hear this racism, because that is surely what it is. I am shocked to hear it casually in the mouth of another – for though I am racist I know where my racism has come from, I know it is moderated by education, is prevented from being a blanket by the knowledge of some history: of the terror and suffering of bodies packed and dying in the holds of sailing ships – and it is only bad experience that enlivens it, that pulls it upwards as a reaction to use it shield-like in the face of stereotype. That is what I tell myself. That is what I will tell those that I can trust. But these men – these sweating and beery gutter wits at the counter – their version seems, well, on balance, entirely less well thought out.

And I must snort and shake my head in disgust.

Interlude

Life as a Crocodile

It's all about patience, at least that is what I tell myself. I wait because it is easier to do so. There is no point rushing in, worrying, until the time is right. You have to wait for the right time. And more importantly you have to be able to recognise the right time for what it is. Too many have waited in vain, patiently, perhaps even nobly, still waiting, waiting, but getting so tied up in waiting that they cannot see when the right time comes. When it does one must strike. And forcefully. No hesitation, no dithering, no analysis. Such action only comes from a deep understanding of the way things are, and to achieve this one must first have ideas, the patience to test them, and the sense to evaluate their benefit.

We are the scourge of many a river. A hated shape. A symbol of some former time when our kind not only ruled the thick reed-grown red banks of a fat lumbering brown river, but roamed the earth, upright, bipedal – small heads elevated above the beating heat of the reflected sun, free to think, to postulate, to expand their existence beyond the sludge from which all came; the cooling airs a spirit of intoxication: condensed oxygen filling a brain with stations above the highest mountains, leading to disbelief among the lesser, contempt within the aggressor, confusion – and yet a strong sense of un-surprise for crocodiles, who have stayed close to the ground, unwilling to risk such headiness or pretension, remaining wilfully effective in all we do.

Did you know some crocodiles live underground? Even I was taken a half-pace aback by this discovery. And not only underground, but underground in lands that are for the most part desert the year round. What cunning! What adeptness! I am proud of these cousins – they are an inspiration. Not only do they shirk the higher air, rich in bodily nutrients and ideas, but they choose in fact to scorn it: digging burrows as their mothers did, deep holes beneath the horrible earth that are cool enough to allow almost a year-long sleep. And when the rains come and flood these holes, do they panic? Of course not. They simply hold the breath they have held for many months for a few moments more and push them-selves along the tunnels and upwards, up into a land of submerged tree trunks and flailing monkeys, a land where once again they become the kings of their dreams – pinnacle, apex, patient unhurried creatures.

Patience.

But what of me? How do I exist? I do not question my existence because I have no need to. I simply find myself on an engorged waterway, somewhere under the sun. At times basking I lift my head with temptation. I lie on the red banks of this place and raise my snout to the sky, flirting with the air above. It is very rich so that I cannot do it for too long – about a month is my record. With my snout raised I begin to have ideas. I have nothing against ideas but plainly any ideas other than complete necessity are flecked with danger. Perhaps not danger for myself, but danger for the river, and the red banks, and the small things that grow or rustle quietly at night thinking how filled they are with stealth, yet I listen, without interest – or so I tell myself, because I am not uninterested – I love the life of others as I love myself, for without their expression of life, without clear evidence that there is something other than me slinking about this place, how am I ever to feel alive?

Perhaps it is a common misconception that the crocodile's thoughts are idle. But who can ever say that while waiting one's thoughts are idle? And we are always waiting for something – waiting for the sun to penetrate a particular patch of armour, waiting for the distant rumble of hooves to become the pandemonium of a mindless river crossing, waiting for those stupid white birds to get a little closer. If ever there was an incarnation of thoughtlessness those birds are it. In the world at large it is widely believed that we tolerate their senseless pecking in our mouths to remove parasites, or barnacles or something. Well, let me tell you the hidden truth, the crocodile in a burrow, under the desert truth, as it were. Or at least my truth. I must make this clear. My brethren, less prone to snout-raising than I, will willingly let those birds attempt a parasite-removing service. And perhaps they benefit from this – I do not know. However, I have found that by simulating the need for parasite removal one can obtain a meal rather easily. Of course I do this away from the others, hidden by reeds and mangroves and such, lest I be branded a caiman.

Because why should one, of course, armed with superior knowledge, or maybe sense, miss such an opportunity? Do I feel guilty, snapping their small benevolent bones, swallowing their unsuspecting bodies? A little. But relish for the final outcome is a stronger motivator.

One time, let me tell you, a very strange thing happened.

For a period of definitely more than one night, and perhaps even approaching a moon, I discovered on my nightly cruise down the river movement on the bank – but emanating from a strange foul-smelling structure that thankfully, in retrospect, my instincts warned me against. I would see this flicker of movement, and smell the living flesh of meat, not unlike gnu, but it came with a price, with a bad smell, something dangerous; and much as I was tempted, I have eaten too many cleaner birds to realise that things are not always what they seem. The feeling I got was much the same as when, according to nature, I pretend to be a fallen leafed-giant of the shore, floating along, unmoving, but waiting. Patiently. Yes, it was the same feeling, but somehow I realised this peril was directed towards me, and consequently, despite the tantalising gnu-like smell, I desisted, preferring each night to cruise a little closer to the structure, until I was close enough to observe that within it was a definite gnu-like animal, tethered at the neck and making some sort of bleating noise.

Oh, how I felt great desire in that moment! The structure lay half in the river, half out of it, so that I only had to swim in and beach myself a little to partake of the dwarfish gnu, and I did in fact turn my massive bulk silently and snake-like in the water to reach the entrance. But in making this turn some hard part of me struck the side of the structure and a strange thing happened – it made a noise of its own – a deep and resonating bonging the like of which I have never heard since, but sounded to me then like the tolling of fate, perhaps even its end. A crashing sound and the front of the structure was no longer open but enclosed, so that the way to the little gnu-like thing to me was barred: it on the inside, me without; and filled with thoughts of how I might also have been trapped within the structure I thought it best to submerge, and made my way from that place, scuttling along the aquatic rocky riverbed.

And gnus themselves. What simple creatures they are! Every year, the same thing. Every year, we're waiting. We know they have to cross, they think they have to cross. Sometimes I feel like telling them to cross a bit further down, where the opposing bank won't send them tumbling back down into the water like calves, to end up hooves akimbo as prone in the river as uncovered eggs. Why does this feeling grip me? I don't know. Perhaps it is because at that time of year it is just so easy that you wish the playing field was levelled somehow – but of course that is selfish, because I am only reflecting my own desires. I have no desires in the direction of gnus other than they try and make life more interesting instead of the predictable slaughter that happens every year. Which – don't get me wrong – I am not complaining about, easy though it may be. Perhaps if they had webbed feet and their horns were sharper and their skin thicker I would not be saying this.

But to dispel a myth – I feel I must. Not as a traitor to my kind but as one who is more enlightened – the whole of the kingdom of beasts, both large and small, are always marvelling at our ability to grip the poor gnu by the nose and shake him left and right, as if crocodiles were as strong as the Great Others, who were taller than the trees and shook the ground with their footfalls.

So many times we hear of this; someone or another will recount the adulation received for this awesome feat. But the truth is, and I don't know why I am revealing this, and even more so I don't know what this feeling is within me that demands that I reveal this – but the truth is that the gnu's bones are filled with air, making him a very light object to toss.

Either that or I don't know my own strength.

Such is life as a crocodile.

Part 2

Finally My Ambulance

This is it, this is my war.

Now I have arrived. I am no longer a boy sat in a swinging chair on the porch, looking up and out over the pure green lawn of the garden, my eyes filling with brightness as beyond it the sudden yellow rising of a stubble crop shines beneath the late sun: a scene of peace and home and happiness – and the weight in my hands, the book I looked up from seemingly the fulcrum of this contentment, container as it was of the finest bond between men, the drama and loss of battle, the terrible war within it sucking me inwards so that every look up at the shorn field beyond is like a minor ecstasy, a relief produced in the tearing away from the greatness spread across its pages, to be struck with the equivalent grandeur of nature.

But what a seed to have stuck in one's chest: a mixed kernel of longing and doubt, roaming the limits of my neat New England town and sometimes along the roads beyond it, a craving for risk and impact to emerge somehow from between the towering trees on either side, to leap over the yellow lines on the asphalt and part me from the content-ment that I could not help feeling, that was growing as my simple adolescent worries were knocked down like bowling pins. Equally, as they fell the chance to strike them all was removed and then further diminished – a worrying absence of pain, of mild suffering that I knew must exist within me if I were to emulate what I had read in those great books – for what may be produced in happiness except kempt gardens, or perhaps a polished and glinting automobile: the perfect house frontage with which in this town I am surrounded? Where would my big feeling come from?

And so I began to buy newspapers, and would listen to the radio, hearing of distant rumblings in Europe, a part of me dreading the machinations that unseen were already grinding bodies to a pulp, but another part of me excited by it, willing the success of Germany, knowing well the rich soil that this was giving the seed near my heart. The wind of opinion in our own nation blew this tender shoot one way and another so that at times I feared for it, at others I wanted it destroyed and the war to remain European – but never this for long – and when it became clear that we would join, I joined also, and left my town. And the action of this: the movement of the bus and of the buildings sliding past was a perfect taste of bittersweet.

A similar movement around me now, except that I am at the prow of the machine and driving, and it is not buildings sliding past but the endless green corridor of French hedgerow, higher on both sides than my vehicle, the sky above grey and the occasional tree still dripping as I rumble under it, but the air warm and for a moment unfilled with the sounds of combat, as if I am passing through the war in a tunnel and will be born the other side. But then another distant thump is heard, the first of which sensed just days ago was a terrifying blow, a noise that shook me all the way to the marrow of my bones – but which through repetition has become only worrying, enriching.

Now, the sound does not jerk my hands at the wheel even if it is close, even if it is close enough that other sounds can be heard straight after it: the hail-like patter of stones and earth, falling from different heights to batter the foliage around me and the top of the ambulance: this ambulance I pilot, my ambulance, its sturdy thick wheels gripping the road's varying surfaces, the luxury of their serrated rubber an initial annoyance upon first discovery, quickly becoming an advantage when I realised that with them I would feel the ground below me, I would not slide over it on thin carriage spindles, to let an isthmus slip beneath.

I am alone and between efforts of navigation can think, can let my mind wander, the compartment behind me empty of the wounded, the seat beside me also empty so that I can fully witness this driving of an ambulance. But beside me is a presence, as if the vacant seat with the worn impression of back and buttock is a negative, an inversion of a thought: that I am not alone, that even though I have my own war I am for ever stalked by those who have had theirs before me.

This is a worry that is forgotten when I see something up ahead: an opening in the hedgerow, a darkness in the green wall that causes my foot to lift from the throttle, the engine and exhaust calming to their lowest revolutions, the exterior sounds that were suppressed by them gradually emerging as very distant thumps and crackling gunfire – and then the droning of an aeroplane heard high and thin as the ambulance rolls to a halt near this gap. And looking down towards it I know it can no longer be where the hedging has merely died or been blasted away, but is what I feared: a road. Not even a small road, no more than a track or pathway that might escape survey, but a wide and good-surfaced road, the grey of it lying like a tongue to meld with the one I am on, to form a junction – and with this I sense that my heart has become noticeable, a new thudding at my ears among the other sounds as I look down at the map, the mass of lines and intersections a sudden intense chaos, the paper ruffled by the breath that has begun to pant down at it.

My finger is fat and feels clumsy, tracing along the tiny lines, the images of turnings and landmarks recalled as the nail passes over them: the places I think I have just been, an attempt to affirm where I am, where I have become lost.

I am lost.

My breathing that tries to heave quicker than I will let it tells me this more than the road that should not be there, as do the faint beginnings of dread, of panic that I try to press down on by the study of map and forefinger. I lean towards the windshield, looking up to the sky for the sun but there is only a solid grey covering, no hint of brightness through it, and when I hear a nearby thundering, the thud of explosions following one another, it sounds to me as if they are approaching: like the footsteps of a giant headed straight for me, towards my vehicle that has been sat here for more than a minute and I think that perhaps there is a German somewhere, his face extended with a pair of binoculars, a beautiful pair beautifully made that are sheathed in leather and that I can feel the weight of in my hands even as I put the ambulance in gear and depress the throttle, the engine spluttering and coughing unhealthily, the wheels gripping to lurch forwards away from the gaze of this aristocrat German with his hunting binoculars, whose favourite sport in the absence of game must be to pick off lone vehicles with his crew: his willing gunmen.

I lock my eyes to the grey of the road, a thin strip walled in by green, an easy enough task to steer the ambulance down it at speed until the straightness of it turns into a bend, a gentle curve that I follow with light and accurate steering, but which suddenly twists the other way blindly so that I must lift my foot and stamp it on the brake, the wheels below locking to make a sliding sound on the wet asphalt, the one in my hands trying to twist so that I must grip it and turn it the opposite way as I feel the back end of the vehicle start to move around and come forwards, the whole thing sliding diagonally down the road: a moment that seems to last a hundred pounding heartbeats before it comes to rest and I can breathe – this time an uninhibited panting, the hotness of it all over my hands like liquid.

Suddenly I begin to laugh. The engine has stalled and the war is quiet enough so that I can hear this noise very clearly and loudly: the elation of minor survival and its torrent of relief flowing through me perpetuating this laughter until I can feel tears at my eyes and am addicted to the sound of it – the sound of my own making – until inexplicably it stops and I realise I am stalled, and with a sudden movement of my hand reach forwards to start the engine. It starts quickly and I nudge the ambulance's broad snout further into the hedgerow, the front wheel lumbering up and over the small verge at the hedge's base, the hedge itself scraping at the windshield until with a swaying drop we are back on the road and I am about to accelerate – except that not far ahead something has sprouted up in the middle of the grey strip of asphalt: a single figure, a soldier, and I think with more relief that this guy will know the way, he will tell me where I am and may even need a lift somewhere: someone who I can share the cab with and tell of my recent near miss, who may in fact have seen how close I came to wreckage.

But in the same instant I also wonder what is wrong with his helmet. Secretly I know what is wrong with his helmet: that he is not an American with a different helmet – yet I am unprepared to admit that he is a German pointing a weapon at me until two other figures seem to leap straight out of the green wall of hedge itself, their appearance very different from the Army I have been surrounded with, their boxy headgear and the spikes of their weaponry a familiar but deformed silhouette, the slenderer shape of their uniforms an instant and vital difference to the one I wear myself.

The engine is rumbling, its vibration felt in my hands, the gunfire distant and sporadic, as too is the thump of artillery, these things sensed clearly while I stare out through the windshield at the three soldiers, who are close enough that their faces have vague features, are not just flesh-coloured circles below their helmets. They stand in a line across the road, all three with their legs slightly apart, their weapons pointing at me and the one to the left holding something large and heavy: something that looks like it could be quickly mounted on the ground with its soldier behind it, that if fired would cut me and the metal ambulance in two – and it is this sight, even more than the fear that has turned my body to a hot and cold stone clutching at the steering wheel, that stops me from reaching down and searching for reverse gear, from attempting a lobster-like escape in the direction I have come. The road is not wide enough to turn; there is no question of ploughing straight ahead, no guarantee that my ambulance would penetrate the walls if I tried to burst through – and combined these things do not panic me, but have a calming effect, because they dampen the need for action: they tell me I am trapped and an attempt at escape would be suicidal, and though I am still afraid and have a deep dread forming as if the pool of a leak for these soldiers and their weapons, there is a distinct part of me that is alive, that is vibrant and prepared to record what occurs, its receptivity un-dulled by any worries of impropriety or cowardice – for what can a man do from within his ambulance, which is not a tank, when suddenly faced with the enemy?

The soldiers ahead seem to know this too, perhaps knew it the instant they sprung out onto the road and are enjoying this knowledge in the easy way they stand, the one at their centre stepping forwards and raising his hand and calling out something that might be a salute – and for an instant I wonder if they have mistaken me for one of their own, if here might be the opening that a braver man would take to plunge the ambulance into gear and attempt a manoeuvre.

But even as the three of them begin towards me, slowly and in formation, their footsteps an audible pacing and their weapons clearly pointed at me – I become confused as to whether that flicker of escape should cause me regret. Because I realise I must be captured – what I am experiencing is the prelude to being captured and their approach means only that: their leader's shout to me not a hail but a halt, and within a week of starting this war my ambulance and I will be parted, I will be imprisoned, forced to look outwards at the world through the grid of fencing and wire, while behind within the compound we will suffer hardship, that may or may not be truly hard, cosseted by solidarity, perhaps by committees and their plans.

They are close enough now that a pair of bright blue eyes is striking out from the soldier in the middle. His face is pale, almost white, tufts of very light blond hair sprouting from beneath his helmet, and a darker reddish stubble around his mouth and cheeks. I raise my hands from the wheel, lifting my arms so that my empty palms will be pale and visible through the glass – and it is a horrible feeling to do this, making me swallow at nothing, a nakedness as I feel the power of the ambulance suddenly sliding away in this gesture, this surrender that brings a smile to the soldier holding the big weapon, who is short but broad and comfortable as he walks with the heavy metal in his hands, his face dark, dirt-smeared and creased, a scar its lightest point: a long sliver of white flesh down one cheek that he seems aware of as he grins, a flaunting as if to temporarily distract you from his eyes: deep-set, not bright but eager – and I think that these eyes have clearly been the mirrors of many French and Polish slain, yet have remained untarnished, may in fact be brighter for it.

And I am watching this man, a separate fear devoted to him and quickly growing when I hear the leader's voice: an 'Aus!' that is not shouted but called firmly, repeated when I look his way, a sideways motion of both his weapon and head that I obey, slowly lowering my hand to the door, getting it open and climbing out. I stand on the road next to the vehicle, facing the three who are a few feet away and have stopped, the helmets atop their heads massively inescapable. The leader says something quietly to the other two who begin towards me, the smaller figure with the scar holding my gaze so that the third is almost invisible, is just a dark shape in the same uniform – but their combined smell strong and complex as they near, of sweat and unwashed human, of the oils and chemicals of weaponry. Their demeanour is almost casual: I am afraid but do not feel as if I am about to be executed, more as if I am guilty of a motoring offence, and when I am asked through gesture to step away from the vehicle I do so without hesitation, stepping from the asphalt onto the grass that curves and lifts me upwards, watching with my hands raised as the two helmets separate and like hungry insects inspect the cab and the rear compartment. The engine is still running, to give a droning accompaniment to this movement.

I turn to the leader when I hear him walking towards me, the small bore of his gun pointing at my chest, the horrible threat of it slowly raking down my stomach and groin, sinking lower with each step until he is standing very close to me and were he to shoot, he would shoot me in the feet.

'American?' he says, his eyes on mine, the intensity of their blueness making them seem very close, as if we are almost face-to-face. His skin is fair and clean below the rim of his helmet.

'Yes.'

'Where are you from?' he says, his English accented but clear.

'Boston,' I say, although I am not from Boston.

'Ah, New England!' he says loudly, and I see the scarred soldier, who has begun rummaging in the cab of the vehicle, lift his head and look out to us, his body invisible so that with the carapace of his helmet he has become a beetle with small eyes hovering in the dark behind the glass, that would perhaps bounce against it angrily were the name of the enemy mentioned again. The third soldier has lost interest in the search and is ambling over to where I stand with the leader, and I turn to him and see him closely for the first time: a young boy with a very thin neck, his eyes large and brown and his face dark, tanned by race more than sun in the places visible beneath the dirt. The leader looks to him and the boy shakes his head. The blue eyes are turned to me again.

'You have cigarettes on you?'

'I don't smoke.'

'A shame,' he replies, and I sense that he enjoyed saying the phrase, that there may have been pride in its use. He looks to the ambulance. 'You can put your hands down.'

He is still not looking at me when he says this, and so I search the boy for confirmation, who looks at me levelly, his weapon pointing at my chest but no clear malice or threat coming from him. I lower my hands, an action that starts with a palpable slowness, but quickens with them suddenly hurrying to a safety at my sides. Then I put them in my pockets, as if to holster the only weapons I have. This done, there is the feeling that I should speak, that I should say something to sustain the lack of aggression between us, which might be broken now as the scarred soldier climbs out of the cab and I see that he is holding my map, a small grin revealing darkened teeth as he approaches, a dislocation of perception when a distant but thundering explosion muffles his footsteps to then dissipate and leave him still walking silently, his boots making not even the smallest sound on the hard surface.

'What is your name?' the leader asks.

'Richard,' I tell him, thinking I will do my best, I will make him work.

Except that he seems satisfied: he merely mouths the name silently and then turns to me, an intensity in his face as if he is thinking, or about to ask a profound question – and suddenly I can imagine quite happily that there is a depth beyond his pale face, that he is far from mindless, and this both interests and comforts me: because now, more than summary execution there is the possibility of fraternity as they take me back deeper into their lines, of us walking together and conversing, perhaps the accidental contact of shoulder as we do so, too preoccupied with our intelligent exchanges and the magnanimity of the occasion to worry about accurate footwork, coming together and parting, both knowing the symbolism of this touch, feeling it most keenly at the moment where I am handed over, to be swallowed up in their barbed stockade.

'I am Stefan,' he says.

'Stefan,' I repeat.

'No. Sven. Sven.'

'Sven?'

'Yes, Sven.'

'What are you, Swedish?'

'Danish,' he says with a slight smile.

'What are you doing in that helmet?' I say, pointing above his head.

'Hmm. It's complicated.' He looks down and nods. 'Complicated. He's French,' he says, an arm briefly coming out in the direction of the scarred solider who has joined us and is stinking potently at my side, the map held slackly in his free hand. 'And he is Romania.' This makes the boy nod. I wonder if this is a joke, a slight toying with me, their freshly captured enemy – but it does not feel to be a cruel product of the Dane's mind – I can tell by looking to each of their faces in turn that they are simply trying to share this fact with me, a moment only snapped apart by the voice of Frenchie when he lifts my map to the leader and says something.

'You are lost,' Sven says.

'Yes.'

'And you are a medic.'

'Driver,' I reply. 'Ambulance driver.'

'Ah. And you don't have any cigarettes?'

I shake my head.

Sven takes the map from Frenchie, looks down at it and then moves around so that he is at my side. His finger is long and pale and I must look down to it, watching the almost clean nail as it traces along one of the myriad roads, as if it too is lost and searching. Then I feel his face turning towards me; I am uncomfortable and in part threatened by its proximity but by some rule must respond in kind, so that our heads are in the position of conspiracy, of sharing a secret.

'Where do you think you are?' he says carefully.

I look down to the map, my head suddenly becoming hot and my eyes blinking, unsure as to his intent in asking this, whether there may be some danger lurking for me within a wrong answer. I risk a flashing look up at the scarred soldier, who in that instant does not look French at all – looks far from French and is watching me with the same slight grin so that his face seems to be only creases of flesh, dark teeth and the white scar. The thought occurs to me that they might gun me down while I stand here next to their leader – this their game or a development of it: to take turns standing close to the doomed man while the other opens up at point blank range, silently daring each other to stand closer, to touch the death that is usually lost from them far away at the end of a bullet's path.

'Here,' I tell him, and point and hold my breath.

'Almost,' he replies, and now his pale finger is close to mine. 'You are here. You think you were there because you are here. You see?'

I start to feel it then: an excitement in the small of my back and around my shoulders: a terrible and wonderful pulsing feeling of joy that I try to strangle for fear that I am still deceived, am misguided by the vagaries of an imminent death. I turn to look at Sven and his mouth, which is small and thin-lipped among his stubble, waiting for its next utterance with childish agony until finally he gives me the gift that I still cannot quite believe when he says, 'You must go this way, and then turn here and' – his finger is slowly moving over the map and then he angles his head as it starts to go upwards quickly – 'then keep going and you will return to your lines.'

We have straightened and when he offers it, I take the map from him. I do not want to look up for fear of smiling, and of finding that their expressions are twisted sardonically and that they look to me as the cat does the mouse – but I know I must, and when I do, the first I look to is Frenchie, and then quickly to the Romanian and Sven who is still close by my side: three pairs of eyes very different but together in their neutrality towards me, a slight satisfaction in the blues of Sven, a seriousness in the browns of the Romanian as if the release of me twists him in some way, makes him want more of the thing we are doing. And even the one they say is French – although he still looks like he would kill me in an instant, it also seems as if he is happy to stay his finger, to not interrupt the silence between us with the sudden leaping violence of his weapon.

Then the sound of the vehicle's engine intrudes, a low and regular murmuring occasionally bracketed by a thump, or the cackle of smaller arms. An urge to be inside the ambulance allows me to step forwards through Frenchie and the Romanian, a nervousness trying to mix with the elation that is making my steps feel like they are not on grass and asphalt but cloud. And yet the doubt that I might still be shot when I have my hand on the door is at its strongest in the action of lifting my hand to the door, quickly gone when I look back to the soldiers and see that their weapons have not moved, that they have only turned slightly to watch me go. Sven is in their middle and slightly behind the other two, his face with a keen intentness: unsmiling but not unpleasant – and I think that his intelligence is trying to understand fully what is taking place, or perhaps looks for some sign from me, a memento of the event, but I have nothing to give except a half-wave, a slight salute as I climb up into the cab. I put the thing in gear and start rumbling forwards, the soldiers stepping back off the grey road and onto the green of the verge to make a line along it. I am pulling level with them when Sven raises his hand and instinctively I brake and lean out of the open window towards him, an action practised many hundreds of times and as automatic to me as changing gear, but that I do now not to my own Army but to the enemy, with hope that one of them has stopped me to impart a final wisdom.

'Don't worry about the gun,' he says, pointing up the road. I look up along the hedgerow but can see nothing. 'It's big, but empty.'

I am not sure what he means. 'Okay,' I say.

It is his turn to offer the half-wave, and without looking to the other two I put the ambulance in gear again and start down the road, accelerating quickly, thinking on what he meant about the gun and then the road widens a bit and at its edge, obscured by hedge and tree there is suddenly the monstrous shape of a large artillery piece sliding past, its huge bore angled upwards but covered with netting, the whole thing hidden by the smoothing mess of netting and camouflage and standing next to it another soldier, the last thing I see as I pass being this man standing there with his hands on his hips, the alien helmet perched upon his large and bright face, the eyes of him widened massively and made only of white until I realise he is crossing them, and at the same time showing his teeth in a huge and exaggerated grimace.

Then this vision has passed and I am only looking ahead and steering carefully, pressing the ambulance forwards as fast as I dare, slowing briefly to check the map and the directions given to me. But I can feel their accuracy and know with a low and wide confidence that they will take me back to the safety of where I should be. And when I have made the turning suggested I find the road has all the characteristics it should, my nervousness ending fully to be replaced with a jubilation that makes me whoop and bang at the steering wheel and shake my head, me driving my ambulance and savouring fully what has just happened: my brush with the enemy, every word and sight a thing to be recorded – even the bizarre physical insult of the last soldier standing by the fieldpiece: even that of great import, of an askew but genuine nobility.

These thoughts and others are the indulgences I let my mind consume along the narrow road, walled in by green and unable to see out, only ahead, this tunnel allowing memory to run up and down it freely as I drive along its straights and bends, the speed of the ambulance lessening as I approach where my Army must be, the signs of it suddenly everywhere: no checkpoint passed through to tell me a general's line has been crossed but merely the appearance of American helmets like mushrooms among the green, as if they were always present but not seen because they were not looked for. Not only them but their machinery begins to emerge in the clearings and along the wider roads, these squeezing encounters past them over verge and against hedge becoming more frequent until I can fully sense the beast of invasion that has alighted massively on this land: its smells, its noises, and the voices of its soldiers a sudden power, a sudden pride and cause of worry in my chest.

Deep within this swarm of familiar uniform and accent, I reach a point when my foot is depressing the brake, bringing the ambulance to a gentle halt among high stacks of dull green crates marked with red crosses on white, a man stood in the path of my vehicle, the sight of whom creates a new fantasy despite my elation: of shifting my foot from the brake back to the throttle and smashing his small, boy-faced, jug-eared earnest little being into the mountain of supplies behind him.

'Norm,' I say, leaning out of the window.

'We gotta go back!' he says, his hands on his hips, his voice high and nasal: a fresh surprise in its capacity to be irritating. And upon hearing it, experiencing again the sounds he is capable of making and having these sounds married to the image of him standing there, I know that I cannot tell him of the great experience I have just had, and that to do so would sully it, would allow it to be digested by whatever miasmic fluids he pours on it through the stupidity of his character – and it angers me that he is the first I should come across, and that the delivery of my event to another will have to be delayed.

'What do you mean, we gotta go back?'

'I mean what I mean: we gotta go back.' He has walked round from the front of the ambulance to stand near the window out of which I lean. 'Move over and let me drive.'

'No.'

'Come on, Dick, move over and let me drive for once, you bastard.'

'I'm the driver, you piece of shit, so you're not driving.'

'I'm a driver too!' he whines.

'Why have we gotta go back? I just got here. Have you got any smokes?'

'Smokes?' he asks me, his eyebrows rising.

'Yeah, smokes, you piece of shit. You got any? There's crates of them around here. Get me a carton and maybe I'll let you drive.'

An idea seems to pass across Norm's face: a slight widening of the eyes and an almost imperceptible nod of his head before he says, 'Get them yourself, you bastard.'

I look down at him, feeling a prickling anger in my shoulders and the sides of my head, my hands gripping the wheel firmly so that they do not fly out and grab at his face as I would like. For I would love to get him now by the cheeks and ears and grip hard and shake his head until something fell out. There is a rule between us, of unknown birth, or authority, but that exists and means that even though I am the driver, if I were to leave my seat here in the cabin in pursuit of cigarettes, he would be entitled to drive us back. It is not that he has me at an advantage that causes my anger, because he does not, but instead what enrages me is the insult implied in his belief that he could dislodge me with such a simple ploy.

'Norm, you really are a thick piece of shit, aren't you?'

'Fug you!' his face is contorted with aggression, so that he looks like a little boy about to start a fight. So I reach out with a long arm and go to pat him on the head saying, 'Easy now, easy,' but he bats this away with a swipe of his arm.

'Come on, Norm,' I tell him, softening. 'We gotta go back. I swear, go get me a carton and I'll let you drive.'

I watch with disgust as the anger on his face passes through indecision and begins to turn to hope – a hope I often see in him: that perhaps we might after all be the best of comrades, that our banter is merely the top layer of a strong bond, the rippling surface of deep water and not the signs of a thick and personal dislike between us. Or at least my dislike of him: a loathing patrolling this same water that he hopes for, like a reptile. And perhaps as I watch him turn and plod away from the ambulance, towards an aisle made by the high-stacked crates – maybe there is a glimmer of sympathy for him, a sudden lifting of the annoyance he causes, made possible by the rear of his head, the small area of his exposed back.

Then he has reappeared and I see a smugness in his expression as he walks over, as if what he holds pressed against his waist is the trophy of some victory that he cannot help smiling at, and not just two cartons of cigarettes gripped tightly, while his other arm swings busily out at his side.

'Okay, move over, you big bastard,' he says on reaching the cabin.

'Give me the smokes,' I reply.

'Ha. Move over and then I'll give you the smokes.'

My hands are in my lap. I lift them and put them on the wheel. Then I look to Norm, at his big face in its fleshy parenthesis of ears, and watch as the realisation crosses this clean and rubbery landscape that I am not going to move over.

'You swore!'

'I swear all the time. Now shut up and get in.'

With that said I bring us to the critical junction of this round of the game that plays out between us, for I have pushed him in the past and he has snapped, and now I wait to see whether he will stomp around the front of the vehicle with what he holds, or whether he will throw them away into the pile of crates, and then get in the cab. But I know that to obtain them he must have asked a favour of someone, and that very asking of whomsoever he knows means that (whether I want them or not) they are already valuable to him – and further, to discard the cigarettes so flagrantly would be a waste and a provocation – perhaps a serious threat to the illusion he guards that we really are the best of comrades, the fear of which I look for in his face, imagining the thoughts feebly crossing to and fro behind his eyes, trying to weigh gain against risk.

'You're a bastard. Do you know that, you bastard?' But he is saying this while walking around the ambulance's nose, so that his voice fades and only returns when the door is open and he is climbing into the cab. 'You're a fuggin bastard.'

'Light a couple of those smokes,' I say.

He stares at me dumbly, his mouth almost downturned at the sides – but to this I respond by turning away from his sadness and beginning the manoeuvre that will take us out of the depot, a task I complete quickly and without bumping anything or over-revving the engine as he would, swinging the big vehicle back and around and through stacks of crates with an ease that I know he admires, that he cannot help admire and for which he rewards me with a lit cigarette held out near to my face, which I take when we can begin in a forwards gear.

'How come we gotta go all the way back?' I ask him through a cloud of smoke, steering slowly around the soldiers, who either hear the engine and hop up onto the verge or stubbornly keep to the road.

'I don't know. He just came in and said we both gotta go back. Maybe somebody got hit.' I flash him a look, his disappointment gone and in its stead the thrill of this phrase: the first time that either of us has been able to use it with sincerity – and as if in complement to this achievement the sight of his head is then framed for me by the deep and loud rumbling patter of artillery: a warning from the nearby front, a message that the war is still present and gnashing around us.

'Who got hit? Nobody got hit.'

The soldiers have started to thin out and the road is clearing: whole stretches opening out where I can press the throttle and hurtle the ambulance forwards, its engine a loud and steady drone to keep Norm quiet and us going fast enough to make him grip the edge of where he sits. We stop briefly to check the map at an intersection, Norm leaning against me and pawing at the paper, his breath warm and smelling of food, his fingers and nails ugly and chewed, their movement a pantomime and thus an extreme annoyance to me because I know he has no idea where we are or where we should be on the map, and yet every time he will do this: he will lean against me and try to navigate through bluster and admittedly adept guesswork, drawing on obscure elements or morsels of knowledge to give the impression, at least to the unenlightened, that he is a good map man.

'Get off me, Norm. I know where we are.'

We start up again, and after squeezing past a vehicle and some last remaining soldiers, plunge into the isolation of hedgerow, that now with the seat filled beside me – and filled with Norm – is no longer a meditative path, but a thin passage with high and close sides that seems unending. A decision was made in me earlier, perhaps before or just after asking Norm for the cigarettes, and it is a choice that will be tested at the next break in the green walls around us: where the hedge will end to allow another road to enter. My elation was lost upon seeing Norm, as if his mere presence was enough to wipe out all that had been gained, but I find myself determined not to let him spoil the magnitude of this day, and instead, I will in fact increase it through the generosity I am about to show him: the experience I am about to provide him with. I risk a quick look down to the cartons between us, their oblong forms beautifully bright and crisp in the dull cabin, the only imperfection where Norm's fingers have burrowed in and ripped the paper to extract a packet – and seeing them there I am further resolved – so that when we come to the next junction I make a turning instead of heading straight, the vehicle suddenly rumbling down what seems a darker road, the thumps and soft cracklings in the air different to my ears, a change I know is figment, but which brings the slightest slicing to my grip of the wheel.

'Whoa whoa whoa!' Norm says.

'What?'

'Dick, you're going the wrong way!' His conviction is surprising.

'Oh yeah? How do you know?' I ask. 'It's a shortcut.'

'What the fug shortcut is this if we're heading straight for the fuggin front?' he spits.

'This is the way I came, asshole. You don't even know where we are,' but I am worried that he does.

'Yes I damn do. You just turned off the route! They've been saying to me back there 'when you're going don't turn right, when you're going back don't turn left' – we just did a big goddamn fuggin left so stop the fuggin truck.'

'Okay, Norm,' I say, my foot still pressing the throttle.

'Maybe this isn't the main route.' I pause. 'But I want to show you something,' and I say this with warmth and mystery, a dull bait that may or may not hook him, and which I augment with a quick look and perhaps the hint of a smile. He does not say anything instantly. So I risk: 'You want to see some Germans?'

He thinks about this for a further moment. 'No goddamn I don't.'

'You can't go the whole war without seeing some Germans.'

'I'm gonna see plenty of 'em,' he says.

'Sure, sure,' I answer quickly, 'but how about some live ones?'

'Live?' he says. 'As in ah-live?' And the way his voice tails off I know that the lure, the glinting prospect must be working away in his small mind: the double opportunity not only for an adventure, but an adventure with me, his good comrade, which he will be able to regurgitate to his buddies over food or a smoke and not have them turn away from him in disgust – for if faced with the doubt of his listeners he will be able to point over his shoulder with his thumb, past his huge ear to where I will probably be standing and say: Dick was there; go ask him if you don't believe me; he was there too.

A quick look across to him and I can tell there is still some uncertainty – but this is fine for the sake of the plan: just as long as we are not reduced to wrestling over the steering wheel it is fine, and I keep him talking by answering his questions about who the Germans are with requests for him to be patient, or assurances that he will see – he will see – deflecting him thus and sensing his growing enjoyment of the bond we are making, the earnestness he is feeling palpable so that he hardly notices another turning towards the front, or the length we travel down this road until I am easing off the throttle and applying the brake, leaning forwards and peering through the windshield, fairly certain I am recognising recently seen aspects of tree and hedge.

'You know I shouldn't even be here, I should be in the Pacific . . .' Norm is saying happily as we come to a near halt, crawling along no faster than a walk.

'Shut up, Norm, and hold on.' With that I pull over to the left, to the very edge of the tarmac, and press the throttle, the outside wheels climbing up the grass verge, tilting the ambulance sideways and me easing it up the small slope until the hedge is scraping my door. Then I turn the wheel all the way the other way so that the vehicle lunges down to cut across the road, bumping up the verge on the other side, stopping only when the hood is sunk in hedge.

'Fug,' says Norm, his arms suddenly moving: a panicked search for fresh handholds.

With a little complaint and wrenching of the gearstick I find reverse and we are going backwards across the road, turning the wheel quickly so that my hands are slapping at it until it locks, reversing to continue the rough three-pointer until it is the rear wheels that are going up the verge, and the road – the road down which we came is coming into view through the windshield.

'Okay,' I say, picking up both cartons. Then I return the opened one to the space between us, making for the door with the one intact.

'What are you doing?' Norm asks, his voice tight.

'Watch,' I tell him, hoping my voice is not nervous like

his, my heart suddenly beating quickly and other warnings in my mind telling me that what I am about to do is reckless: the same feeling an echo of which I suddenly remember as being a boy having climbed high in a tree back home, sick with fear, but also the determination to leap and catch hold of the branch on the tree next to me, the outcome a mixture of uncertainty and hope until the bough was gripped in both hands and I knew I had not fallen. A brief but pure joy followed then: the reward for transgressing the sensible – and perhaps it is the same line I foolishly wish to cross right now and the same reward, at base, which I seek. But this is a minor hesitation, and I turn away from Norm, who was only half-seen during this reverie, my hand working to open the door, pushing it open slowly and climbing out to let it shut incompletely as I come to stand on the road, facing the rear of the ambulance.

I walk along the side of the vehicle, its dull green flank changing brightly at the side of my eye to the huge red cross on white and then back to green again, until I am at its end and must step away from it and into the open grey of the road: a sudden immense and threatening expanse, nothing visible in the hedgerow on either side, no movement or sign and yet I am fairly sure that if I were to run for a few seconds I would be able to see the fieldpiece – and thus Sven and his band must be nearby, guarding their empty weapon.

A sound startles me: a crunching of metal that could be anything before I realise it is just Norm getting out and slamming his door. 'Stay there,' I hiss. And spurred by fear I edge forwards away from the ambulance, holding my hands up high but not too high, the height I believe to be of peace but not surrender, the carton a white rectangle in one of them until I have taken a fair few paces along the road, the point where my nerve will fail me fast approaching, and just before this point is reached I crouch down slowly to deposit the cigarettes, leaving them in an upright position, a small white obelisk hastily built and that I retreat from backwards with my hands raised again.

Norm is standing at the end of the vehicle, his brow furrowed and the rest of his big face sporting a quizzical and stupid look – and with a brief flare of annoyance I realise that here before me is the face of someone witnessing something they do not fully understand.

'What the fug Dick are you doing?' he says.

'Let's get in,' I tell him, skipping quickly to the driver's door and climbing up.

Norm joins me in the cabin. 'Dick?'

I ignore him, concentrating on the pedals and the stick to get the thing in gear and accelerate, the ambulance lurching forwards to put a rough fifty yards between us and the offering. Then, hoping I have not gone too far, but have gone far enough I brake back down to a halt. There is an awareness in me that I should keep driving, that the risk already taken has been high – but suppressing this reasoning is the desire to let Norm see fully what is happening, not to impress him, but to depress him further into the ground, to stamp on him finally so that in his brighter moments he will not be tempted to assume supremacy between us as he sometimes does, but instead will remember what I produced and put before him: a thing of ultimate largesse and from which I hope he may never recover.

'Dick?'

'Let's see what we can see,' I say hopefully, and reach for

the door with one hand, pointing across at his own door with the other. Then I am climbing back down onto the road, hearing Norm doing the same on his side, both doors closed with near simultaneous clanks and then our heads visible to each other across the cabin through their windows: a quick look shared that is almost meaningful, before together we turn to look down the road to the small white carton sitting very tiny in its centre.

And then, like wildlife, one of them emerges: the lean shape and the odd helmet coming through the hedgerow, which even at this distance is clear and alien.

'Jesus fug a German!'

We watch as the figure creeps out onto the road towards the carton, doubled over in the combat position, the stutter of nearby small-arms fire that we can hear perhaps the thing that is making him nervous – and I find that watching him move like this, beyond wondering which one of them he is, I worry that he will merely scurry back with the cigarettes, that there will be no acknowledgement, no great sealing of the value of these events in my and perhaps Norm's mind for ever. But I am not disappointed, because when he gets over to the cigarettes he picks them up, and straightening a little waves them above his head: a clear sign in our direction and one that I respond to with a lifting of my own hand, which prompts a final upwards twitch of the white box before he turns and moves quickly off the road.

I turn to Norm. His face is passive. I know that my own is beaming but I do not care if he sees this, because I am flushed with belief, with the happiness that I am on the road: the true path along which I can begin building the great pillars of my own experience. And here is the first one: a gleaming giant of munificence in just the first few days of the war – and with the enemy – while the huge resource of wounded that I will have to pilot to and fro lies almost completely untapped: the vast blood-greased hand-clutching humanity of it all still yet to come.

The soldier has returned to the road, a thing I see while climbing back up to the ambulance, which makes me stop half in the air to watch as this soldier runs across and dives into the opposite hedgerow, others trying to follow him but falling in the road, the sound of gunfire no longer a distant background crackling but suddenly attached to these events, and shouts coming that might be German but become without doubt American when the first GI appears, his legs moving quickly below his normal helmet, he the first of a squad bursting out onto the road and firing their rifles at the corpses, or near-corpses, so that none of them except the first over complete the crossing from hedge to hedge.

'You see that?' says Norm from the other side of the ambulance. 'You see that? That's our boys coming through. Fug yeah! Our boys.'

I do see it and am transfixed: am frozen in my perched position as the squad increases in number on the road: moving low around the corpses, their heads turning to look about them, quick movements hungry for awareness so that they must see us as clearly as we see them – and suddenly it occurs to me that we should wave or make contact somehow before they mistakenly fire on us.

'Wave, Norm! Wave!'

'Hey! Well done there boys!' he shrieks, his voice suddenly high and girlish.

But they do not respond, and I cannot see even one of

them look up, or turn in our direction. Perhaps they saw us earlier, had confirmed us as merely a red-cross-emblazoned ambulance before beginning their attack, and ignore us now because they have no wounded; have no use in recognising us non-fighting men. The uncertainty is unsettling, is more worrying than if a pair of them had split from the squad and come charging down to investigate. 'Come on, let's get out of here,' I say, starting to get in the cab.

'Wait a second,' Norm replies.

'What?'

'Can't you hear that?' And I can hardly hear him because he is speaking in just over a whisper, his half-voice almost lost in the whirring and crackles, the constant swash of battle noises that seem to live in the air around us, the same way that creaks and snaps live in an old and sun-baked house.

'Hear what, Norm?'

But even as I say this I hear what he means: the sound of someone running towards us, the footfalls not clipped as they would be if made by boots on asphalt, but muffled and crunching, as if made on earth or similar – and this fast pattering has a clear direction that makes it impossible to doubt where it comes from: the hedge to our left, the same side that the one lucky German helmet dived into. For a moment I imagine the fear he must have as he runs, and the pain that will be beginning to rack his chest as he tries to distance himself from the unexpected slaughter behind him. I look across to Norm and see that he is smiling, that there is a pleasure in his eyes and face, an eagerness for me to share his pleasure before the beginning of a grand joke, and I have already hopped down off the ambulance and am running around the hood when I hear him start to call, his voice rising into falsetto with the importance of it all before he has it under control, by which time I am around his side of the cabin. He turns confusedly to see what I am doing there, and then I take my big hand and make a nice fist and punch him fairly hard right in his big forehead, watching as he pitches a bit away from the ambulance, cocking my fist to be ready, moving on my feet a little to strike again. But there is no need, because his eyes have gone and he is sliding down, a weak hand reaching out to grip the ambulance and missing, then his body thudding onto the tarmac.

The footfalls from behind the hedge have stopped. He must be very close, and though I turn and peer at the green wall, looking for some sign – for differences in the light between the leaves perhaps – I see nothing. There is no sign and when I speak softly I feel as if I speak to a merely imagined presence.

'Sven?'

There is no answer, just a rustling and then the resumption of quick footfalls pattering unseen along the hedge, away from me, away from the squad behind and I try to track the sound as it recedes, but quickly lose it.

'Hey!' calls a voice from behind. I am startled and turn and there on the road is a GI, his rifle held relaxed across him and his helmet slightly askew, the straps loose at his ears. His face is young and bright and he is smiling, even though he must see the unconscious Norm at my feet, may even have seen me hit him. 'Ain't you Dicky Yates, the Division Heavyweight Champ?'

'Well. Yes I am,' I tell him, pleased at this recognition. 'What's your name, kid?'

The kid tells me his name, where he's from. Then he says, 'What happened to him? He hit?'

'No. He's not hit,' I answer.

Below, as the two of us stand over him, Norm is coming around. He is groaning and his hands are beginning to move.

'You got any hit?' I ask the kid.

'Nope.'

And then I am helping a groggy Norm into the cabin, slapping his back and telling him that all good buddies, all great comrades have fights – to not worry about it and boy what a sight that all was, wasn't it? And there's a good Norm. Sit tight, Norm, you're gonna be just fine. There's a good boy. Well done, Norm. That's right, you sit there, you piece of shit.

The Shipwright

The oarsman, an old fellow in a soft dark cap and shirt, should have known better. I could enjoy the dipping sound of the paddles, were it not for his habit of twisting his neck to the side before pulling at the stroke, thus inadvertently causing more force to be transmitted through his left oar, so that we were making a slightly yawing progress across the river. The river itself was unusually calm, almost glassy, and the day was ending, but these incidental conspirators had no plans for my happiness or contentment, because it had been another day without promise: many doors had I knocked upon and been refused; there had been no messenger waiting for my return to the office overlooking the wharf, holding a sealed document that to him would mean nothing, but to me could be all.

Verily it all.

'Oarsman!' I shout.

'Yes sir?'

'Put your back into it, you unhitched gig.'

He looks at me, taken aback. Perhaps he thought me meek and cow-like, a person small in stature, of moderate and unadorned dress, that would be unable to hurl insult so freely to the lower classes; perhaps he would think I had only barely emerged from them.

'Beg pardon, sir?'

'You're rowing this boat like a tasselled barmby.'

'I most certainly am not!'

'The north bank looks like it's drunken from where I'm sitting, I tell you.'

His gaze, bright and attached to mine, stays affixed even as he takes another stroke and his head and neck twists to the side, so that for a moment his eyes appear to roll in his head with madness or menace. Then not only does the failure of the day weigh upon me, and the deviation of the boat, but also his grumbling, which is incessant until we reach the bank and I pay him.

'Thank you, sire,' he says.

'You pull harder on the left oar, did you know that?'

'Aye! My right arm is shorter. Been that way since birth, I'm told. That's why I give it a tug on the left. If I didn't we'd be going round in circles mid-river.'

I look at him for signs of mockery, and finding only a trace, am moved to ask him his name.

'Barrington, sir,' he says, with a touch of pride.

'Barrington.'

'Yes.'

'See you anon.'

He nods and we part, perhaps a little better understood on both sides, a small bonus that does nothing to ameliorate the cold and muddied trudge up the bank, the steep and worn steps away from it, the walk down the tight and foul-smelling streets with their constructions looming woodenly over the thoroughfare, and in the half-light very few lamps lit to give it all a severe and dim coldness, so that I must walk as if through the manifestation of my heart and mood, towards my own tenement among the filth, the sight of its irregular and bulging overhang only part comfort for the warmth it might bring, but mostly dread for what I might find within.

When I enter I have barely got off my overcoat when I can feel her standing behind me in the passage. I turn and in the gloom that is almost darkness her face is expectant, enquiring, but in a way that has lost most of its warmth and licence, so that now I cannot shrug and say that the day held nothing, and be assured of a smile and understanding, of her patience. From further in comes the sound of miniature coughing.

'How is he?' I ask.

'Worse,' she says. Her darkened face is hard and unattractive. She will not ask me but there is no point in withholding from her, it is best to get it over and done with.

'Nothing today,' I tell her.

Her eyes flick sideways and she nods, then they are wetted and I see that she tries to control herself. 'We must get him away from here, from this filth!'

'I know, Anna,' I answer, using her name in a hope to placate. 'Let's go through.'

She turns and I follow her down the passage, out of it into the soft brightness of the hearth in the kitchen, the pair of candles low and disfigured, they squat in their own demise upon the tabletop. The boy is by the fire and turns to me. It pains me to see him, as if I am shoved in the chest: his weakness evident in the fascia around his eyes, the thinness of the wrists that poke from his shirt, the delicacy of his fingers clasping the edge of the table. Still he smiles to see me, the spirit of his youth emerging from the shell of his ailments, so that I am flushed with both pleasure and shame.

'Hello, Son.'

'Hello, Father,' he says, for a moment his voice clear and strong. 'How are you?'

I am about to respond but he begins coughing, his eyes become large and watered, a convulsion along his body that is horrible to watch because it is practised: he has found the exact method with which to hold his body and cause himself the least pain. We have not taught him this, the useless and money-sapping doctors have not taught him this, it is his own design, which Anna and I know intimately, that beyond the cramped rooms in which we live, the dirty street behind me, the thin and meatless stew that is our nightly fare – beyond these things it is to me the most terrible manifestation of our penury. I look to her, to where she stands at the other end of the table, and when she turns up from watching the boy to face me, I am surprised that she is not hardened and demanding, that for a moment we can only share our barely hidden pity for him.

And when I am at the table and eating, watching the flames of the fire expire into embers, listening to the faint but proximate sounds of Anna and the boy as she prepares him for the night, I think of nothing but the mistakes I have made, how every taken path from a certain point seemed destined to turn me maze-like into this stagnation, which verily is like the doldrums, with its thirst and pestilence and hunger. The window is open, and I get up to close it, to stop the cold and liquid-like air seeping into the room. My hand has finished this task when another knocks at the door: a loud spirited knocking.

Anna appears in the doorway. 'Who could that be?'

'I don't know,' but automatically I fear it to be bailiffs, an irrational thought since I have not yet defaulted; yet this inevitable future seems to reach back and again knock loudly at the door. A muffled voice is heard, perhaps calling my name, its tone eager rather than threatening and I begin to make my way towards the passage, squeezing past Anna into it, this brushing of arm against her waist perhaps our first physical connection of the day. Then I am lifting the latch and opening myself to the dark and rank street, to find one figure poised and near to me on the step, another behind him standing with his hands behind his back.

'Mr Fenner?' the man who must have knocked says. He is young, and neither burly nor threatening.

'Yes?'

'Please excuse the lateness, sir, but my employer wishes to speak with you.'

I look beyond him to the man in the street. I do not recognise him but he stands calmly, still with his hands clasped behind him. It is dark and I can barely make out the features of the young man near me, but this does not prevent me noticing that his employer is dressed in at least well-tailored clothing, and standing like that he appears either confident in who he is, or what he is about to do.

'My employer is Mr Samuel Horace, sir.'

I hear movement from the depths behind me: Anna must have heard the name also. Excitement is the wonderful thing that must illuminate my face and raise the corners of my mouth, that makes me quick to open the door wider and begin gesturing and saying, 'Come in! Come in! Please, quickly, come in!'

The youth passes me and there is congestion in the passage as the three of us slowly make our way back towards the kitchen. I am muttering nonsense in greeting and about the dreary state of the weather; I am flustered watching the two men emerge into the kitchen until I am in it myself, and see that in only seconds Anna has somehow transformed it into a humble and almost cheery venue.

Before we have offered them anything Horace has turned to me and removed his hat. In the dim yellow light I can see his greater age and a delicacy of feature, but also that he too is excited and can barely hide this, or the joy that floats upon it and makes his pale eyes sparkle and crease.

'I have had good fortune, Mr Fenner,' he begins, 'with my last voyage. Today the *Avon* returned, do you know her?'

'Of course.'

'She has returned successfully and two months before her, the *Green Dragon*.'

'Yes.'

'They are good vessels but old and burrowed. They are also small.'

He pauses and we regard each other. We are standing quite close. Anna and the youth are completely silent and there is no sound from the boy, who must be listening, the still-sharp acuity beneath his illness making him silent.

'I want you,' says Horace, 'to build me a new ship: the next incarnation of the *Dragon*, but bigger, one hundred feet long!'

For a moment I say nothing. Then I am smiling, and feel

my arm being lifted, because Horace has gripped my hand in both of his. 'Do you accept?' I look to Anna and see that she stands very erect, is very still and proper, which tells me that inside she will be screaming with happiness and relief – and this is confirmed in her eyes, which look to me with a defiant brightness and exultance.

'Of course I do, Mr Horace. Of course I do!'

'Excellent! Then let us celebrate. Andrew,' he says to the youth, 'go out and fetch some wine, and some hams and meats, that sort of thing.'

Andrew departs, and in the few minutes that he is gone Horace tells me the details of his commission: a vague outline of his vision for a beautiful ship, drawn for me with his hands moving only inches from my face, and with movements of his body, contortions which captivate the boy who spies on him from the passage. There is innovation, and difficulty in what he wants, and I am glad of this, because my reputation is weak in the standard lines. And I am still disbelieving of my good fortune to have befallen such an ideally suited patron when Anna goes to the door to readmit Andrew, and they spill forth together into the kitchen carrying flasks and wrapped packages.

It is a great pleasure to sit with these two new men, to lift liquor to my lips and then watch as the boy enters the kitchen and formally introduces himself to Horace, who cuts the boy a perfect arcing slice of gammon and gives it to him. And in this gesture towards my son he shows complete comprehension of what he is doing: that although he may be giddy with his own success, he understands the seriousness of conferring his favour upon me, and the consequences it has for my family.

When the pleasure visibly rises on the boy's face as he chews the meat, I think Horace will look to me, but in the last instant he controls himself, and instead is content to ruffle the boy's hair.

The next day Andrew and I are in the light of the window at my desk, which is awash with papers and plans, most of which Andrew has brought. He has also brought money, in a purse which sits in the drawer of the desk, the soft smoothness and weight of which I can still feel pressing into my hand, despite that now it holds a pencil.

There is the sound of movement in the stairwell, a slow and heavy shuffling in ascension, and I wonder what distraction has drifted from the quayside and into my office, until the figure appears: an old man with a mass of silver hair, stooped and hidden beneath his cloak and hat, who stands as if to totter before raising a grey and ungloved hand towards us to say, 'A chair, boy. Give me a chair.'

'Master!' I respond. Andrew has risen and is behind his chair; I motion for him to take it over. The old man shuffles further and then collapses into it, and after a brief recovery is lifting his head, so that I can see the familiar face, very old and deathlike, but the eyes alive and critical.

'Master Langdon, a pleasure that you are here!' I tell him. I cannot remember the last time he visited my office. 'May I present young Andrew Watts, an associate of mine.'

The Master looks up to the young man near him, almost sneeringly, but this is a deception because his voice is soft. 'Hello, Watts. Thank you for your kindness.'

'My pleasure, sir.'

'How are you, how have you been?' I ask him. He is

positioned halfway between the doorway and my desk, with Andrew stood at his side in the middle of the room. He is distant and I would like him to move closer, would like to say that it has been too long since we have seen the other, but cannot for fear of sounding reproachful.

'Fine, boy. Fine,' he says, with a wave of his hand. 'I hear you have a commission.'

'Yes, sir. Mr Watts here is the representative of Mr Samuel Horace.'

Again he peers up at Andrew, as if to see him afresh with this new information. 'Finding times hard?' he says to me.

'Yes, Master, I was.'

'Yes,' he says, and holds my gaze. 'I do not think you should do it.'

I am surprised that he says this, but not shocked. 'Why not, sir?'

His hand waves again and he screws up his face, and when he speaks it is to the corner of the room behind me. 'These new vessels, boy, their design is awkward,' he shakes his head, 'and compromised. You wish to make your reputation upon a mere dray? You have a feel for the wind, boy, a magnificent feel for it! If you build this sea-barge you will be sucked into that trade for your career. You will never escape.' His eyes are now upon me. 'And you will regret it.'

He stops, the passion fading from his face. He must know that what he says is useless. We observe the other and I think that he has made the considerable effort to come here and display professional disapprobation not for my benefit, but in large part for his, so that he can return to the immobility of his retirement and know that he was understood. By me, his finest pupil.

When we begin talking again his manner is less formal, but he refuses to be drawn into comment on the project. He does not stay for much longer and I am sad to see him go.

'Goodbye, Master,' I say to him, helping him up into the cabriolet.

'Fenner,' he nods. 'Good to see you, boy.'

But watching him diminish away from the wharf and back up towards the city, watching him and turning, I have many unclear thoughts about succession and modernity, that do not need further refinement, for I know that nothing could stop me building this ship.

Finally Andrew has left, and I am alone at my desk, the morning old and not particularly bright, but the window clean and unclouded with condensation – I have the stove burning powerfully – and this is enough that the expansive page I look down upon is dazzling, is frightening and awesome in its blankness. The sounds of men working, of their industry, the call of a gull enter my mind mutedly, and I am happy with pencil poised, for the brief is clear, and each time I think of an aspect, it is as if a chorus of ideas blossoms in response, so that I am both excited by them and afraid that they will slip away, and cannot lower the pencil to begin a careful sketching until I have breathed deeply and thought in private incantation that this is what I do, this is what I do.

Then my hand is moving over the page and lines are left in its wake, the form of something appearing, its birth interrupted as I rise and move over to the bureau, extracting old and worn plans of magnificent vessels, checking what I am about to create against what has been created before. And in this way, in the reaching back to what is known or has been done, and pushing forwards into what is to be, I begin upon the path, that within only minutes, if not seconds, has its starting point – the moment where I was poised but had not begun – sealed off and lost for ever, and I am grateful that the only course is forwards: forwards unceasingly until resolution.

I have sketched a basic keel and hull and the opposing arrangement of masts, I have done these things and can look upon them with satisfaction. But it is tempered, because throughout this purer process it had become increasingly evident that the inevitable experimentation and mock-ups would have to be done sooner rather than later, that in fact they would have to be done *first*, so that the rest of the vessel could be designed around their results. And as I look to the window, and to the quayside scene below, where some men appear to be unloading a barque, I have to concede that I knew this from the start, and had drawn out of faith for past methods – but a malignant, inverted faith.

Thus it is in fact a relief to lay down my pencil and prepare myself for the wharf: a donning of hat and overcoat, and a moment spent before the stove with hands outstretched, before turning to descend the stairs and enter into the blustery cold and the raised voices of physical men.

First I visit the carpenter's yard of Mackay; the ship will not be built here but in the west, yet I want to check that he is available to start work if not this afternoon, then tomorrow morning. It is good to arrive at his gates without fanfare, but quietly and brimming with purpose, his yard empty and seemingly lifeless but not unkempt. There is a hut with a chimney, from which puffs of smoke appear briefly before dispersal by the gusting wind, and it is from this hut that he emerges, a few moments after I call for him, a short and stocky man who does not cover himself against the cold, but walks bow-legged and patiently in nothing but an undershirt and trousers.

'Ah, Mr Fenner,' he says from a worn but open face, the eyes deep and a subtle intermix of blue and green, a softness that is contrasted by all else about him: the powerful arms and thick wrists, the hands that are caked and pale with scars and nicks. His head is below mine as he opens the gate, his short-haired skull exposed and hatless – yet it does not seem prone as it would be with other men. I pass through and we shake hands; his grip is strong but he does not seek to crush me, and as our connection is broken I begin to tell him what I want, and he steps back and places his hands on his hips, so that between us there is two feet of space in which I place structures with nothing but words and numbers, married to this the occasional gesture, while Mackay stands and nods and grunts and then interjects to confirm the length of something, the thickness of another.

After perhaps three minutes of this we stop; Mackay is nodding and though he does not smile, I know that he too is infused with the happiness born of our ability to under-stand the other, to share this object that has been conjured out of the realm of nothingness, which he will go on to make concrete.

'Aye, Mr Fenner, it is a worthy arrangement,' he says. 'Will be no bother.'

We shake hands and I pass out of his yard with my chin set against the cold, but this is perfunctory, or habit, because my step is light and springing: I do not feel the wind as anything other than clean refreshment, an invigoration, and thus engaged in perambulation immediately following the minor achievement with Mackay, it occurs to me that it is perhaps in our dealings with people that the most professional happiness is to be sought, rather than the idealised and cosseted environment of the drawing desk.

And what I am about to do now will take me furthest from the realm of ideas, because I walk towards the shabbier limit of the wharf, to where it abuts the city and forms a dim band of idleness and waiting, of sailors and roustabouts, mostly vagrant and drunk, who somehow survive quietly in stupor among the low and decrepit buildings, in the long stretches between their employments. If it were near dark I would not dare to come here alone, but buoyed by daylight and purpose I am unafraid walking down its close and foul-smelling passageways, peering down thin and wet channels between the hovels and drinking houses, to be peered back at by children or dogs. I am grateful for my own squalor, as compared to this, and am absorbed and downcast in this thought when I hear footsteps ahead, and look up to see a familiar figure, clad in a soft cap and shirt too long for him.

'Barrington!' I call.

He is picking his way over the brown puddles and rivulets of the passage, with an exaggerated care that I suspect is inebriation. When he looks up his face is contorted and squinting, he stands looking this way at me with his arms hanging down almost to his knees, and I note that his arms are of the same length. His face relaxes and he nods. 'Ah, it's you, sir. How de do?'

'Not on the river today?' I ask, picking my way over to him, so that he is only a few feet away. Surprisingly, the scent of alcohol does not assault me.

'No, sire. Good day yesterday so day off today.'

'How would you like a good day tomorrow, and no rowing?'

He looks at me, as if with one suspicious eye, and the other perceiving opportunity. 'Doing what?'

So I explain to him that I need him and eleven of his finest harbour-dwelling confederates to turn up tomorrow at Mackay's yard, and in return they will be paid two days' work for just a few hours. 'Can you do that, Barrington? Can you find the other men to bring with you? You must bring the other men otherwise no one will get paid, understood?'

'Yes, sire,' he says, but I can sense that a large part of him is still wary, is perhaps distrustful of the person before him. So I reach into my overcoat, and feel for a coin, which when extracted is the brightest thing in the passageway and seems to glint and sparkle even when there is no light to bounce from it.

I hold it up to Barrington, who takes it delicately and without touching me. 'Another three of these for you if you bring the men.'

'I'll bring them, sire, tomorrow morning.'

'Good. Now I have no further need to go on this way,' I say, pointing behind him, 'so if you don't mind I will walk with you for a while.'

'I'm going back that way,' he says, pointing with his thumb over his shoulder, the other clutching the coin in a fist. He has the happy look of someone released, of a man about to do only what he wishes.

'Just make sure you're there in the morning,' I warn him.

His teeth, surprisingly bright and orderly, become visible in a grin. 'I will, sir, yes.'

'Good, good.'

And we turn and part oppositely, and I retrace my voyage down the middle of the dark and stinking passageway, but with a light, skipping step, and emerge back into the open air, away from the low shacks and hovels and onto the wharf proper with hardly a mark on my boots.

Dinner that night is proud with ale and meat, while Anna is in the best of forms, generous with smile and glance, busying herself in the kitchen that is aflame with fresh candles, the fire of the hearth a bright red so hot that I am in shirtsleeves, that I must open the window for air. Even the boy does not cough; he can sense the spirit of his parents, which must seem to him like something powerful bursting upwards, as between us we discuss possibilities of new lodgings, perhaps even a house, sometimes turning to him to ask the rhetoric of whether he would like a garden, with an apple tree – or tell him how he will have a room high in the house and overlooking this garden, so that on clear summer days the sun will rise and stream through the window with a golden light – and I tell him that he will have to squint against this brightness as he opens the window, and then with its warmth against his face he will be able to breathe in great lungfuls of sweet air, health- and vigour-giving air!

All this I say to him, and there is no falseness in positing these things: I do not feel any constriction at my chest to think of them and thus the possibility of their denial, and it might be the ale, but more it is the palpable reality of my good fortune, to know that these things will come to me and my family, that already I am on the path to success: the ship I build will be such a fine one and others will follow it. With this thought I retire to bed far earlier than I have in months: suddenly in a desperation, but only to pull the morning towards me faster.

The next day is warmer and with little wind, there is even some sun in patches but I am nervous the entire trip down to the bank and across the broad river, my walk through the wharf on the opposite side quick and distracted, the sound of the men working, of their oaths and fraternal invective more a threat than a symptom of vigour, and I establish that I feel this way because today's experiments are now more than creative exploration: they are the fulcrum upon which a minor greatness may balance – namely my own – and it is this uncertainty, this possibility that I may have struck profound innovation that makes me fear for it, as if it might be taken from me.

What I am glad for is to see at Mackay's gates a healthy assortment of men; I count sixteen heads in total, a cluster populated by Barrington, who must relate my identity, to turn their heads as I approach.

'Well done, Barrington.'

'There's four extra,' he replies.

'No matter, everyone can partake.'

Inside the yard is a bright structure of pale yellow: the fresh young wood that Mackay has used smelling clean and sappy, in contrast to the uneven gang of men that filtered through the gate, who now gather around me at the framework, occluding its scent with their squalor-wrought own.

The carpenter is present but aside, observing without expression as I get the first man to sit cross-legged in the corner of the structure, and then direct another man to sit next to him so that their knees touch. Soon there are nine men seated in the structure's footprint: they are silenced by expectancy and confusion as to purpose, and even show a little fear when at a gesture from me, Mackay starts laying long planks over their heads, these lengths of wood resting loosely on the highest of three horizontal struts skirting the structure. When the roof is in place I squat down, and ask the men to sit up straight. The tallest of them has about two inches between the top of his head and the bottom of the wood.

Then Mackay and I begin removing the planking, the spare men assisting eagerly in this, and when this is done I tell the men to remove themselves from the structure – all except one – and when he is alone I tell him to lie down, so that his poorly booted feet project towards me out below the skirting.

I gesture to Mackay. 'Middle?' he asks.

'Lowest,' I reply, and he places four planks over the man, so that there is less than a foot between his nose and the wooden decking. The man's feet twitch as the last plank is laid.

'You are not going to bury me, I hope,' he says in a quiet voice.

We laugh at this and I am happy to do so, because there is clearly enough room for him in there, if anything the strut could be lowered further, and I am excited, perhaps laughing a little too long, overreaching in familiarity as I get more of the men to re-enter the structure and lie down as the first, to cover them over too with decking, until from standing, all that can be seen is five pairs of feet sticking out from the end of a low wooden box. 'Nail it,' I tell Mackay, who works deftly, hammering in each nail with no more than three strokes, his mouth and eyes creasing slightly in response to the men's moans of simulated terror; also their criticism of his technique, of how he cannot count to four.

Again I squat to peer into them, crouching over and then finding I have to lower myself onto a knee to get a line of sight all the way to the back, where their far ends exist as stubbled throats and cavernous apertures of nostril; in my own nostrils the smell of these unwashed and alcoholic men a sudden and sour assault. One of them has his hands pressed against the decking above him, and I note that his arms make right angles at the elbows. Although I am convinced, there is one final component of the experiment that must be undertaken, and so I ask the men to slide themselves out of the low space, which they can achieve without too much collision and concordant insult, and when they are all out and milling around I choose the five tallest of them to crawl in again, and get another five to place themselves on the decking, so that in the end there are ten sets of worn footwear protruding, and space above for another deck.

It takes Mackay little more than a quarter of an hour to build a second deck onto the structure, equal in height from the first deck, as the first is from the base, so that by midmorning it is only Barrington, Mackay and myself standing with our hands on our hips in the desultory sunlight, while fifteen men lie in a space which originally fitted only nine. A few more minutes and Mackay has tacked in planking at the sides of the structure, and climbed to its top to give it a true roof, the only opening that remains being where their feet are. We have one more trial of everybody getting in and out, and then I declare that the day's work is done, and happily I pay the men and thank them, because the investigation has been a success – except there is one element that bothers me, and that I am reminded of as each man breathily clutches the coins given him: it is their smell lodged deeply in my nostrils, and which was at its most powerful standing with all fifteen of them enclosed upon the structure, their feet twitching or their toes tapping together in boredom, their voices, once loud and jocular in conversation, quietened when the light was blotted by Mackay's industry – at least one of them having fallen asleep to begin snoring – but the air coming from this arrangement foul and thickly: a miasma that any healthy man breathing must soon succumb to, and find himself in sickness.

No, no, this will not do, I think upon leaving the yard, so that my journey home is brooding and isolated, is made after success, but a success that seems only to rest upon a caveat, and when I am at the door and Anna is standing there with the boy peeking from behind her, I must conjure a false hospitableness, and enter inwards knowing that I am hardly with them, but remain deep in a place of thought that is now exhausted and lifeless.

Throughout dinner I am quiet or else miserly with my responses, and though I am aware of this and repeatedly try to become emergent and expansive, my mood is such that these attempts fail, and eventually I must declare myself to Anna as preoccupied with the day's work, and in response to this she soothes me and strokes my arm, a contact that at first is pleasant and then becomes overbearing. It is hot again in the kitchen and I rise over to the window, pushing the hinged square out into the small column-like space between the tightly packed buildings that leads up to the breezeless sky above.

Then from the depths of my mind it comes to me: the inexplicable and mysterious sense of rightness, of recognising a problem and solving it in the same heartbeat. For tonight there is little air coming from the window – just a trickle of cold on the fingers of my outstretched hand – while on other nights when the wind is right the air barrels in as if pumped, and I look at Anna, but merely in order to make a calculation, to seek support in her quizzical face for the process of numbers I set against the practicality of a delicately curved sail, and of wind direction and its variances; these things not to push the ship, but to funnel air down into it.

She must see my brow furrow and my head dip with the occasional nod, signs that she will recognise, that she will be able to contrast neatly with my reservedness of earlier.

'Anna,' I tell her. 'I must go back to the office.'

'Now? But it's dark, Robert.'

'I will take a cab across the bridge.' When I see she is still against the idea I add, 'I'll only be an hour or so, and I will make the driver wait for me.'

'The cost!'

'We can afford it, and this is important.'

She holds my gaze for a moment, and then in rising I know that she has conceded. 'Let me get your coat,' she says.

'I would not sleep otherwise,' I say at the door.

'I know,' she says, and now she smiles. 'Be careful. You paid out money today; people know you have it.'

'Here,' I reply, and take out the money bag from my pocket, emptying a few coins into my hand, before passing the rest of the bag to her.

A kiss from Anna and then I am walking down our street, a rare expedition into the night, the little yellow lights from the houses so few and dull, that without the moon it is powerfully black, and I am grateful to turn onto the larger road and hail down a cabriolet, to step up onto its gentle swaying and into the light of its little orbital lamp, away from the street and the imagined yet sinister growths of its hidden shapes.

Rare too to pass through the city this way, its strange nocturnal activity emergent: men and women either with destination or none in mind, and the beginnings of drunkenness, its speckling of shouts and laughter intensifying as we near the bridge. I am neither entranced nor distracted, but listen to the sound of the animal's hooves, which have changed from their patter on the lesser dirt-tracked streets, to the current clopping on paving, and as we turn and begin climbing the gentle slope of the bridge, I do not look outwards to the darkened vista but down at my hands, which have begun to stroke and intertwine the other, and when we arrive at the wharf, and pass through a section of it to reach my building, I am eager but calm in alighting, I do not bound up the stairs or rush in lighting the lamp but do these things carefully, as if not to disturb the work that is to come.

And I intended to stay an hour or two, but within the drawing of a few lines I feel a huge vigour, as if a fountain of it directly beneath me, and shaking, taking a breath and looking to the black square of window I rise and go down to ask the driver to come up and light the stove for me, then I pay him for what he has done so far, and to go back and deliver a note to Anna, to tell her not to worry, that I will not return until the next day.

Then when he is gone I set about it: I start very steadily and with great control, but this is in bad faith, for in truth there is no need for caution now, and whereas I came here this evening to draw a single component, now that I can feel the wholeness of the ship before me like a solid thing, I do not hesitate or limit myself but with free hand draw it in its entirety, working faster and faster, feverishly, but without significant error, with hardly any error and each part fitting into the other so that by the very beginnings of dawn, when the black window's upper half is tinged with grey, the ship – my great ship – is born, in everything but the smallest detail.

I am exhausted, but elated, and check the stove quickly before leaving, passing through the wharf as the earliest man abroad in it, a wildlife of rats and their predators benign in their scampering, and though I could pay a cab upon arrival at home, in order to prolong this moment I walk to the riverbank and watch the London sky lighten to a grey-blue as I wait for the first oarsman to appear. It is done, I think. It is done! Each time I indulge myself with a reflection on this, a great happiness wells in my chest, because I know the work is good, that Horace will be pleased with it even before he understands the innovations, which far from being cosmetic, may in fact usurp the very standard across the world.

'Yes, sire,' I hear a voice say from behind.

'Take me across, will you?'

'Certainly, sire,' the man says. He is about my age, perhaps younger, and for his trade at least, neatly attired. 'My boat is that one over there.'

I wait for him to unhitch his boat from the small quay, and step in when he signals me with a look upwards.

'Out early this morning, sir,' he says.

The cool air is good and I take a deep breath of it as we move off, the boatman leaning over to one side and pushing the wood of the quay with his oar. 'Yes, I suppose I am,' I tell him, and the journey across is languid and pleasant.

Anthony and I are in the garden, the late spring weather being so warm that we had both scoffed our breakfasts and burst out into the bright stillness, a thin fog giving the stretch of lawn with its spotting of trees a golden haze. I stand and watch the boy run into this with his feeble but utmost speed, thinking how his pale limbs propel him with a new power and vigour, how I cannot recall the last incidence of a severe coughing fit. He is calling to me and I answer perfunctorily, but happily, very happily because the sun is warm upon me, and will be warming the great hull that sits only a mile or two south from here, the ship that began with only keel and rib, and has passed untrammelled through the long succession of craftsmen, to become presently the short-lived domain of the sailmakers, who install the last of the canvas even now, as I run headlong and gut-packed after the small boy who has turned to bait me from a distance.

Then I am at the front of the house, the sun still upon

me as I stand between the white columns of the portico, the large black door open and the sound of Anna approaching from within: the swish of her garments and her soft steps on the tiles. I turn to her and take the basket she carries, which is covered with a cloth and will contain little bundles of her efforts, both from the kitchen and its garden.

'Here he is,' she says, and I can hear the sound of horses' hooves on gravel, and before turning I reach for her forearm and squeeze it, and we say nothing, but indulge the other with a long look, the bright light making her squint and angle her head so that for a moment she is girlish and deeply handsome.

All this in only a second or two, for the driveway is hardly long and the carriage is almost at the house: an elegant structure with larger wheels to the rear, an enclosed chamber and pulled by two fine grey geldings, now halted by the driver who sits high at the front of it. The small door is directly before me; I can see an arm in its window and then the door opens towards me, and Horace is peering out, his face and hat framed by the aperture, his expression like that of a man who has just been laughing.

'Good morning, sir,' he says to me. 'And madam! How are you, Mrs Fenner, on this fine day?'

'Good morning,' she replies. 'I am well and happy, sir.'

'Excellent. Ah, provisions,' he says, pointing at the basket. 'Well, seeing as we are thus prepared, let us depart.'

I stoop and climb into the carriage, and when the door is closed it feels as if I am gone from the world and have been swallowed by a leather-mouthed whale or similar. 'What a carriage!' I tell my benefactor, making my way over to sit next to him, feeling the pleasant tug in my stomach as the horses move off. We wave to Anna, who shades her eyes with one hand and lifts the other in response, and then when we have turned a silence descends on us that remains until we have left the driveway and have joined the Bristol road, and I say, 'You should have gone directly there, Sam. I could have joined you at the yard.'

He turns to me. 'Nonsense,' he says, and shakes his head with eyes closed. Opening them he says, 'Has she changed much?'

I look from him to the black wall of the carriage facing me: a suitable void on which to project the images of the ship in all its stages, before I remember the exact timing of his last visit. 'Yes, she has. By today she will have all her canvas.'

He merely nods at this, and this gesture is affected, but only by its limitation.

The geldings make short work of the journey to the town, and as we approach the yard I feel a nervousness that manifests itself as a tapping of my foot, and stems from an irrational fear that sometimes grips me, that the ship will have been consumed by fire in the night, or a discovery has been made of a grievous flaw in its design or build, and that the first face to greet me will be one bearing news of disaster.

Faintly, the sounds of gulls and the smell of saltwater penetrates into our black cocoon, and when we turn the corner to begin on the road upon which the pregnant yard resides, Horace has opened the door and is leaning outwards even as we move.

'Sails are up, Bob!' he says, and I too am compelled to leave my seat and join him in precarious clinging and balancing at the door, extending my head through the gap below his, to see suddenly in the blue of the sky, not a cloud but a purer white square of sail set against it.

'They must be finishing off,' I tell the head above me.

'Yes.'

We arrive and alight and there is no messenger of disaster, just the ship itself lying huge and splendid, the flanks of its hull not yet hidden by waterline, the smooth curves visible to the base of the wooden box that protects it still from the harbour waters, and at the bottom of which a man is wandering around, as if looking for something, who then stops to remove his soft cap and lift it in greeting. This figure is Barrington, whom I brought from London to Bristol, and has proved himself a trustworthy watchman, sleeping through the cacophony of the day's work in his little hut, to awake in the evening and find that the thing he shares the dock with has grown yet again.

On deck there are many more men: I spot the agent from the victualler among them, prominent in his better clothing, quietly directing lesser-dressed labourers who are bringing a stream of goods from a cart parked ashore, up the gangplank in a neat line like ants to then disappear with their sacks and caskets into the hold. Above these workers there are men at the masts and in the rigging, who are as loud and brash as the circling gulls, for they are the sailmaker's men, and their work is not only the final part of the construction of this ship, but in their eyes, at least, the most important. They have completed the main and foremast, and now work on the mizzen, and I note that the twin ventilation sails are up on their scaffold, looking like two huge white flowers sprouting up from where they are attached to the deck. Looking further aft I see the exhaust port, to allow the air captured by the elegant canvas blooms, and made fetid belowdecks, to exit freely.

'She's a beauty,' says Horace, as if he speaks not of a ship, but of something that is beyond his power, and forces upon him a humility. 'She'll be the finest slaver in twenty years!'

'Yes,' I say nodding.

She will that, I think, and together we walk down the slope from the road, and then up the gangplank and onto the ship.

The Stove

There is softness and a heat beneath me.

I am covered and warm under blanket and fur, and the air is dry and tastes of the wood that burns in the stove that I am lying on, which I have been laid upon for so long now that I have lost count of the days; I do not even know whether it is evening or morning. When my sickness is not so strong, when my head has stopped its wild spinning I open my eyes to see the beams and slats of the roof above, bleary and indistinct, prone to movement and disfigurement so that I must close my eyes quickly, to revel in the brief darkness before different monsters emerge: faces that flow one into another, their expressions desperate or angry, their features alien but then suddenly recognisable and I must gasp their name, to beg for forgiveness.

In the quieter moments, when the precious darkness remains behind my eyelids, and the stove does not feel like the back of a galloping beast – this is when my stony hunger emerges, to press on my stomach, to reach up from there to my chest with its desperate scrabbling claws, which have scratched so long that their sharpness has gone, to leave instead a dull but powerful ache: an emptiness inside me that has changed from something rodent-like to become the burrowing of a fat worm – a blunt-mouthed thing that maybe feeds on hunger – this the only thing of me containing strength.

Before, illness was always accompanied with a streak of pleasure, especially in winter, because it meant the shaky but happy climb up into the high nest atop the bulk of stonework, the delicious lick of heat from the fire on a bare leg, and the gentle but insistent hands helping you upwards, to find the arranged fabrics and skins clean-smelling and warm like the owner of those hands – my mother – who would quietly attend you without the slightest trace of resentment for how such attention would affect the burdens of her day. Once settled you would look to her, her face would be at the same height as yours, but sideways: she standing smiling and for a rare moment completely still, happy to see you so ensconced.

Now, though, I do not remember climbing up here, and I have no pleasure or any happiness for the luxury of not moving. I am not safe, none of us are safe in this homestead, or in the next, or even the next after it and beyond, because my hunger is not unique, it is rampant across the country as far as you could possibly travel: a sick wind over barren earth to make us drop to our knees and dig for the last roots, the land already stripped of anything green that is not poison. And in the town, when I was still walking and able to range in desperate hope, I imagined I heard the voice of this wind: a soft and wavering call that terrified me in the dim afternoon, before I realised it was the sound of the town's young children whimpering in unison, their voices emanating from the darkened houses: children much younger than I but who must still sense the reason that there are no dogs, no cattle or horses, who must have an idea beyond the pain in their own stomachs, that a beast beyond the most horrific night-time tales of their menfolk is circling the world inescapably.

To think that the famine both exists within me, and spreads outwards to every border makes me shudder with fear!

And only a short time ago, before I found myself upon the stove in illness, I can remember perhaps the greatest happiness of my life. I cling to its memory: my father coming when he knew I would be away from the others, how his face beneath its cap had silently ordered me to get up from my luckless foraging along the edge of the woods. I had stood and used my trousers to brush the dirt from my hands, fearful to be rebuked for finding nothing; but instead he turned his head to lift his sharp grey eyes away from mine, and I watched as slowly he surveyed the land around us. When he had seen everything he wanted, he turned to me and in his look was the flash of recognition I always craved: the sight of which was always my greatest thrill, because it meant that his far-reaching gaze was focused not on his labours, or on things I did not understand, but for a short while would favour me, his son, to change any day – even one spent starving – into a moment filled suddenly with prospect.

'Come on!' he had said and led me into the woods, our first few steps together, the gentle roughness of his thumb and forefinger at the base of my neck, their strength something I could borrow to shake the stupor of hunger into a faster movement, so that when he lifted this contact and strode ahead of me, I was able to follow; felt able to streak past him in a run.

He had led me deeper into the woods, the earth sloping down as it followed the base of the valley, and then we arrived where the trees stopped and the earth curved sharply down to allow the stream its passage, both slightly breathless, the sudden halt from movement and the gulps of cold, clear air making my head light, allowing hunger to resurge in my stomach. 'Down here,' he said, and I followed him along the edge of the bank, stepping where he stepped carefully, wondering at the purpose of the adventure, but also just content to move with him, us together alone above the trickling and folding of water.

Suddenly he stopped and put his hands on his hips, not a natural gesture of his and I watched as he looked around us, as his waist turned with the movement that would allow no space between the trees to go unseen. Then he crouched, took his boots and foot-cloths off, rolled up his trouser-legs and jumped into the stream. The water was at his thin bare shins, moving quickly so that it rippled around and downstream from these pale blades, and though I feared the coldness of the water I too began to release my feet. But I heard a grunt from him and looked up to see him shake his head.

'Look,' he said. He waded over to a large stone towards the middle of the stream, the water rising up his shins and darkening the band of rolled fabric below his knees, but he showed no care for the discomfort this would cause, instead bending to put his hands on the stone, to push and slide it sideways in a smooth movement, as easily as if the stone was floating.

Quickly he rolled the sleeves of his shirt up and plunged his hands into the stream. He worked invisibly beneath the water's surface before his straining expression softened and he straightened to standing, to my surprise holding a pot: a small squat object that I recognised as one of many from our home, but distorted by the arrangement at its mouth of what appeared to be a dirty cloth and a wooden lid, lashed several times around with cord.

My heart was beating quickly as my father waded back over to the bank, and I edged forwards to receive him, to see what was inside, his head and the smell of him close to me as he released the lashing, then with effort twisted the lid away from the heavily waxed cloth that was perfectly clean underneath, to reveal the grain in the pot, sitting intact and unblemished, moving as good grain should when he gave the pot a tiny shake. In disbelief I looked to him, to find his grey eyes on me, a smile appearing as he replaced the lid and rested the pot on the bank.

He waded back out and carefully replaced the stone, and then on the bank, while covering up his feet, he said, 'There is another one under that stone. I will show you two more places. I'm showing you in case anything happens to me. Not even your mother knows where these are; you must not tell anyone – not even your brother!'

He was looking at me as he pulled on his boots. 'Do you understand?'

'Yes.'

Of course I understood!

I understood that we were saved, that we had been saved by the guile of my father. We carried this grain home with us, taking it from the pot to fill our pockets and then carefully discarding the pot. That night all of us stayed awake watching the fire, waiting until the dead of night when my mother finally risked making the bread, the agony of its baking scent making us squirm and moan, and my father worried that the smell would carry all the way to the next homestead. My mother assuaged him that this was nonsense but their discussion made us all fear a sudden knock at the door, this terror felt most keenly when finally the bread emerged from the stove, a small golden dome that we waited for to cool, before the brief and unforgettable ecstasy of its consumption.

And as I ate, I caught my father's eye, and the knowledge that passed between us was that he was trusting me with our lives, and he was not afraid for this trust. He had chosen me and not my elder brother, and while I did not want to inwardly gloat on this, I could not help but feel a great happiness: in part for the reserve of food hidden in the stream, but mostly for the affirmation of what I had suspected – that between my father and me there existed a purer bond – had been proven true.

For a few days I lived gloriously in the belief that we alone would not wilt or suffer death, that I would not see in my own family the unthinkable void of loss through starvation that had already afflicted those we knew of nearby. I felt guilt that we could supplement our meagre foraging while others could not, and I mentioned this to my father, whose impassive face told me he felt the same. He then spoke and said perhaps he would take a pocketful of grain here and there, and it was the day after this that the men came: one in a tunic that looked like a uniform, the other in the black clothing of the city, both of them arriving in a vehicle that we heard from many miles away, that froze us to the spot as we all sat around the table, my father pinning me still with the grey of his stare. I looked away from him many times, to the other faces around the table, to return and see that he was still staring at me: a silent flow of command that I understood, that I tried to show I understood.

Before the men arrived we went out to meet them, to stand in desolate array: my mother and father, my brother and my two young sisters, making a neat line with me at its end, to watch with curiosity the approach and halting of the lumbering car, the dark figures emerging from inside. The man in black stepped forwards: he was tall and broad, bigger than the other, and he did not look comfortable in what he wore, as if it was stiff around him. My father asked him what it was he wanted, and he explained bluntly that they had had reports that we were hiding food. And though expected, I felt shock jolt through me like the sudden kick of an animal, to fade and be replaced with a sickening fear, that appeared in my legs as an uncontrollable trembling.

My father protested; the man ignored him and motioned to his aide, they walked past us and began a slow circle of the house. Between them the talk was quiet and efficient as they pointed out features, inspected areas of ground with stamping and prodding.

'We have given everything already!' my father called after them, but he was ignored, and together but disjointedly my family followed the men as they circled the house, watching silently as they investigated the empty byres and storehouse, following in a fearful trickle through the door behind my mother and father when the men entered the homestead, to begin a violent upheaval of all furniture and bedding, checking every part of the floor, looking in every pot and earthenware container and smashing a few in the process.

'Please!' my mother said. 'We have hidden nothing!'

Still they did not answer, even when my father began again to implore them, moving close enough to sometimes bar their way. They would move around him as if he did not exist. His voice, the rough and frightening sound they made with their search and the crying of my sister: these were the sounds I listened to, trying to control the trembling of my legs, looking at the floor until I heard the man say, 'Sit down,' to look up into silence, and see my father being offered a chair at the table.

Our home was destroyed: chairs and stools were overturned, sheets of bedding were strewn over the floor, mingling with broken bits of pottery and cooking tools. Behind where my father sat down at the table was the stove, its smooth pale mass unblemished, its metal door hung open to reveal the flames inside; this object too large and impervious to any damage, and which gave me hope as the larger man seated himself at the head of the table, having waited patiently for his aide to stoop lithely and lift him up a chair. It felt perfectly normal to see my father and a man sat at the table before the stove – this a thing I had seen many times – and now that the search was over, the storm of it all perhaps had passed: the men seemed no longer unreasonable brutes, but could again become men – guests even – if they might merely make good in some way.

'Well, we have not found anything,' said the man in dark clothing, sitting stiffly and with a slight grimace, as if the chair pained him.

My father said nothing, and my mother, standing with her hands clenched at her navel, stopped leaning forwards so intently.

'Comrade Commissar,' my father said. 'We are hiding nothing. We have contributed all we have.'

'So you keep saying!' laughed the man, who my father had named as Commissar: this a title I had heard of, but never heard in application. It was no surprise to me that the owner of this rank was the large man sat at our table, the giant hands of whom had just ripped through the innards of our home. 'You may well say that again and again, but I know you are lying.'

'I am not lying,' my father said quietly.

The Commissar raised his hand, to stop further protest from my father with its palm, then his fingers relaxed so that a fist remained between them. 'I have had not one, but two reports,' and his thumb and finger appeared, 'that you must be hiding grain.'

My father did not answer immediately. 'Your reports must be . . .'

'Wrong?' said the Commissar, his face shocked. 'Perhaps they are lying.'

My littlest sister had stopped crying; I saw my mother shift her position where she stood. It seemed to us as if our fate would be decided on what my father said next, that the Commissar was fair enough that the right answer would assuage him, and the men would leave. My father did not speak for a long time, and when the silence became much too long I looked to him, to find that in that moment the profile of his face looked very weak, and I felt a pain in my stomach and chest to see my beloved father suddenly reduced to become childlike, so that it was like watching a sibling and not a man, squirming before a cleverer tormentor: his mental struggles obvious in the heavy breaths he was taking, the swallowing and the erratic movement of his foot beneath the table.

'Comrade Commissar,' he said. 'The people who told you this must be wrong.'

'Do you deny that you gave grain to the Zautashvillis? To the Griners?'

The Commissar said this eagerly, and it was shocking for me to hear the names of these two starving families: they were the ones my father and I had discussed the previous day.

'No.'

'But you said you held nothing back, that you had given everything.'

'I found the grain. I admit, Comrade Commissar, we had some, and we gave some away.'

'You found it! Where did you find it?'

My father did not pause. He raised his head and said, 'In the nest of something. Some rat or vole in the woods that I was trying to catch. I dug up its burrow and found a handful of grain it had stored.'

'A vole?' said the Commissar leaning forwards, his eyes wide.

'Or similar.'

'Well! Of course! Yes of course,' replied the Commissar, and I felt relief beginning to soothe the shaking of my legs, and a renewal of admiration for my father: the weakness I saw in him dispelled totally by this explanation, which was one based heavily on his suspicion that rodents stored food, and meant that he repeatedly told us to excavate any burrows we found. The relief was not only in me, but in all of us – even my youngest sister, because even she could remember squatting with a stick, widening the walls of a small tunnel in the earth. We all seemed tied together by this lie, so that when the Commissar looked expectantly at each of us, he found young faces full of confidence, and also my mother, in stillness, regaining ownership of the ruined home around her.

'What a lucky find!' he said, turning back to my father. 'Come then, Peter,' he said to his aide. 'Let us leave this lucky, lucky family!' He stood up from the table and my father rose with him. The Commissar and Peter made their way to the door, passing obstacles of their making impassively and we followed, the separate figures of my family coming together so that we were close and I could feel my mother's hand on my back as we watched the two officials walk out into the morning, begin to make the short distance to the car. We followed my father outside, brushing and bumping each other as we passed through the narrow doorway, to see the two men paused at the car's open doors and turned to us as if about to wave.

'What are you waiting for?' the Commissar called out. And I was about to lift my hand uncertainly, but stopped the movement when he said: 'Come along then!'

'Comrade?' my father asked, and there was fear in his voice. To hear this made my heart pound, made my legs begin to shake again and I prayed – I prayed that somehow nothing more would be said, that the men would only leave.

'Don't act surprised,' the Commissar said. 'You don't expect to stay here after lying as you have, do you?'

'Comrade . . .'

'No, no. Don't protest. Come on! Come here and get in the car. Peter?'

Peter leaned to reach inside the car and when he straightened, he was holding a rifle. We watched as its barrel came slowly down, the tiny black eye of the muzzle clearly pointing at where we clustered, to make us all afraid of what might spit from it, my sister hiding her face against my mother.

'Come now, or Peter will shoot you where you stand.'

I looked to my father, to see the side of his face, to find in it not weakness but something far worse: an expression of resignation, the same one he might have if a sick animal could not be revived, and he would have to make the walk to the storehouse for a club or knife. He took a step forwards, away from us, and from silence my mother screamed: a shattering and ugly sound that terrified me and my brother and sisters, because it did not sound like her at all, it held no warning nor anger but was senseless in its distress, and I wondered with panic and confusion how a single step of my father could turn her into something so alien and frightening. Then, to cause a pounding in my head and chest so intense that I thought I would collapse, I realised my father no longer belonged to us, but was being ripped from us by these men, perhaps for ever, and without him, without his strength and guile, we would all perish.

'No!' my mother shrieked, a sudden clarity from the incoherent noises she was making.

My father stopped and turned, to be suddenly rushed at by my little sister: a tiny streak that he squatted down to cling to, and the sight of them clasping one another was the trigger for all of us to rush forwards and embrace him, each of us straining to feel more of his firm warmth with our arms and heads, with our faces pressed against him. Then my mother descended like a soft covering to encircle us from above.

'It will be all right,' my father said when he emerged to stand, his hands moving quickly to stroke our heads, feel the curve of an ear or grasp a shoulder. 'It will be all right.'

And I remember how we had been like stunned animals: a small disordered herd yet all gazing dumbly in the direction of my father walking to the car. His head was angled down and his arms swung lazily at his sides – this his gait when he had no task or purpose – and it still seemed possible that he was walking over to join some friends or similar, that things would be all right as he had promised, that our world was not ending and our family about to begin a slow passage towards death.

'Wait!' the Commissar called out, the tone of his voice high and uncertain, as if in discovery. My father had to stop again and lift his head. 'Why should it be that you leave your family? It does not have to be.'

We waited silently, but each one of us must have shook inside with hope. I can remember exactly how it felt: it was a pain and a happiness that stopped my breathing and seemed to stop my heart; I stood perfectly still as if any movement might distract the Commissar from a course I craved, we all craved more than anything else.

'Yes, yes it is quite simple. You do not have to come with us!' he said, opening out his arms. 'All you need do – all someone needs to do is tell me where it is hidden.' His face was not unpleasant, he did not seem to act out of malice. Suddenly I realised why it was that my father had shown me the pots in the stream: it was because he knew that I would be brave enough to speak up, that my small form would emerge with the courage in a moment such as this, that I would be daring enough to intrude into the adult world – it all seemed so clear to me!

I writhe now on the stove remembering that moment: great pulses of regret and sorrow making me twist and gnash my teeth; hot flushes of shame to think of the small step I made forwards, full of the glory of being the one that would save my father – and then the bovine swinging of the Commissar's head in my direction. I had raised my hand and said that I knew where they were, then turned in victory to my father, only to find his grey eyes staring at me coldly, the rest of his face impassive and its features completely limp in the hidden rage that had turned his hands into fists.

Instantly I realised my mistake. I wanted to look to my mother, to find comfort there, but the burning confusion around my head and face meant that I could not, for fear that her sympathy would be absent. And now that I had spoken, the Commissar and Peter were very different: they had left the car and moved quickly towards me, their faces had the same expressions as when they had torn through our home, and I cowered as they approached, felt fear at their advent against which I had no hope of defence, and it was a relief to hear my father's voice call to halt them.

'Wait,' he said. 'I'll show you.'

The two men, my father and I then crossed the barren field to the woods. No one spoke. For me every footfall was one made in deepening horror and realisation at what I had done, so that when we arrived at the stream, although my legs shook uncontrollably, elsewhere I was numb: I heard them speaking but did not really hear them, I watched dully as my father climbed down the bank and retrieved the first pot; can remember him doing the same to lift the other two from their hiding places, his movements indistinct, unlike the clear dark water still bending and rippling over itself, this the thing I stared at unblinkingly.

After that, the days that followed were long, filled only with hunger and silence. I felt the constant wrenching of the disaster I had caused, and the few words my mother spoke to me were of no comfort, because they did nothing to mask the desperateness of our situation; they could do nothing to change what had happened, or even begin to hide the desolation that had befallen my family. These barren and hateful days turned to perhaps a week and our hunger worsened enough that my sisters became like the children of the village: keening almost constantly with pain, a sound they soon learned could seldom muster my weakening mother from where she sat blankly at the table, and which they reserved for when she showed any signs of movement.

And it was during these days that I fell ill, having staggered back from another unsuccessful forage with my head spinning. I returned home and told my mother I was sick; she looked up from where she sat, and then to the top of the stove, this permission the only assistance she was able to provide in my retreat there, so that the climb upwards felt like an endless task, peppered with long periods where I did not know what I was doing, why there was suddenly warm stone against my face.

The illness – its feverish twisting swoops of thought and image – are the only respite from the guilt that now presses on me more than hunger, because when my mind clears, when the sounds of the homestead emerge and I am awake I think for an instant that things are different, before I am plunging downwards in the horror of realisation, to see most clearly the vision of my father as he was pushed roughly into the car, his face turning, the grey eyes brightly alighting on me.

Now I writhe and clench my fists, I bare my teeth and grimace in the hope that the look he gave me at that moment was forgiveness!

To think that I may have killed him, that he is suffering the lingering death of the journey to the north and all its horrors, is enough that I think I wish for death myself, for this illness to take me; and sometimes when I am able to lie very still I can feel its approach, I will it towards me but then find myself suddenly gasping for breath, abrupt noises that will raise my mother's head, to look up in surprise to see that I am still alive and am looking down at her in search of something.

I hear a shuffling from below and open my eyes, the roof briefly flaring with light, then the sound of the door closing. It will be my brother, returning empty-handed from his scavenging, or digging, or begging in the town, except that when I roll weakly to the side I see that my mother is standing at the table and my sisters are making their high-pitched whimpering, and this activity tells me that my brother must have succeeded, must have come home with something edible. I think that I will let them eat it without me, that I do not deserve to partake, but then above all else the hunger that lives in me flexes violently and I struggle to get up, find that I cannot and so instead turn over onto my front, begin to slide to the edge of the stove and then down its side.

When I have reached the ground and stand, my legs shake and try to topple me, but I am able to turn by holding on to things, to see them clustered at the table: very close, yet unaware that I have descended. By staggering I move forwards, each step an effort of balance, a fight against weakness, and I worry that they will eat whatever it is before I can reach the table, but it does not seem right to try to call to them, and so I quicken my stagger, bringing the table towards me, arriving at a free edge of it in a stumble to make them all turn to me, their faces a little startled except for my mother, whose surprise suddenly turns to anger.

Before her, near her fingers on the table, is a tiny piece of dark bread. I watch as she carefully breaks it apart, giving a piece to my two sisters, and then one to my brother. I wait for her hand to extend to me, but it does not come. I look to her hands to see where the rest of it has gone, seeing how the worn fingers are closed in soft fists, and I think that the last of it must be hidden there, and sway at the edge of the table wondering why she delays, listening to the agonising sound of chewing coming from my siblings.

'Mother,' I croak.

She does not look at me. She takes in a huge breath that makes her shoulders and head rise and fall, and when this breath comes out of her I realise it is not a breath but a sob.

'Mother.'

She turns her head but is still looking downwards, not at me but at the part of the table I cling to. In this position she shakes her head. Then her hands are moving in front of her: the wrists revolving and the fingers opening like the end of a magic trick, and I watch intently but without excitement, because I realise she holds nothing, that she is doing this because she cannot bring herself to say that the food is gone; she is showing me her empty palms to tell me silently that I will not eat, that I have been passed over.

I stand here, starving and swaying before my mother and am abandoned! She has turned from me, the side of her face distorted with pain; she is crying and I feel the tears at my eyes, my breaths beginning to stutter into sobs. There is a cold pressing against my chest and everything around me is slippery and menacing. Then this danger seems to fade, and I am left standing only in a great emptiness.

'Is it because I told the men?' I ask.

'No!' she gasps without turning.

I am relieved at her answer, but only for a moment before I am gripped by terror, because then I understand why I was not given some of the bread: it is because she sees that I am too ill, that I will die, that to feed me over my brother who can still forage, or my young sisters and their mewling, would be a waste. The coldness thuds against my chest – neither hunger nor illness, but a deep and desperate sadness for both myself and my mother, who stands and shakes with silent crying, and who I would like nothing more than to hold, have her hold me and feel the press of her kiss. But I know that to do this would increase the pain that wracks her, and so I turn away from the table, a movement in which I have never felt more alone or afraid, and stagger back to begin my slow ascent of the stove, to collapse into the mess of tepid coverings there.

I lie on my back and look at the roof, the pain in my

chest fading, becoming a numbness in both my body and my thoughts. Soon, or perhaps after days, I find I have little care for myself, for how I have been excised from the world that was my family, somehow torn away from the protection of my mother's love. But what I am afraid of, and what repeatedly grips me with a terrible strength is the thought that I must pass utterly alone into death; it is enough to start my heart beating furiously, this pounding and the blinking of my eyes the only movement I am capable of.

There is light on the roof and I hear someone calling. The sound of their voice is distant, but excited, and this excitement is enough that I find some last strength to twist my head to the side and upwards, so that lying I can see the doorway, and standing there a figure. For a brief and wondrous moment I see my father returned, before the figure steps forwards to resolve into the form of my elder brother, who is holding something above his head and shouting 'Bread! Bread!'

Exhausted, I release the twisting effort at my neck, but am unable to turn my head away from where it has slumped. There is darkness and I realise that my eyes have closed. In this blackness I feel my breathing, shallow and whistling, and to think of it suddenly makes it very difficult, so that I must concentrate intensely to bring the air in, to push it out. There is a noise, a wailing, like a bird or small animal, and something is against my face: something cold but alive pushing against my face to turn my head. I open my eyes and there is my mother above me; I find it is her making the wailing sound: her face is scrunched and creased and wet with tears and at its side hovers her other hand, the fingers extended like a beak, the point of this beak coming towards me so that together with the sound, it is as if she tries to make a puppet, except that her fingers descend to my lips and gently open them. Suddenly I am tasting bread soaked in water, my body convulsing with an instant response to raise my head and begin sucking at her fingers, her tears dripping down onto my face as she feeds me, the sound she makes not a senseless wailing, but an endless repetition of the word sorry.

Interlude

The 38 Bus to Tel Aviv

I t's not all it's cracked up to be, that's for certain. There are still pleasures to be had, of course, but the initial excitement has passed: it is now so distant that it only exists as flickers of memory, and I wonder sometimes if these, even, might be illusory.

But it is my lot, and for that I am eternally grateful. Tonight, for instance, I think I am beginning a new chapter – I think that finally I have found the correct path. I will begin again with Number 1. She is by no means the prettiest, or the best endowed, and there are many features of her that I find distasteful. I will take her, however, safe in the knowledge that in four nights' time it will be 'Number 5 Eve', which is an event to look forwards to for sure, because in terms of beauty she is incomparable to all the others; her hair is as black as a raven's wing, her eyes are like two giant pools of seawater, and the face around these portals to bliss is smooth with barely the first flush of womanhood, while beneath, past the perfect curves of her breasts, beneath the flat plain of her stomach, deeper than all this is the Holy of Holies, for here in magic fold of flesh exists my Shrine of Olibanum.

Already I find that I cannot wait! That my jaw is tight and my heart pounding for her.

Perhaps I should abandon the plan, discard the correct path (which may be illusory) and go straight for Number 5 tonight, for surely in this mood that I find myself there can be no chance for disappointment, it will be as good as it was when first I took her, for she was indeed my first – oh what bliss it was afterwards to lie beside her, every light brushing of her finger like a pulse of something pure and secret, a power that only existed between us, that belonged to us and was yet above us and ungraspable.

But no. No no no. I must not deviate from the path, I must be as strong as I was when climbing up the steps of that bus, even though my heart pounded and my palm was slicked with sweat – in fact I felt parts of me sweat that I did not know could sweat.

Besides, I have learned my lesson. I have learned more than one lesson, have tried many different techniques and systems. In the beginning each night was a wildness: I would have them parade before me and then select whichever one took my fancy; it was an unbridled joy then because of my innocence, and also theirs, and we partook of each other as life on earth partakes in spring, with nothing but a forceful desire to bud upwards, to burst outwards, to unfurl and express lest the dream conjured by the warming sun turns out only to be a dream.

The dream does not end; I found it did not end and soon the nightly selection became more difficult, the parade less enthusiastic, the chaos of passion becoming replaced by a sense of imbalance, that some Numbers were being chosen more often than others, and there was even some embitterment from Number 28, who had not been picked at all. I made a point of selecting her, and do you know what? The very next night I went back to Number 5, and my! How I was rewarded! It was as if all the old magic had suddenly flooded back. It came back with so much force as to be a mystery where it had gone in the first place.

And so, inspired by this, I invented the 'High-and-Low' scheme, which ran quite successfully for a while, and was based on the simple premise of picking one of the uglier Numbers, in order to provide contrast with my favourites (namely Numbers 5, 7, 22 and 29. And Number 14 too, she's good). Then an innovation: I found that if I went Low-Low-High, the contrast was even greater, to much joy all round. A brief experiment in Low-Low-Low-High proved, however, to be too much of a grind.

During this time I did look into the possibility of whether one could transfer Numbers, but was told that this was (unsurprisingly on reflection) banned.

So the High-Low scheme operated for a while, but there was a flaw: on some of the nights when I was due to go Low, I would find that my lust for one of the better Numbers would be uncontrollable. Sometimes I would even break my own rules, and this was a double-edged sword: it could result in a wonderful evening, it could also end in disaster, with feelings of guilt, and self-disgust – for it is always a terrible thing to have to abandon one's own plans.

After long reflection, and many a pleasant stroll, I realised that what I needed was a way to give every evening meaning, and while it would not be possible, or indeed desirable, to guarantee the ultimate highs of exultation and ecstasy every night, if I had a system that meant everything belonged to a greater framework, a higher order as it were, within which I would be guaranteed the occasional highpoint, then surely this would be preferable to the casting about of former times, the tired, lazy parades, the meaningless selections, the disappointing, draping mantle of one person's flesh on another, which I must confess had become the norm.

And the beauty is, the new system is brilliantly simple. It is simply a question of going through the Numbers in order. I am excited, as I always am at the beginning of a new system like this, but this time I think I really have it. Already I see great possibilities: for instance, once I have gone through all the Numbers, I will go through only the odd Numbers, and then only the even Numbers, and at the end of each sequence I will take time to reflect – how was it for me? This system is perfect because it is unthinking, and yet will create natural and interesting patterns.

I can't wait for *Prime Number Only* week. That way I'll get 5, 7 and 29 in quick succession, with very little chaff in between, magnificent.

Sometimes, though, I wonder if all this planning, all these ideas are again, illusory. And that once again, once I am into the system, once its flaws become apparent, I will begin to think that it is not a good system after all, and will start upon the path of betrayal in my mind, even though going through the motions of the established system. Then, as has happened before, I will stick to it for a few more days, may even try to formulate a development, using complex mathematics (the possibilities are endless) – yet I will do all of this with the knowledge that deep down, in the fundaments of my soul, I have already rejected the Path – it is dead and merely awaits its replacement. Then will follow the usual dreaded period of unorganised choice, with all its pitfalls and self-loathing. Perhaps what I need is some sort of penalty mechanism, to make it more interesting – I don't know.

Ach, but these thoughts are those of the doubter! If I had had such thoughts when I was on that bus, I would never be in this position. But I did not, and BANG, here I am. One must believe in the system!

Here they come, then.

They must sense from my bearing that a new system is at hand, for they are alert and seem excitable. There is Number 1, standing at the end. Steadily I approach her, the others are watching me, and Number 1 thinks that I will walk past her down the line but no! I stop before her and calmly, wisely, with the certainty that what I do is right and correct, that I stand on the right path, the true path, the only path, the path above all others both now and in the future, I raise my hand out to her, and she takes it.

And as we depart I am aware of the nodding heads and accepting sighs of the others. I know that they are happy, and I am happy, for together we are the strands in a huge fabric of meaning, some of it by my design, so that every movement we make is once again a wonderment, is ablaze with a glorious light shining all around us, the light of glistening pearls that lie strewn across the golden path of our righteousness.

Part 3

The Eagle and the Pit

When they are finished, he is just a bloody stump
sprouting from the ground.

This blood is bright red against the dark earth
and what remains of his dark skin. I take a clutch of frames
where the blood shows gaudily in the sunlight, an orange
hint of unreality to it as if a scene from early Technicolor,
then I move so the colours are hidden, and instead what is
visible is not what leaks, but the slumped bust of his profile:
a silhouette of head and shoulders that has many possibilities. I work quickly to capture these, kneeling, squatting,
stepping sideways to change the casting of shade, and I do
this with a slight excitement: the same excitement that I
always have when working near violence, but augmented by
the rarer knowledge that the product will be both very good
and sought after.

Sometimes this knowledge, this feeling can be wrong; at
other times the brute fact of it unequivocal. When Hanif
and I arrived at the village the signs were not yet present,
and even when we were taken to the clearing at its edge and
allowed to survey the shallow pit – a look of peering disgust
from Hanif, perhaps a dozen shots from me – there was still

no indication. It was only a long drive wasted until I saw a group of people being herded down towards us: a mixture of ages and sexes not overwrought with fear or desperation, but a reluctance and quiet dread in their faces visible to me, and that I caught with a reaching zoom, pressured as they were by the two men with covered faces, who did not shout or push but walked beside them with every intention of delivering them to the clearing. This was when it registered that something would happen, that Hanif's information was good, and I took no more shots of these herds of people as they were brought down from the hovels and decaying public spaces, to collect in the open space as a loose cluster, not quite a throng, but an audience nonetheless.

And when they brought him down I would have sensed it if my eyes were shut, because the people were suddenly made quiet as if flattened, not by an order but by the sight of him half-struggling against the two that held his arms, his steps laboured with reluctance so that he bobbed up and down between them; this the sight before the sound of his crying reached us, and we realised that he was begging those who held his arms, that he did not want to fight too much for fear of offending them further. There was no obstruction to my lens in seeing this, the people around me kept away so that I had clear pathways, the children even running with fear if the black eye of the device seemed near enough to encompass them.

His begging continued as they lowered him into the hole, a constant flurry of a language I could never master – and why should I because I do not deal in sound but image – and as he begged and implored but did not struggle I photographed him; when the earth had risen up to his chest and he was completely pinned within it, I had already made a complete circuit, him not seeing me move around him, the fact that I was completely invisible as I moved and squatted and clicked a further indication that truly, he only faced his own death.

I heard Hanif's voice: an echo of a sudden guttural command from one of the men with cloth around his head and face, probably an order for me to get back.

'They're going to start,' he said.

But I did not move, because I do not follow commands, and only turned the camera to look for them, those who were about to start, to see with one eye a group of men standing near a pile of pale stones that must have been brought, as I did not see them only minutes previously. These men with covered faces were clustered around the stones, some of them squatting as I did, their hands in positions of selection, and I got several shots of this, moving backwards on my haunches until the man in the earth began to appear in the frame, his head nodding and swaying as he spoke and cried or perhaps prayed, and I hoped fervently that at that instant no one would grab me or put their hand to block my lens, because the composition was very good, the light was perfect, and I was working quickly and without effort.

There was another shout, and again Hanif's voice interpreting, his voice sounding warped and urgent. Obediently, then, I stood and moved away, dropping the camera from my eye to quickly encompass the loose crowd, looking for interesting faces and finding none, returning to the men without faces and then walking an elliptical path towards them, raising the lens when I saw the first step forwards and throw his palm-sized rock: not a great picture as the throw was tentative. The second man was seemingly more practised and launched his stone with a fluid and powerful technique, and I captured him leaning forwards on one leg with his arm fully extended, his neighbours surrounding him sportingly in the frame, waiting their turn; and this one I felt was sure to be an excellent photograph.

This done I turned from the throwers to their target. He was already badly blooded and had stopped babbling, and I thought with a sudden relief that he was unconscious. Except that there was a sort of rhythm to the throwing, and he must have been able to detect the spaces between the throws because then he would look up quickly; the next man would step forwards and hurl his stone, and he would see this and tuck his chin to his chest in futile defence of his face. This too I captured, but without the same smoothness, and in the knowledge that the greatest shots had already been taken: what must be done was to close out the sequence as professionally as possible.

That was a few minutes before. Now he is certainly dead and I photograph his ruined bust. Hanif is unhappy and wants to leave immediately.

'In a minute,' I tell him.

As I finish I am also watching the approach of one of the executioners, who Hanif does not notice until he is standing right next to him. I stand and put the cover on the lens, because now I have finished.

'Ask him what did this man do.'

Hanif speaks to the man, then turns to me. 'Adultery.'

'The woman?'

'She will not be killed, but she will be punished.'

'It's a bit extreme, no? To kill someone for adultery.'

Hanif gives me a long look. Then he interprets for Mr Headscarf, who turns to me, and in slow English says, 'This is God's law.'

'Yes, I guess it is.'

Then we are in Hanif's van and driving back to the city.

The evening light is low and orange, and even without it the scrubby naked earth on either side of the dirt road is the same colour, as if we whine and rumble through an illuminated amber liquid. The light means that I cannot check the day's produce during the drive – a pleasurable ritual of mine if the work has been good – but no matter because I am content to smoke and look out at the flat and ugly scenery of this stupid country, and I do not need to see the pictures on a tiny screen to sense that they are going to be very good, and the response from colleagues and editors instant and congratulatory from around the world.

The land changes from wild to become outlying, and then progresses to urban, with a sudden rush of decrepit buildings and the people of the city surrounding the road and then filling the road itself, the orange light having departed and been replaced by night, a darkness not banished as it would be in a real city, but lingering every-where in windows and alleys. Soon we are in the centre and have stopped at the hotel. Together and in silence we unload from the van, agree that Hanif will telephone me in the morning to see if he is needed.

Then, with my key obtained I am climbing the steps away from Reception up to my room, rushing slightly to get the door open, to pull out the camera and marry it with the laptop that I must extract from its place of preventative concealment, flipping it open on the small desk and waiting for the pictures to make their way from one technology to the other. There they are on the screen: a large screen unlike the back of a camera, and I can see truly that the pictures are very good; I can hear how they will say that I have done it again, and am flushed with a happy clumsiness as I fumble with a third device, which will connect the pictures skyward out of this hole of a metropolis and into the consciousness of the rest of the world.

With the pictures sent I leave my room and descend the stairs towards the bar of the hotel. I feel agile and skip steps downwards, each jump a minor flight – and seeing my shadow on the thick carpet, split by the different points of light above, I am reminded of the way the shadow of a flying eagle can look on very high ground: enlarged and rippling over mountainside, fast outlines that you never see, or could hope to capture lower down when the angles are not in your favour.

The bar is a short slab of stone in front of a mirror, between which patrols the white-uniformed barman, who is allowed to make drinks for foreigners. Alighting in this small patch of the Reception area, I order from him and take to one of the high stools, which revolves pleasingly to enable a view of the front entrance and most of the stairwell – in fact I can see most of the front area of the hotel. When it comes, the drink looks good and I also notice that there is a redness and slight dreaminess to the barman's eyes: his movements are not slow but are very contained; he is clearly quietly but profoundly drunk.

I turn from him because there is noise behind me: a sudden bustle at the entrance of the hotel, a mix of porters laden with flight cases and the bright colours of expensive Western apparel, worn by a number of men and women who are slowly filtering through the door, talking with each other, with the porters in broken English and hand gestures. I was not expecting company, not from the world's media, but here they are, heading straight for me, and I wonder what has happened to bring them here, a momentary panic that I have missed out on something, before I remember that their visit is premeditated, is linked to the visit of a dignitary in whom I have no interest.

Some of them have made their way to the desk and are talking with the attendants, others are ignoring the logistics and heading straight for the bar. Among them are faces I recognise, and one I know well: a handsome man who is flanked by two women, one of whom looks very young and a little frightened by the country, and who instantly commands all my attention – a slim and golden-haired girl whom I quickly see is plain in some angles, quite beautiful in others, and especially beautiful in profile: her hair tied up to reveal a delicate ear when she turns, the small area of neck behind this ear and down around to the throat a sudden inexplicable source of desire in me – for the softness there – to have it available to senses other than sight.

The man in the centre looks up as they approach, must see me perched at the stone because his expression changes from the passivity he held in listening to the girl, into something more wary: a creasing at the sides of his eyes and the lifting of his chin, but tempered with a small upturning at the ends of his mouth.

'Ronnie,' I say. The girl and the woman have stopped talking. Ronnie steps forwards and offers his hand.

'What are you doing here?'

'Not holidaying.'

Ronnie smiles, uses the hand that I have just shaken to gesture on the left and right. He tells me that the woman is a journalist, whose name I recognise, and I nod to her; then he says that the girl is called Emma, and she has just started out: 'This is her first field trip.'

'Not quite the first,' she adds.

'And this, ladies,' Ronnie says, 'this is world-famous and award-winning photographer Mr Nick Carrera.'

The older woman moves closer and puts a hand on my arm. 'I knew it was you, but I was looking forwards to Ronald's introduction.' She lifts the light contact from me, which I did not resent; her face is worn and noble, she is seasoned and of good reputation, and I tell her this last part – and in that way we become friends. But the young girl's eyes flit and her bearing is nervous: small movements of head and hands that others would not pick up but I do, because I am watching her.

I order drinks for all of us and we move away from the bar to one of the congregations of seats. A younger man comes over and I think that he will join us, but he merely passes a key each to Ronnie and Emma, explains where the rooms are and leaves the hotel with another man who is waiting for him.

'Your ilk,' Ronnie says, after he has gone.

'They are not my ilk. They may hold a camera, but they do not take pictures.'

'And they never win awards,' says my new friend the journalist, who is called Helen. 'Unless they die in battle. Then it's the Military Cross or better.'

'Without those guys you'd be nothing,' I tell them.

'Without us they wouldn't know where to point it,' Ronnie replies.

This garners laughter and Ronnie is encouraged. He orders more drinks. Their rooms are organised, the cameras and lights they have no responsibility for and they have no commitments until the next morning. Also they are isolated in a country where you cannot drink, except in your hotel foyer. I am with them and on the verge of another great success and soon we have had several drinks, we are happy with the alcohol and the location and I am edging closer to the girl Emma: this is her first trip working abroad and she did not expect to meet me but she has. She has become aware of who I am and she is falling for it.

'You took that shot?' she says at one point. Her eyes are brown and I study them carefully. I am searching there for judgement but cannot find it, cannot see anything but a guarded admiration in her plain but well-structured face.

'Yes.'

'I'm impressed.'

'Be careful,' says Ronnie to her. He leans forwards. 'Be careful, Emma, because Nick here is like one of those TV detectives. People around him have a tendency to die, so that he can take a picture of their corpse and get famous, isn't that right, Nick?'

'You're not on the idiot box now, Ronnie; you don't have to talk complete garbage. You are just the same as me: we fly in where the story is good.'

'Like vultures!'

'Like eagles,' I reply, spreading out my arms with the palms facing them.

'The awards have gone to his head.'

Ronnie says this while I still have my hands in the air. But it is easy to slowly retract them and reach for my drink, to not sit so straight in my chair and then relax back into it, turning to smile quickly at the girl Emma. Her expression is quizzical but not without warmth; she is not yet convinced by me but certainly interested, and when first Helen and then Ronnie stand to retire to their rooms, it is simple to ask her to stay for one more drink at the bar, to share with her the knowledge that the barman is shamefully drunk but much the better for it. As are the drinks, mixed by a man who might mix them for himself, and we have several, before together we go to my room.

Hanif's van arrives the next day without a windshield, and we must travel using sunglasses and shirts wrapped around our heads to protect us from the flying specks of dust and sand kicked up by other traffic. At mid-morning we stop at the edge of a hamlet, while Hanif speaks to the locals. I inspect my equipment in the back to find it partly buried in orange-red sediment, which I scoop out with my hands, reaching through to the black plastic bags and looking inside these to see if the cases within are protected.

'Yes, this is looking good,' Hanif says when he returns.

'Okay.'

I am mostly satisfied that my equipment will be safe and we drive off, back onto the straight dirt road bordered only by more flat, featureless orange scrub, some hills in the distance to one side and occasionally the sign of habitation clinging to the road, but mostly just an empty, pointless country.

Earlier in the morning I had shown the stoning pictures to Ronnie. Emma had left in the night, and even though, while at the bar I had offered her a preview, she had not then asked to see them.

'They're very good,' Ronnie had said. 'Are you leaving today, then?'

'My fixer thinks he has another lead. The rebel bunch up in the northern plains. Thinks he can get me to one of their leaders.'

'I'm sure he can,' he said, leaning over the desk in my room, his body still but his hand moving as he manipulated the images that angled back up at him. His face was impassive, but his attention keen and unbroken by our conversation. 'But you don't want to go up there, Nick. Not on a wing and a prayer. Very tough country, hey. They're crazy and they don't like the media at all. Besides, you've got these.'

Then he stood and faced me. 'Your work here is done.'

'Come on, man, a chance is a chance.'

'It's risky.'

'It's always risky!' I told him.

'Not for me any more,' he smiled.

And we had accepted this difference between us: he must have left with his small crew to pursue his diplomat, while I had packed my case with what cameras I thought I would need, and stowed the computer in its nominal hide. I had stood waiting for Hanif outside the hotel's main entrance, watched his aged and rusted van appear among the heavy and chaotic traffic, could tell even from a distance that part of it was missing.

'What's this?' I asked, when grindingly he pulled up.

'An accident last night. You'll need something to wrap around your face.'

'Someone taking pot shots at you, Hanif?'

'No, Nick,' he replied. 'Just an accident.'

That had been in the cool of the morning; now we are in the beginning of the afternoon and have arrived at some sort of village. There are the ubiquitous huts and hovels at its edge, but closer in some brick or mud buildings, and the road is dirt but very hard, and there seem to be too many people here, as if it is a festival or market day. And although it is nothing but people, I feel the beginnings of an excitement in my chest. No guns or tanks nor anything of the like but I can sense the village is incorrect, is hiding something even from itself, and while Hanif drives I climb over into the back and swipe the dust from the cases, carefully picking out two cameras before resealing the zippers and the plastic bags around them.

When I return to the front I remove my headscarf, lift my sunglasses to the top of my head and, after checking the first camera, put it to my eye and begin shooting. Instantly, some of those who see the lens react, and they react badly with angry faces and a violent waving of hands; also by calling loudly to others: a man who is leaning in a doorway hearing this call and turning to look for me, starting out in futile but threatening pursuit of the van.

These are all signs I recognise and am grateful for, because more often than not they lead to the event – whatever the event may be – which I can feel is most likely nearby from the trickling nervousness in my stomach, and the sudden and strong desire I have to use the camera: to frame the things around me, the lack of windshield a sudden advantage, allowing full range and clarity for the stubby black turret that I swivel.

'I think this is it,' Hanif says, after we have continued down the main road a short while further. He turns off and parks the van in front of a small white building that looks both recently and badly built. We get out and slam the doors behind us; I stand in the sun and wait, my cameras hanging around my neck, looking very Western and it is not long until I am approached by a native, an older man who flees when I lift a camera and try to shoot him, an incident that triggers two other men to appear and quickly come towards me with aggressive aspects of body and face, jabbering angrily and making swipes for the camera when they have got close enough.

'Press,' I tell them. 'Don't touch my camera or I'll have your boss kill you.'

It is the usual scenario, and though I am not unafraid and do not speak a bit of their language, it does not take me long to show them that they cannot simply take the cameras from me as they had hoped, that they might get in trouble if they touch me or the technology, and that I am here on very official and important business.

'Smoke?' one of them asks, pointing at the packet he can see in my shirt pocket.

'Sure,' I say, and when Hanif comes out he finds all three of us smoking.

'The Chief, he says he will see you.'

'Chief? Great. Let's go, then.'

I give my cigarette to one of the men, and am about to turn to go with Hanif into the building when a shout comes from it, a sound that brings the two men to sudden alertness –

and I know something is wrong because immediately Hanif is trying to talk over the man who is giving orders, but does not succeed, and suddenly all three cigarettes are on the ground and the men have grabbed my arms. Their grip is strong and their faces lack none of the speculation of earlier; they have their orders and though I protest and threaten they walk me towards the building, lifting me so that my reluctant steps make little difference to our progress.

The building is dark and cool inside: an empty corridor to echo my imprecations for the men at either side, and there is no sign of the man who gave the order for me to be seized. Hanif is behind and saying something to the men that hold me while I shout at them, so that this group of us noisily tunnels down the corridor into the building before I am turned and made to pass through a doorway. Inside this room is an old desk, and behind it sits a large man in combat dress: not a uniform but the typical amalgamation of dark greens and khaki of the self-proclaimed freedom fighter, no ornament or badge to denote high rank. But the way he does not look up – despite the fact four men have just burst in on him – the way he waits and leaves us standing and breathing before glancing upwards pointedly is enough for me to suspect his local authority.

He says something and the two men release my arms, only to quickly snatch at both cameras and begin pulling in earnest, snapping the strap and coming away with one of them, while the other belt holds and I can twist my wrist and hand around it, devoting all my strength to holding on to this remaining camera so that now the man pulls at me rather than the strap and we struggle silently in the middle of the room.

'He just wants the camera, Nick,' says Hanif distantly.

I am determined that the man will not take it from me, but then the other rejoins and they can prise my grip open and finally get the strap over my head; then both cameras are on the desk and the men are holding me again so that I cannot retake them.

The boss or Chief or whatever he is lifts one of them up and turns it over. It looks small and alien in his hands and his fingers begin to pry at the back, as if trying to open it, and I realise that he wants to rip the film out before me, he wants the satisfaction of reeling out the thin strip into the all-destroying light: a bit of theatre for our edification.

'Tell him it's digital, there's no film,' I say into the room.

Hanif translates, and the man's expression does not alter much, but enough that I see he has been caught.

'Tell him that I have come to take pictures of him and his men, so that his power and legitimacy will be known around the world.'

Hanif speaks again and I watch the Chief listening, looking for signs in him that the offer appeals.

'Tell him who I am, Hanif, how people know me, how I can promote his cause.'

The Chief continues to listen impassively to Hanif's voice, which emanates quietly but urgently from behind me, and continues to do so, so that I think he must be elaborating, which is fine, for Hanif knows his country and its people. He is a good fixer and can talk people down – this I have already seen in the previous days – and when a look of shock passes over the Chief's face I think that Hanif must have struck home, must have got through to this ignorant and simple-minded warlord. The Chief straightens in his chair and then says something lowly but with anger.

'Hanif?'

'He says that there has not been a stoning here for a generation.'

'What does that mean?' I ask, twisting against the grip of the men to look over my shoulder at Hanif, who is standing in the corner of the room, looking small and worried. 'What the hell does that mean? Did you tell him we'd come for him? To take pictures of him?'

'Yes . . .'

The Chief has spoken again and this time it is an order because I am being dragged out of the room and back into the corridor. 'Hanif! What's going on?' The men's fingers are like steel cords on my arms and they march me down the short stretch of corridor remaining until we are outside again, but the other way, away from the road, back into the bright sunlight that momentarily obscures what is around me, before a rough and stone-strewn yard or clearing becomes evident from the glare: a place that is not walled in but is secluded, that I recognise from either fear or experience as having the potential for atrocity.

The three of us stagger over this ground until we come to a mound, behind which is a pit, a sight that is no less than a kick to my stomach for the shock it causes. Then I feel strong and lithe snakes slithering around me and into my pockets, which I realise are of course the hands of the men hunting for my possessions: a thin wallet and my mobile phone, cigarettes and plastic lighter, an inexpensive wristwatch. One of them puts these things neatly on the ground, and this action I watch with a paralysing mixture of acceptance and detachment, thinking it right that my things should be put neatly onto the ground, that this is a good sign. I look up and around: I cannot see Hanif or the Chief or anyone else and there are only the two men, and the one with the items on the ground finishes arranging them and says something to the other without looking up. Then he has moved quickly and got hold of my legs around the ankles, so that I am lifted from there and from under the arms, to make me wriggle worm-like while kicking and shouting my disbelief. Suddenly they are not holding me and I am falling, a scraping and several impacts soft and hard from earth and stone as I drop to the bottom of the pit.

My first thought is that the pit is too deep for stoning, and perhaps instead I will be buried. I am able to twist my legs under me and stand, lifting myself gingerly, a passing concern for broken bones. The pit is deep enough that when I look up, the entrance is as a rough circle of brilliant blue sky, at least my height again or more from the top of my head. The base of the pit is small enough that my feet are cramped in standing; I cannot sit but must lean or stand. There is no movement from the circle of light above and I make several attempts to climb the walls, but they are earth and crumble instantly when I try to grasp at them, or dig fingers in for purchase.

I shout long and hard for Hanif, then shout to the blue circle of sky about all the dignitaries and public figures who I know and that will miss me and seek revenge and justice for my loss, threatening this blue light above until my throat burns. But no one comes, no one is listening, and in silence I turn instead to considering my fate, wondering with repeated waves of a violent and nauseating fear whether they would actually execute me, and if they did, how would they do it? Hanif's words, echoing those of the Chief, run cold and sharp around the pit and into my head and I realise that I am more afraid than I have ever been in my life, that what I face is not typical, is far beyond my experience and may well be the prelude to something deadly.

In the time that passes I pepper the silence with hoarse shouts, but otherwise there is nothing to do but occasionally crane my neck upwards, and trigger minor but painful slides of rock and dirt with unsuccessful bouts of climbing. The opening at the top of the pit is suddenly darker and for a moment I think that someone has come for me, but then I realise that it is the sky itself dimming, and that my repeated glances to it have brought the beginning of evening unnoticed.

With this awareness comes a sharp thirst, and hunger, and perhaps it is these two things coupled with my fear that start it: a procession of images that unsolicited begin to form on the close walls of the pit and the back of my eyelids, snippets and flashes that begin indistinctly but become stronger and clearer as I understand what they are – until they are so strong that I can think of a scene or event that I have pressed to my eye with the aid of a camera and have it appear on the wall before me, as if a projection, a strange private show that I soon discover is inescapable and will not stop, no matter if I close my eyes or look to the darkening blue above.

At first they are a comfort, these images, because they are witness to what I have achieved and I am glad for them, even if they are bloody and violent, and often show the desperate suffering of others. But then I begin to fear that their presence, their recollection from memory may be indicative of my own impending suffering and death, and the two begin to fuse so that each new image – which with lessening control my mind seeks out and displays – brings with it a fresh and varied horror that I realise is not entirely for my own life, but also for the people I have photographed. The process of detachment I thought I understood and had mastered, to leave an instinct and gaze not blocked or shaken by compassion, and thus allow me to look where others were afraid to. But perhaps the subjects themselves – the people or their corpses – were screened from me in the purpose of taking their picture, as if by the use of a crystal lens I could hide from what was seen, and now in this pit without device, and with my mind running wild with fear, I have no defence against the shifting wash of misery paraded before me.

As night falls it deepens the unreality of where I am, of what has happened. The profound darkness, the inability to orientate from what must be a starless or clouded sky makes the images stream faster, totally without my control, so that they threaten and bombard me with their contents, they swirl and become disfigured before changing into something else. And behind them, always present in these war zones and torture cells is now an eagle: its wings slightly opened as if emblematic, its eyes very clear and golden, as from behind what it is that I see, it stands and watches also.

I know that this eagle is not me, is not symbolic of any talent of eye and spatial arrangement that I possess, but is the harbinger of something more dangerous, and I find I wish it would depart, would flap its wings and up because

I know which memory it pulls me towards, one that I try to avoid with thoughts of other things, but that suddenly snaps my chin to my chest and causes a heaving breath as I remember it: the grassy airfield, a building like a shoebox of concrete at its edge and the people streaming towards it, none of them quickly, some of them staggering, a ragged bunch of stick figures that had emerged from the trees. We had landed only seconds before and I left the unloading plane behind me to walk closer to these people, who were congregating at the building where the supplies would be meted out. I took a few uninteresting long shots of them as I neared, knowing no one would want very much the familiar sea of gaunt starvation that their faces portrayed.

I was still some way from the building when I noticed movement to the side: a small figure sitting on the ground far behind the others, a very young child that with great effort got to its feet and began staggering onward, would fall every few steps and have to begin again the process of standing. I moved quickly in its direction, walking smoothly as if stalking something, becoming quickly aware of the surroundings of the child and how it could be framed, and when I had got close enough I slowed and began to crouch and shoot, and noticed that the child had begun to weep, that it was sitting weeping with its tiny hand palm up in its naked lap, while behind it, behind her shoulder, in the patch of dark open ground there suddenly landed a bird: its beak large and aquiline, but the rest of it far from graceful – instead the bald-headed dirtiness of the carrion eater, its eyes dark and piercing, watching the girl with a sudden cocked head and then hopping closer.

I can remember the elation I felt: how quickly and silently

I moved to get the perfect shot, and how I knew the first one taken was the best, that all the others would be superfluous, that the first one alone would be enough to explode onto the world.

I did nothing wrong! I was not the catalyst of that scene and did not call down that vulture, and though I did profit greatly from that day I have never felt guilt for it. Not until now, and as soon as I admit this I become awash in it, the images and their accompanying raptor dissipating into a blackness, leaving me to nurse the pain I feel in my chest and stomach, to fight against the heaving of my breaths.

Then it is dawn, and the jagged circle of the opening turns to a grey away from black, and when it is no longer grey but tinged with blue there are noises, and my heart jumps to hear them turn into what is definitely a voice. I look up to see a figure peering down, his arm moving and an object flying at me which uncoils to become a rope. I grab it and begin climbing, while it too is being pulled, and by this dual effort I emerge from the pit and into the morning, to find one of the men who held me standing by the rope and grinning, another man that I do not recognise, and Hanif standing a little apart.

'Hanif,' I croak.

'It's okay, Nick,' Hanif replies, and for a second I think that he might be readying me to face an ordeal. But then he holds out his hand and in it is one of my cameras, the one with the broken strap. 'They want you to take pictures now.'

'How about some water?'

Hanif says something and the man I am familiar with produces a bottle of water, twists the top and hands it to me. I take it, spin the lid the rest of the way off and then suck the water from it. I cannot suck it quickly enough and with my head tilted back I can see nothing but the end of the bottle and the blue of the cloudless sky all around me, unrestrained by a border of earth. Suddenly I feel very high, a happiness pushing me upwards into the air, and when I detach the bottle from my mouth and look down, I turn to the man who passed it.

'Where's my stuff, hey?' I ask him, gesturing with thumb and little finger, tapping my front pocket and the back of my wrist. He grins as if he does not understand. Then to Hanif: 'Tell him no pictures of his boss until I get my mobile phone back.'

Hanif speaks and the man grins and nods; I do not know whether he will bring the things back and do not care, they are all expendable. I turn and trudge over to Hanif, my body stiff from the enforced position of standing and leaning, and taking the camera from him I look to his face to check for any sign of amusement or pleasure at my detainment, but to his credit I see relief and mild concern – if perhaps only for his pay cheque. 'Where did you spend the night?'

'In the van.'

'The cases?' I ask, taking a cigarette he offers.

'All safe.'

'Let's go, then.'

We leave the yard and re-enter the building, going along the same corridor and emerging out into the front where the van is still parked, but also waiting for us is an old military jeep with a driver and heavily armed passenger in the front, a large-calibre mounted gun and attendant gunner standing in the back. Hanif points to the jeep and I get in one of the two remaining empty seats. He has already stashed food and more water there and I thank him before flicking the cigarette and eating and drinking, watching as he goes to the van and extracts the cases, bringing them over to squeeze them in at my feet. Then he gets in the other side.

'Where are we going?'

Hanif turns to me. 'There is a camp a few kilometres from here. I think their General wants to meet you.'

'The General wants me to take his picture?'

'I think so.'

'Outstanding,' I say.

And I am in wonderment at the change in fate: from fear of death and short subterranean imprisonment, to a chance to meet with the man here that no other journalist has met with. But as we are driven through the early morning – as I pass through the bare and open land, no longer cornered by the pit and its images – I am shocked to find that where there should be the space in me for elation and laughter, there is nothing but an emptiness.

After a while we stop so that I can urinate at the side of the road. I find that when I get back in the jeep my thoughts have returned entirely to that day at the airfield. Something turns in my stomach that feels like revulsion. I replay my every action and look for fault, and though I can find none it is suddenly apparent to me that while I did nothing wrong, I also did everything wrong at the same time. When we start off again along the dirt road and I look up and out, I am for the first time perplexed by the nature of what it is I do.

'Are you all right, Nick?'

I turn to Hanif and then look away from him. Suddenly I

have a huge and basic desire for alcohol and women that is laughable in its baseness, but so real that it has my hands clenched into fists. In truth I do not know what it is that I do. In truth that day, when I had finished taking pictures of the child, I had stood and the vulture saw me and flew off. The child was weak but had nearly reached the centre. I did not help it because I did not have to: it made it there, she made it there by herself and I did not frame this event, not because I am unsure as to whether it really happened, but because it was not relevant to the original picture taken.

That picture helped those people, I say to myself.

'What?' asks Hanif.

'I didn't say anything,' I reply.

I ask him how far he said it was and he tells me. And in the minutes before we get there, already I start to feel whatever change the pit threatened on me loosen its grip, so that when we arrive at the camp, which is large and looks to me to be a full-blown staging area, I am free of its talons, and have my own grasped perfectly around my camera as I jump out of the vehicle and descend to the trodden ground, ready to stare unflinchingly and birdlike at the next atrocity that offers itself before me.

A Lunch in the Sun

S
o there we were, having lunch to celebrate the rising of Christ. Less than a dozen of us sitting around a table in a mock Tuscan villa, the hills beyond arid and sloping, and through the tint of brown sunglasses looking like it could be Italy. But then the brilliant-white-clad waiter leans over to place some more drinks on the table, his eyes pale and red in his black face, his mouth opening to utter an almost silent word in deference as he brushes the arm of one of the women.

A while ago everyone was wearing sunglasses, standing away from the shelter of the parasols in the sun and talking and laughing while the same waiter moved silently between us, ignored. Everybody was talking and hiding behind their sunglasses and now that we're not wearing them it's all suddenly more interesting, as if we're meeting each other for the first time, seeing each other's eyes and having to rethink our judgements.

But I keep my sunglasses on. Perhaps by this people will leave my acquaintance with an unconscious impression of furtiveness on my part, not being able to see my eyes, staring at the smooth and lifeless lenses as they would the eye of a fish. But the truth is the sun is so bright here that if I took them off my eyes would hurt: that white African sun blasting off the pale walls of this counterfeit palace.

The waiter comes and goes with drinks and food and drinks and more food, all the time stooping to the table with the same terrible deference, ingrained or practised I don't know, yet perhaps with an honest sadness. But not sad enough to make me think that it's spoiling this afternoon, this great moment of Christ's ascent from death, this wonderful day of celebration where all man must rejoice for the forgiveness of his sins and the mercy of Heaven, this day of sunshine and laughter, of wine and the water flowing below in the fountains and the distant stream beyond.

Because to my left and beside me, in front of me and to my right, there are beautiful women and good-looking men, and we're all sat here already sated but ready for more. One of the women is still wearing her sunglasses and I find myself respecting her modesty, despite her strapless dress that reveals her neck and shoulders and a hint of the top of her breasts in a golden smoothness that looks like caramel ice cream. She is the most beautiful here and perhaps she knows this, but it does not show. I decide I'm not in love with her.

But I do fall in love when a stranger approaches, bringing with her a small girl whose eyes are already as hard as stone and with a face in astonishing and perfect proportions. What a beautiful thing! Like a jewel, like ivory, a little walking idol to spark in me a strange and alien impulse of greed, of a desire to somehow possess, to keep her for myself, and only myself, as you would a stolen artwork.

'What a beautiful girl,' I say.

She looks up at me like lightning and then looks away

pretending not to hear. She did hear and must press her face into her mother's leg to hide her smile. And this deception, careful and childlike, is enough to dispel the illusion, and force forwards the fact that she is human, that somewhere there is flaw and stench, there will be occasions of cruelty, and that even now the crone in her patiently waits its chance to strike, is already around the eyes and lips of her mother.

I look up, away from this pair and out over the hills, which have been planted with lavender in places and vines in others. Did they move the earth itself to make it look like this? Perhaps they mounded it up higher and higher until it completely blocked the township that you see on the drive in: the rough and flapping abodes of the poor, where no doubt our waiter lives, as do the kitchen staff, the cleaners and porters. And going past the township there had been small boys selling sand art in discarded bottles and jars, layers of different sediment placed (glued?) to make pictures or patterns to hawk to the white people passing through to the palace on the hill. Also, in the hot sun, and blazing white, there had been a procession of men and women, singing a hymn and clapping and stepping, on their way to church and pumping a steady flow of harmony and what must have been a form of happiness into the air as they went, for they certainly sounded happy. How is it in these poor and dirty places they manage to get white so white? The waiter is immaculate in his whiteness, he wears not a single crease or blemish.

'George!' a young voice cries. It is the little girl, and I turn to find her filled with happiness, because she has spotted the waiter. Has she made some mistake, in childish befuddlement taken him for one of her own house staff?

The waiter straightens and turns, then extends his hand and with the palm downwards flaps his fingers against his palm. The girl runs to him and now she has a new leg against which to press her face. George pats her lightly on the head.

'Isabel, you must let George work,' calls her mother.

She hugs his leg fiercely once more and then retreats, and I look up to see that George's refined demeanour of sadness has left everything but his eyes, which – though filled with someone who seems to love him plainly – cannot quite forget and should not forget the bitterness of a nation that will be like a hemlock root in all that it makes for many years to come.

I turn away from George, and for a moment I imagine the scenario: that he was gardener or similar for the family, the family moved away abandoning all their staff to penury, and the mother would have struggled valiantly to find them employment elsewhere. It would have been a great stress for her, and poor old George ended up here, tending pale humans with alcohol, lest they wilt in the sun.

Or lucky George perhaps.

Beyond him and everyone the crickets and insects chirrup and whir, as they do anywhere I suppose, and when a warm breeze gusts the dry grasses sough against themselves. It does not matter that everything here is fake, not when you are drugged by what you imbibe, to become involved in a feast and worship worthy of ancients: that of the sun, universal and all-seeing, bright enough to make us hide our eyes.

Death to Football

There he is beside me: how I hate him, God forgive me. We find ourselves unlikely neighbours, as I suppose all hospital patients do – except perhaps in maternity wards – but there is certainly no birth here and much more likely death, for we are in this strange Victorian enclave of London, the entrance to which might be that of a hotel or embassy, except that if you know its gates and portico and must walk through them, or be carried through them as I suspect he was, the chances are you will not leave by the same aperture.

He is resting now, probably asleep, his head very large and bald and tilted on the pillow, a tube or two headed for the blood of his arm. Even in this repose, and in his dire illness, the face of this man remains brutal and stupid, so that you know the brain behind it contains little more than the rudimentary tactics of a pointless game, stores memories of vast luxury both material and carnal, perhaps tries to count the figures of his salary that weekly – weekly! – could end the suffering of great tracts of humanity on the other side of the world, who must toil endlessly for food, or water, to avoid disease; who might have to watch their family members die, their children die or their partner go blind, who live in stench and filth and could be lifted bodily from this almost in an instant, but for the likes of him, who is given wealth as a giant whale is given plankton by the sea: inexhaustibly! And for what is he given all this? To use his feet and not his hands (you must not use your hands!) to push a small ball from one end of a field to the other.

For this, not only does he receive riches, but the adulation and attention of the masses, who find his meanderings and occasional kicks and headbuttings of the ball somehow, and completely inexplicably, important. So important that huge stadiums are erected and filled with people, of all ages, not just children; huge cathedrals to the non-god of other men, golden calves in shorts and shirts, how I wish that I could cast their wretched giant cups and plates of silver into a ravine, a righteous abyss!

Meanwhile the newspapers: those red-bannered whores, and the broader-sheeted higher-class whores their cousins, they too drink from this cup of madness, so that this man, who lies with death awaiting him, I have seen him many times, looking out like Cro-Magnon man from newsagents' stands, linked to headlines I am, in my disgust, compelled to read: he has done this, he has done that, this team wants him and they will have him, and they will pay an amount of money so vast that I confess on seeing the figure in print I gasped aloud, and spent the rest of the morning in a stunned disbelief, a torpor of disillusionment.

I thought to myself: after all these years, after how far we have come, how much we have pulled away from the merciless barbarism of our collective past, how is it that we can still be so utterly perverse?

And I suppose I should speak to him. We have exchanged only the most cursory of greetings, a mere acknowledgement as one must, when in such a situation. I confess that when they brought him in, when I recognised his massive head even beneath the oxygen mask, saw the fatal concern of those who manoeuvred and installed him next to me, it occurred to me that God does in fact, move with mystery. But to look at him now I feel nothing but hate, and rage! An anger for this man, who is the symbol of all that is wrong with the world, its mindless avarice and misdirection, these twin fangs of the devil serpent that prevents the Kingdom of Heaven's rightful expression here on earth! I sit up, swing my legs out of the side of the bed and grasp my hands together, and then with my eyes closed I pray fervently for calm, for instruction, for love to enter me and give me strength.

Of course, when I open my eyes, I find that he is awake and watching me.

'What you doing?' he asks. His eyes are large and clear, they appear massive even in his large head, which is resting enough against the pillow to almost distort his words.

'What was I doing?' I respond. *Beatus es bardus.*'

'What?'

'I was praying.'

He blinks. 'Religious are you?'

I take in a big breath. 'I'm a priest,' I say, and sigh, perhaps affectedly.

'You ill?'

'I was. Not any more. At least for now.'

'I'm ill,' he says.

'I know.'

'You know who I am.'

I nod. 'Yes.'

'Are you going to try and convert me or something?' There is some spittle at the corner of his mouth. I watch as it droops downwards, to then make contact with the fabric of the pillow, a tiny dark patch forming. He appears giant but weakened; he has been brought low into the realm of simple mortality like any other man, and I wonder if now like this he still holds dear the things he has accumulated: the fat-wheeled fast cars, the disgusting and most likely colonnaded palatial spread in Beaconsfield or similar, the jewellery – which will include diamonds in both ears like a woman – and the oversized watch, all these petty symbols of nothing but a desperate cavity in his heart.

'You do not believe in God?'

I expect him to snort, or smirk, or sneer even, but perhaps his medication is too strong to allow him pathos, for he only whispers: 'Don't know.'

I smile, and nod a bit. I do not know either; what to say at least.

Because to look at him is to feel again the pulses of rage in my chest, and also a triumph, that this man who has evaded righteousness for so long now finds himself utterly at the mercy of God's will. Of course I am aware that these sentiments are wrong, that I should feel pity for the man, that to feel any flicker of victory is a great sin, especially in the face of suffering. There he lies, my Levi, and I must attend to him. And I reflect on how he mentioned conversion, albeit defensively. If there is a single thing that I have learned in my years at home and abroad, it is that all thoughts of another's intentions come from one's own.

Then slowly, it is as if I am raised up from the bed: pulled up inwardly by a strength and certainty, which flowers all too briefly and I know as the bliss of God's presence, for suddenly it is evident to my simple mind (amazing that I did not see it sooner) that He has willed this encounter, that it is my duty to bring this man whom I despise into his fold, to snatch him away from Satan and deliver him unto Jesus Christ lamblike, to help him in his last days.

I find that my hand is tapping against my knee, and I look down at it, and use this fidget in order to prevent full voice being given to the other realisation I have, that this would be *one hell of a scalp* – little old me scoring a deathbed conversion on none other than Seth Bascoe: superstar prodigal footballer, mourned by the nation. Likely it would not be made public (unless he were to make a statement, perhaps through a publicist), but it would certainly become known – and this sort of information would without doubt wing its way all the way back to Rome. These things I should not think of, but I am not perfect: I am a weak servant after all! Try as I might to banish them through breathing, and silent incantation for strength and forgiveness, the thoughts remain, so that when I look up from my tapping hand I find that I am deeply nervous, and ashamed of my weakness; yet also profoundly desirous to convert the man before me.

'Have you ever prayed?' I ask him, playing it safe.

'No.'

'And yet you think there might be something there, a power up there.'

'I didn't say that,' he says.

'You said you didn't know if you believed.'

'Yeah, I don't know, you know. About any of it.'

'Any of what? Belief? Theology?'

'Yeah that stuff.'

'Stuff!' I exclaim. 'It is more than stuff, I assure you.' I feel a heat at the back of my head. 'It is more important than wealth, or success, or having the latest gadgetry and clothing. We are talking about the soul of man, about your soul!'

'You see, that's why I don't know anything about it,' he says.

I pause. He is eyeing me levelly, as best as he can from his reclined position. 'No, I'm afraid I don't see,' I tell him.

'Because it's people like you who are selling it, stuck-up people like you. Know what I'm saying?'

He rolls his head a little on the pillow, so that he turns away from me and looks up at the ceiling. In profile his head is bulbous and the lips full – from this angle he looks vigorous, just resting – and though I know that he has ended our conversation I search for something to say, but can find nothing.

It occurs to me to apologise, but this is forestalled by a commotion at the entrance to our room: nothing other than the penetration of it by his entourage, which consists of a woman who looks to me only just lifted from the gutter, and then pasted with expensive clothing, and a professional-looking man in a suit, and three others, who each, in their own way, have a genetic resemblance to Bascoe. The oldest of these last three, and most likely Bascoe's father, is the only one to acknowledge my presence, and I nod and purse my lips in reflection of his greeting. Then I lift my legs up onto the bed and slide them down the other side, to seek out my footwear, and my gown on the chair, so that I can exit the room and leave them to it.

It being an old building, there are no long corridors down which to wander and reflect on the complete hash I have just made of the scene behind me, though I find the shorter distances and occasional stairwell perfectly adequate for this personal recrimination. I had the chance and fluffed it! God forgive me, I was unable to do your bidding, I am unworthy of the bliss your presence engendered in that brief moment, please forgive this weak soul of mine that was unable to control its own prejudices.

I find I am aghast at myself for stuffily losing my temper with a dying man.

And this headshaking and regret continues as I make my way slowly back to the room, a part of me hoping that the entourage will have departed. (A part of me hoping to deny a dying man the comfort of his family and friends, God forgive me!) When I turn onto the corridor the young woman is standing in it, near the entrance to our room; her hair is big and tied up strangely to look like some sort of insect edifice atop her head, and she does not stand correctly but slouches, as if crumpled in the whiteness of her trousers, battered in the crisp blue and white stripes of her blouse, weighed down by the gold around her neck and on her wrists. These, to me, are the signs of grief, and I wonder if Bascoe might have slipped away during my perambulation. But when I approach her, it is to me she looks, and there are not tears yet, but a question, which she posits in a matter of fact voice as, 'You're a priest, are you?'

'Yes.'

'You know who he is?'

'I do, yes.'

Even now, I think, she cannot refrain from name-dropping, from a sort of celebrity-rank-pulling. Perhaps they want me to vacate the room; this is likely what she wants from me, and I feel the beginnings of a belittling shame creep into me, as if the corridor has become unbearably hot.

'He hasn't got long, you know,' she says. Her voice is without inflection and only contains a little accent. Her face, though, on closer inspection, bears the marks of a slowly crushing pressure.

'Yes, I understand.'

'He says you're not ill any more.'

'For now,' I say.

'Maybe you could talk to him, you know.'

For a moment there is a flicker of sly coquettishness about her: a brief dipping of the head and looking upwards almost from under her eyebrows, which far from disgusting me, I have to admit I find appealing and childlike, as if she has retained the mannerism that procured cookies and sweeties, and uses it now, in death-chamber apotheosis. Also, a second chance! Another chance to put right what went wrong only minutes ago, is before me. God is generous and kind, I think.

'Of course I will talk to him,' I tell her happily.

'It will be less busy in a minute, some of us will be leaving.'

'Yes. Wonderful,' I say. 'I mean. You know.'

But she does not notice my gaffe, and feeling naked and meek I follow her into the room, where the mother and the businesslike man acknowledge me, so that this time I am the recipient of a blend of looks and nods and pursed lips and pained smiles. I walk to my bed, aware of being watched, an involuntary clumsiness in the few steps this takes, the short time of which I spend upon wondering how many of them will leave, for it is far easier to talk to a man when he is alone, perhaps not so a woman, but I have found that a man will only let himself be open to what he sees as weakness, if he knows its perception by others is limited.

Then lying on the bed with eyes closed and my arms beside me, I listen to the confusion of departure, their voices in farewell and with the repeated promise to return varying in degrees of self-control, which I can hear far more plainly without the buttressing sight of strong and set faces. Heard isolated like this they are all edged with unease and worry, especially the young woman, who I am surprised to find sounds very desperate, but realistically so, as if I have just switched on the radio and cannot tell whether what I listen to is a harrowing news report, or award-winning drama. Terrible that again I cannot seem to refrain from prejudice! But what does a woman like that bedecked with gold and diamonds truly know of love? What is her exact concept of loss, beyond no longer hearing the clacking shut of strong-sprung jewellery-case jaws?

Be still, darkness in my heart. And while I wait for things to quieten down I pray for wisdom; yet before I have finished I hear the last farewell, and sense the room's peace and silence, which is deep enough that I think we might even be alone, so that I am flushed with a sense of opportunity, of a rare door opening, the excitement this triggers making any further prayer futile. I open my eyes and sit up to find that the lights have been dimmed for evening, the only segment of entourage remaining being a mature woman, who sits in the darkened corner: clearly Bascoe's mother. She looks at me and nods, and I surmise that in her at least,

in her ageing frame of sadness and well-cloaked despondency, I have support for what I am about to attempt. I half-
smile and nod back once.

'What's your name?' Bascoe asks suddenly, to make me
jump and then turn to him.

'My name is Francis.'

'Do I have to call you something, like Reverend?'

'No. Francis is fine. Can I call you Seth?'

I move from my bed to sit in the chair next to him. His
eyes follow me: they glisten hugely and are very alive, the
last redoubt of his power here on earth.

'Doctors say I only have a few days, a week maybe.'

I nod and look askance, breathe in deeply before saying,
'I'm sorry.' The old woman is in the edge of my vision; I
think I hear her shift in her chair.

'How long do you have to stay here?' Bascoe asks.

'I'm leaving tomorrow,' I tell him.

'Through the front door.'

I snort involuntarily; I had not expected him to say something like that. 'Yes. Through the front door.'

'Upright!' he says, an exclamation that is closer to a gasp.

I nod, and watch his eyes in search of bitterness, but see
none in them: they lock to mine and do not move until they
are looking at something behind me, and then he is blinking
a quiet and intimate greeting, to the young man entering
the room: who I turn to find is a less powerful, younger
version of the footballer. I think that he will dismiss me
from his bedside for this person, but he does not. When my
eyes meet those of the youth in question I see only hostility,
and these dark orbs that brim with menace for me I find I
can hold much longer than those of the mother, following

him as he walks around to perch insolently on the end of my own bed, so that he will be directly behind me.

'At some time, did you think you might not make it?' asks Bascoe.

'Yes,' I reply. 'When the doctor first told me.' His eyes widen, and I can imagine his own version of this moment: after some test or scan, and then back in the office of the expensive consultant, the moment when all hope for a recovery was taken from him, the memory of this still able to punch through the haze of his medication and startle him. Fit and powerful as he was it must have been quite far down the line before he realised truly that he could not fight it, that it would beat him, and I find (with some relief) that I pity him for this. 'I thought it was all over as soon as the doctor told me.'

'I would like,' he says, 'to think there is something after this.' His voice has tightened, is hoarse and no longer in its deep bass. 'Do you really think there's something after this?'

'Yes.'

'What is it?'

What is it indeed, I wonder. I have spent many years of study and prayer trying to understand this, and now this unworthy man asks me for it on a platter, or more appropriately in a neat little pill, that he can gulp down easily. Behind me the youth sighs impatiently, and the woman in the corner is affecting impassivity, yet when her eyes rise from her hands I see in them a barely hidden fervency. Perhaps the youth behind me is right to express his displeasure: he senses correctly that I might easily feed a dying and uneducated man a fairy-tale vision of Heaven, to sweep away the many years of their common unbelief, of an understanding that they must have shared, even beneath the glare and incantation of their devout mother. He is too young or stupid to understand that his brother does not betray him, but has progressed to a place where youth is not yet ready to follow.

I breathe deeply, not knowing what to say, and then in a flash the words come to me, so that it feels as if they are the sudden exposed tip of all my study and searching.

'It is there, and it is good, but it remains a mystery,' I say.

I had pointed up, then placed both hands on my chest, then opened them out with palms upwards and shaken my head with a puzzled smile – gestures I have never performed previously, but which came so naturally as to leave me suspecting something other than me, moving my body.

'Amen!' says the woman.

'Amen,' says a voice behind me, not the youth, but Bascoe's father, who must be standing somewhere near the doorway.

I do not turn to him, but remain fixed upon Bascoe. There is more noise behind me: a muted clipping of heels on the floor which will be the young woman, the girlfriend, trying to totter quietly, sensitive enough at least to see I am in session with her provider, that I am *through on goal*.

'I never thought it would come to this,' Bascoe says, still focused upon me, and I suspect he is now deeply clouded in medication, and may not have even noticed the latest arrivals. 'I never thought I would be talking to a priest like this.' Again there is the impatient sigh from behind me; and I think upon the unsurprising marvel of blind and self-obsessed youth, that this boy must pump his own lack of belief outward in an attempt to swamp his dying brother's nascent and final approaches to the afterlife.

'It is not so rare, that people see things more clearly as the end of this life draws near.'

His eyes still hold mine but are hazy, and he gulps with the effort of swallowing, and his eyes widen and his face softens as he does this, so that for a moment the man is eclipsed as if by a child, baffled and questioning. But he seems to gather himself within, and then after a long and careful breath he says, 'I thought I had finished being afraid, but I haven't. That's the only reason I'm talking to you.'

Yes I think, the final hedging of bets. 'When the doctor told me, and I thought it was curtains, do you know what I considered?'

He does not respond, but there is a tiny movement of his huge head.

'My first instinct was to get very, very drunk, which I did, and then while drunk I considered leaving the priesthood and spending the next few months doing everything I possibly could to make up for having joined it, which after that bottle of whisky, I must confess presented itself to me as an idealistic, continuous binge of gambling and alcohol.' What I omit from this confession is that this fantasy also contained women: it contained the opposite of every sexual privation that decades of monasticism had produced, so that I had lain there in a drunken stupor, squirming at the thought of every depravity I would allow my dying corporeal frame to indulge in.

Bascoe exhales. 'You like a drink?'

'I am afraid I do.'

'I did too.' His jaw hangs limply for a moment and he is very still. I wonder if he is at the stage where he refuses all food and drink, and if he knows what this means, if his silent family around us are aware of what it means. 'Why didn't you, you know, go on your bender?' he asks.

'Money!' I lie. 'I would have had to steal. And stealing is . . .'

'A sin!'

'Most certainly.'

He becomes disconnected, as if this small maintenance of banter (an art he is surely well versed in) has drained him. For a moment he is not breathing and his eyes drop to my chest. But then he says: 'But you didn't do that.'

'No.'

'Why not? I would have.'

I look up away from him, breaking contact with his supine form for the first time since sitting down next to it. 'Because I was afraid. I was afraid to destroy. To deny everything my life comprised, just as you think you will now, by letting God into your heart.'

'I'm not afraid of that,' he says.

'No?'

'I'm afraid of losing it all, everything I have.'

'And what exactly do you have?' I ask, suddenly feeling the pity I had nurtured for him evaporating.

'I have everything!' he says, and in his eyes now there is an arrogance, and a sneering that before was absent, and I begin to wonder if he has brought me by his bedside to bait me in front of his family, to put in a good performance one last time, if not on the pitch, then at least in front of a home crowd. 'I came up from nothing and I took what the world had to offer, you know? Why is your cancer-making god taking it from me, eh? Why?'

'Seth,' calls his mother quietly.

'No, Mum, I'm going to tell this priest what I think!'

'You tell him, bro,' says the brother.

'Why should I let something into my heart that's robbed me blind?'

I feel a hot pulsing in the back of my neck, a terrible urge to shout at him that he deserves his downfall, that his useless, pointless, sports-based life is nothing but a sham, and it is God's gift that he is stripped of it. The girlfriend is tottering about again behind me, perhaps nervous at this change of demeanour, and I reflect with regret on what carnal delights he must have known with her, and from very early in his manhood, joys of the flesh that in my drunken weakness and fearing death I claimed a brief and merely conceptual subscription. Except that even now when I am on the eve of discharge, have been given the all-clear and have returned to the path of God, the beast that was awakened in that moment, though caged deeply within me and made drowsy with prayer and ritual, still I feel it thrash against the bars to sense this woman, opposite of all the women in my acquaintance, selected primarily by Bascoe for qualities I have never savoured.

That is why I hate him so, God please forgive me, for he makes me realise that I am like all the other idiotic men (and women) in their cantilevered domes and bowls of senseless idol-worship: my interest in him comes purely from envy and from Satan, who is not in the young brother sitting behind me huffing and puffing at what I say, and is not in the man before me who does not wish to let his greedy fingers slip from all he has accumulated, but is of course in me.

'Could I be alone with this man for a few minutes, please?'

I say to the room, while looking at Bascoe. For a moment there is a silent stillness, and I think I will be forced to ask again, but then his mother rises, and the others follow her lead, so that it is surprisingly easy and quick to have the room cleared.

I have delivered many a good sermon in my time, and now as I take a breath and prepare to bring forth another for this dying man, I feel the strange calmness that sometimes comes in these moments, where I have had notes before me, entire texts even from which to recite verbatim, and found that they are suddenly superfluous, and that what must be said comes from a different place: unplanned and, dare I say it, mysterious.

'Seth, I must admit that I have found it hard to think other than this of you: that you are merely the exhaust of a tired and floundering society, that what you do is parasitic and meaningless.' His breathing is steady and his eyes do not stray from mine. 'You have devoted your life to nothing more than a game; you have procured great wealth for yourself and maintained your body as a vessel for this, to sneak this bullion into your keeping, but you have neglected to maintain your soul, which has become atrophied, empty!

'And the youth that follow you: they do not see the emptiness but only the trappings, and thus wish to emulate you, so that in the period of their crucial formation they are already bent on the path of avarice, and will drift from the hard learning of virtuousness to instead seek fame and wealth, even steal it through crime and rioting. You are their dark priest! Their figurehead! Just as much in Satan's grip as the tin-pot dictator, perverting other minds to senseless values, doing no good but for yourself!'

I pause to find calm; the anger is rising in me but it is strangely hollow, is tempered by doubt. Because I must admit that while there have been sermons springing from mystery, as if God-given, equally there have been others that suddenly lose all meaning, even at the height of lectern-gripping earnestness, to leave me standing and facing expectant faces with nothing to say, yet worse no voice from within and a doubt about all of it: of God and Heaven, of Satan and Hell, of the Creation, of angels and saints and sinners and miracles and crying statues and people springing up out of wheelchairs – sometimes it all bottoms out and seems every bit as ridiculous as the worship meted out to a game and its players, a crazy, crazed game where everyone agrees only to kick the ball, because you are not allowed to pick the ball up.

You must only kick the ball; why this madness?

'And what about you,' he croaks. 'You. You're a husk of a man. A shell of a man. You know you smell bad even from here? You smell of dust and books and that smoke shit, what do you call it?'

'Incense,' I tell him. He must be hallucinating the smells because I have not been near a church in days, am wearing none of my own clothes.

'Yeah, that stuff. You stink of it. Every week you're standing up and telling people what to do, what to be, you know? Look at your body, it's a rotten old husk. How can you tell people what to do when you can't even look after yourself?'

His passion has risen to replace the bewildering loss of my own, and I must concede that he is right: my body is decrepit and has been for decades. Hunched and withered as I am, it was little surprise to learn I was in mortal sickness. The surprise was to have recovered, ostensibly so completely. 'The body is merely a temporary frame for the soul,' I reply, not liking the words as I say them.

He looks away and attempts to laugh at this. 'Yeah, keep telling yourself that.'

'Look at your own body now: it is dying but there is the part of you that is not. Can't you feel that?'

His eyes rotate from their wanderings to fix upon mine. They are drugged and sleepy, but not yet completely lost to the opiate dream-world; there is still enough of him here in the room for me to work with.

'Can't you feel that? That there is a part of you that'll never die?'

And again I dislike my own words, because what I really want to ask, and am afraid to, and not to him but to myself, is whether I might be a man that has never lived, and have used the Spirit and its cloth to deny myself, to insulate myself: many years of abstention and virtuousness spent wasted in the belief that in the end I will be rewarded, I will have glories in Heaven the likes of which no amount of glory on earth, be it material or carnal, could ever hope to match.

But if none of it were true, if it were just an invention, an elaborate and widely shared game of the mind; if after death it is only an eternal oblivion, a non-being for ever after: the type of permanent non-existence that will roll mercilessly and without end into the future, years upon years of nothingness for the very thing that was me – if that is our fate then what have I done! What have we all done, those of us who have not chewed up life as this man has?

I lean back and look to the ceiling and inhale. A surprising weakness of the self this, when I should be strong for him, for God. 'Seth,' I say. 'You are right, I am a husk, a tired old man. I have my doubts also, you know.' His hand, at the end of an arm fed by tubes, is near enough that I reach out for it, and when my palm rests on the back of it I say, 'I am sorry if I have judged you; I have no right to judge you.'

'No, you don't,' he replies.

Then I find I am praying, mouthing silently for strength and forgiveness, and for the soul of this man, and for my own soul, a flow of words that begins automatically but quickly accumulates a passion and feeling, so that slowly I can feel the warm glow of God's presence, once again an ember in my heart, the void becoming distant, lust in its cage no longer thrashing but silent, the fear of a life wasted, of its corporeal element unfulfilled, now so minor that I think it ridiculous, that it could ever have been strong.

'You're praying again. What are you praying?'

'I am praying for you, Seth. And for me, and for the glory of God.' And this gives me an idea. 'You yourself have known glory.' I nod and lean forwards. 'Yes. On the pitch, shooting goals, winning matches!'

In response, weakly, he nods, more with his eyes than his head.

'What does it feel like, to shoot a goal?'

'It feels like nothing else,' he says. 'It's the best feeling in the world.'

'Better than sex?'

His eyes widen. 'Yeah! Everyone knows that.'

'Better than driving a fast car?'

'That's not better than sex.'

'Oh.' I pause. 'Well, that glorious feeling, like when you shoot a goal, where does that come from? Do you think that only footballers feel that, that they have a monopoly on the best feeling in the world?'

'I don't know.' He pulls a long breath inwards. 'Maybe.'

'Of course not!' I hiss, and then calmly, after smoothing the back of my head with my hand, the same one that had been resting on his: 'I have had that feeling too, that glory, that sense of exultation.' His eyes are fixed to mine. 'I had it only a few hours ago when I awoke to find you still in the bed there, and realised what it is I must do.'

'Then I was right: you do want to convert me.'

'I do not want to convert you, Seth. God wants you to allow him to love you. That feeling when you shoot a goal . . .'

'Score!' he croaks.

'What?'

'Score a goal. Not shoot a goal, you fool.'

'Yes all right then, *score a goal*, that feeling, it is just a drop of God's love; imagine what it would be like to bathe in that for eternity!'

What sweetness it will be indeed, I think, rocking slightly in the chair and my hands coming together to rub one against the other. I am almost disappointed to be healthy, to not be on the happy final approach myself, preparing to slough off this old and flabby skin and exist as spirit, in a wondrous and hitherto unknown state, only glimpsed during the better moments of a lifetime spent in the service of the one true God. 'If I could change places with you, Seth, I would!'

'Yeah, amen to that,' he replies.

'But I cannot, so you must change places with yourself, as it were. You do not need to have some sort of big faith, you just need to open the door.'

He does not move but stares back at me. His chin has sunken into his chest so that he looks strangely hunched forwards, as if about to receive a blow. He rises and falls with his breathing, and then after a long exhalation he is still.

'Seth!' I whisper, and look to his face, which has not moved or altered and the eyes of which still stare out at me. I am flushed with fear: my heart pounds with the childish terror of having broken something valuable, and I am suddenly hot with the feeling of being in very deep trouble. I can hear the voices of his family coming from the corridor – what will I tell them? That he passed mid-conversion?

As if a valve is opened he suddenly shudders and draws a deep breath inwards. Merciful Father in Heaven, placing miraculous breath in this man so that I might finish my work with him! But urgency now: these could be the last hours, minutes even, of his life, the clock is definitely ticking. I turn to the doorway to see if we are still alone, to find that the noises coming from the corridor are now a silent crowd of anxious faces peering in at us; there is even a nurse or two watching.

Thus ostensibly under pressure, I turn back to the footballer and slide my chair closer to his bed. For a moment I close my eyes and breathe. When I open them I feel very calm inside, and a happiness I cannot explain. Far from being in a hurry, it feels instead as if time is a thing that I control, that everything around me is moving slowly, like escapes in nightmares, while I alone am awake.

'Seth,' I call to him, across the gulf of age and culture, of the difference in our outlooks that is wide between us but made insignificant by the power invested in me through the grace of the Holy Spirit. 'Seth.'

He looks to me. 'What do I have to do?' he says quietly.

'Open your heart. Open it to the possibility of grace.'

'I can't, I don't know what that means!'

'There is no great secret,' I tell him kindly. 'The things you have done wrong in your life – as we all have – how do you feel about them?'

He stops to think. I watch him contentedly, neither concerned nor hurried, as if the outcome of our conversation is already decided, and all that's left on my part is to enjoy the ride.

'I'm sorry for them. I wish they'd never happened,' he says after a while.

'Good!' I say, smiling broadly. 'And what do you feel about the greatest moments of your life, the best times, the happiest?'

'I feel like they've been taken from me, you know?'

'I know. But you would rather have had them than not.'

'I've had some great moments.'

'Now,' I say, leaning closer so that I am almost above him. 'All you need do, is see that the bad and the good are linked, through you, in God. That which is bad, be sorry for, and ask forgiveness for, and He shall forgive you. His love for you is so great that He wants to forgive you! Can you feel that, isn't it amazing?'

He is looking up at me and breathing steadily, and

although his expression is fixed, it is fixed purposefully, in an aspect to block and hide what I suspect will be a great emotion swelling in him, the upward effects of nothing less than the awakening of his soul. 'I can feel something . . .'

'Yes.'

Behind me a woman's voice from the corridor: 'Praise the Lord!' it says and another says, 'Amen,' and finally a happy hissing of 'He is among us!'

'That feeling, let it come out,' I tell him. 'Don't try to block it.'

He gulps and writhes as he lies there, not with the pain of his illness, but of his soul, and as I have seen it before I watch it again: the process by which a man is consumed by the bursting forth of remorse, a regret for all the foolishness, sin and evil of his life, the purging of which is like a vomiting, and now produces a pair of large round tears to make desultory progress down his face, the mouth of which is being pulled down spasmodically at the sides. I do not say anything but nod my head and close my eyes, a few words of prayer for him, but not too much because I want to catch the moment when the relief washes over him, for this is the best time to pounce, when they have just emerged from self-judgement and are completely laid open, suddenly undefended by will or former conviction.

After a minute he has stopped crying and has calmed. I pat his hand. 'Seth, I want you to pray with me.' He does not nod, nor blink even, and yet there is no protest, no censure from his eyes. The small noises from the corridor, from the huddle in the doorway, have been replaced with an utter silence. 'God in Heaven, forgive me my sins.'

'Forgive me my sins,' he repeats, almost imperceptibly.

'Thank you for the great life you have given me.'

'. . . life you have given me.'

'Please accept me now, in the eleventh hour, into your love and the love of your son, Jesus Christ.'

'. . . son, Jesus Christ.'

Then I stand and return to my own bed, for the water jug on the table and after pouring a little on my hand return to Seth and make the sign of the cross on his forehead, a momentary pulse of doubt as my skin touches his, so that I pause, and the audience in the doorway must see me pause and wonder why: a bit of theatre for them, a bit of suspense as to whether their man gets the keys to eternity, he who lies here giant and crying, a crocodilian monster prone on his back in white bed sheet swaddling and small-bore hydraulic peripherals, he of the great nothingness of his life or the great everythingness I do not know. Standing here, leaning over him with dripping fingers, seeing his pitiful gaze turned upwards to me and inwards to the quiet bliss he is probably feeling – I confess I have my doubts as to his worthiness, and so perhaps for expediency more than anything I finish the baptism quickly and without fuss, to a minor response of contented sighing behind me.

Then I am kneeling at his bedside and praying, sometimes closing my eyes tightly and pressing my chin to my chest, at others staring at his face which is close to mine and in the thick and fleshy profile appears at peace. Looking at this bulbous forehead, the large nose and full lips, the full cheeks now sunken, and taking this man's hand in my own, to grip it and feel it grip back, I cannot help but think what a good job I have done.

Well done me, you did it!, you got him, exceptional stuff.

'Francis,' he whispers.

'Call me Frank.'

'Frank, I've never felt like this before.'

'God plus morphine is a pretty heady brew,' I say.

'How can I thank you?'

'You don't need to thank me. No not at all. But you could' – how to say this? – 'perhaps maximise your atonement.'

'I thought that had been done. With all the crying and stuff.'

'Yes it has been done. Yes.' I pat his hand. 'But Jesus taught that it is harder for a rich man to enter the Kingdom of Heaven than a camel to pass through the eye of a needle.'

I watch him digesting this. He must of course have heard this saying before as everyone has, but not until now could its true meaning become apparent – and with a shocking and infinite clarity – for now at the point where the roads of fatal illness and salvation have converged, he is on the very edge of that Kingdom, he is peering into it, and yet with all the senseless wealth he has accumulated he must now fear that the gates could be barred for him, that even though he has cried his eyes out like a child and felt the pain of remorse, and through these acts felt the love of God become proximate, it might all be denied him at the last moment.

'You're saying because I've got money I can't get into Heaven?'

'I'm not saying it,' I tell him. 'Jesus said it. It's quite clear, there in black and white in the Gospel. But, Seth, consider this: what a small price to pay for eternal happiness! Do you know what that means? A bliss that is never-ending, that is not even constrained by time itself! Free yourself from earthly constraints, prepare for . . .' and here I hesitate. I had been looking beyond him, to the darkness behind the curtains, but when I look down to him I see that he is captive, he is like a child listening to a good story. 'Prepare for paradise!'

For do you know what the alternative is, I ponder, a reactionary lifting of my hand to stroke the rough underside of my neck. Oblivion for ever, no more you, no more me; and yet in the face of that here is a man who would on his deathbed baulk at the leaking of his funds. He has already had it all: in his young life he has feasted and had his fill, he has gulped down the adulation and esteem of other men, the sex of women, of many beautiful women like that one behind me now in the corridor, that temptress of earthly pleasures, who even now as I contemplate the afterlife is the sign, the siren that deceives or warns me that there might only be one life, one chance of existence, and not to spend it for gain and pleasure as this man has, on all-fours like a beast at trough, is to waste it, is to be a fool!

'You must atone for your sins!' I hiss.

'Yes,' he says, swallowing labouredly and tears forming at his eyes. He is afraid, and so he should be. There was Heaven, dangling in front of him, and now it has been snatched away. 'I want to,' he whispers. 'I want to do that. But how?'

I hold his gaze and take a slow breath.

'Give away your wealth before you die.'

He does not move. 'To charity,' he croaks.

'Yes,' I say. 'To charity.'

There are minor convulsions in his chin and neck and then fresh tears at his eyes. Suddenly he is the small boy asked to give back what he thought was his.

'I have seen many people cry, Seth. From bereaved women, to grown men, even superstars.' Here I smile and raise my eyebrows. 'And all of it I can take: I sympathise, but I am not affected by it myself, you know?'

'Yeah. I'm sorry.'

'If I was affected by it, I would fall to pieces. But I must not fall to pieces, I cannot, because when people are emotional often that is their time of greatest need. That's what crying is: a signal to others saying I NEED HELP.'

To this he nods agreement as best he can: supine, massive and very weakened.

'If I were to cry with you now, I would not be able to help you in this,' and I raise both hands to then point downwards at the space between us, 'your hour of very greatest need, as you strive to pass safely from one world to another. Do you understand? I hope you can understand this, Seth, because you are in grave danger. For how can you expect to gain the love of God if you still cling to material wealth, earned through a life rejecting His love?'

He looks to the ceiling, blinks away a few tears. 'I did leave a bit, in my will that's already done. All signed and everything.'

A bit, I think. Yes a bit. For him what would this be, a few thousand? That might equate to some new equipment for a children's ward, or maybe an entire school: some flimsy thing erected badly somewhere in the band of desiccation that strangles Africa. Mere gestures when he surely has so much to give! And not enough for his salvation, or my own designs: which are to rescue hundreds, if not thousands, or even hundreds of thousands by channelling the might of his posthumous wealth to the poor and the sick, a golden flow diverted away from the claws of his socially improved family, away, even, from any tenuous claims that guttersnipe woman might make, no longer able to flex her tottering sex against him.

'Well,' I say kindly. 'Do you think that a bit is enough?' I would like to huff and puff in accompaniment to this but here I must be careful. If he detects anything other than friendship and benevolence from me now, the chequebook might close with a snap. Yet looking down at him, watching his eyes wander from the ceiling to mine, to then retreat for lengthy periods behind the thin flesh curtains of their slowly shuttering lids; seeing this mixture of fear and hope that he dwells in, it seems clear that he is close to a summation, the necessary dawning of himself as man in the shadow of the true power of God, and I begin to feel again a wonderful sense of inevitability for this, our discourse. The bounty it shall result in will be munificent; I can see it as if it were already an evident reality before me.

'No,' he croaks. 'It's not enough. I could give more. But is there time?'

'Of course there is,' I say. I can feel a tingling at the back of my neck. 'Who's that chap in the suit with your family?' I ask him quietly.

'Who?'

'The man in the suit, he was here earlier.'

'Yeah, that's Del, my agent.'

'Ah.' I shuffle forwards on the chair and whisper, 'He could call your solicitor, get him to come here, couldn't he?'

He blinks to accentuate a tiny nodding. 'Yeah. Yeah he can. Can you call him in for me?'

'Of course. What's his name again?'

'Del.'

I turn in the chair and twist to face the doorway and its small crowd. 'Del?'

The agent steps forwards and strides in, a man of average height with dark and bushy hair, well clothed and groomed, or at least appearing so, the slight signs of dishevelment, of stubble and a loosened tie perhaps intentional rather than the multiplying creases of strain. He looks at me expectantly, as one waiting for further command, and as I point to Bascoe I think that maybe I was wrong about him being a Jew, he might even be Catholic.

I move the chair back to allow him past, a strong waft of aftershave and the glint of a gold watch as he crouches down at the side of the bed, to lean his face close-in towards the footballer's. I cannot hear their whispered exchange, and merely concentrate on trying to look as neutral as possible, lest Seth's request is treated with suspicion. Perhaps I should pray, yet I know it would be impossible, as I cannot stop the beatific thought that I am on the verge of a great and lasting joy, a God-given reward here on Earth for the labours of my own path: a fairly long life spent mostly quiet and prayerful, filled with many small moments of weakness, some larger than others, but never enough to knock me down, to cause more than a stagger beneath the burden of righteousness. I have been strong overall – I have been strong! Despite the vertiginous pull of ignominy on either side, I have never fallen.

And to think that weeks ago I lay on the ground, drunken and believing I was dying, filled with base, animal lusts to make me writhe – yet now here I am blessed with more life, administering to one of our mistaken society's supposed greatest sons, this man an idol in a society that values wealth above all else, that does not blink at the perversity of showering him with gold for the playing of a stupid game, when only half a world away the blink of an eye might cause constant and excoriating pain to a child: a child who must exist in its own little pain-world every day and every night and may do so until death because those with money are too busy throwing it at the likes of this man, are incapable of diverting even a little of it to end another's suffering.

Truly, Seth Bascoe, I was right to say what I did: you are the high priest of a society that rots, a toppling occidental citadel with walls high enough to mostly block the moans and screams from outside. And the people of this place, how they loved you! How they will mourn your passing: there will be a mound of floral tributes, a frenzy of flash photography, a myriad teenage tears on television as your hearse makes its steady cruise to wherever your useless body is interred.

'Christ forgive them!' I hiss through teeth that are clenched, above fists that are clenched, and look down upon him as he whispers yet to his aide, the big man still swaying the attention of others, but a man like any other levelled by the approach of death, and whom I now have a little command over. And by hell, I think, I will suck every last ounce of lucre from his wasted person. He has no need of it now. Then he may part this earth, to await stern and uncertain judgement at the foot of his and everyone's God.

The Champion

In the bad old days, when I was still an unrighteous motherfucker pushing a pram, I often ended up in the supermarket.

When you are young and unsuccessful and have to cross the road at a zebra crossing pushing a pram – when you must turn and thank through drilling rain the person snug and smug in their German rear-engined sports car for allowing you this shameful passage – you do not generally arrive on the other side of the street a happy and fulfilled man. Then you enter the supermarket, outlet branch of a national chain it may be, but which appears to be staffed only by first-generation immigrants of the shelf-stacking caste, and this does nothing to cheer you up. Because the rain may have stopped by way of roof, yet now begins a worse assault: a foreign language completely indecipherable, yelled over your head as you are stooping beside one of the workers, looking in their domain: for something low down.

It occurred one day in this place that I could not find what I was looking for. There is a reaction I saw that morning that I have seen since: when the face to which you make your enquiry is contorted with wretchedness, partly by an extreme regret that they cannot help, but chiefly with disappointment in you for asking. It does not anger me now, this face, because I know it and expect it. I do not mind it even, can understand it might merely be a cultural difference, or just an inability to understand English.

But that day it did anger me – to reiterate, I did not know success – everything then was an insult or conspiracy against which I struggled. In those years it felt as if motorists would deliberately not stop for me at the zebra crossing, or the Polish men drinking at the end of our street would wait until I passed to toss their cans into the gutter – cans that in the morning I would pick up and throw back against the shutters of the Polish shop. This was my world beyond the front door: the miserable angry face of the pointless, heartless urban street as seen from the bottom rung, and I hated it, and I hated the man that could not help me find the product which I knew (I did know) they must have.

I was angry and about to give up and leave the supermarket when I heard his voice. It was stentorian and delivered so plainly that it immediately commanded my attention, so that I turned to see who was producing it, and saw a very tall man in the next aisle – effortlessly tall (I am not tall) – talking to someone about how the shelf was stacked. He was telling them how it should be done. It was a detailed plan, almost obsessive, but it could not be denied that he was in the process of realising a vision, no matter how prosaic. He did not speak with an accent; he was dressed smartly in a suit rather than the drab uniform of the others, and augmented to his height there was about him an air of success: he was clearly the manager, he spoke English and this was enough that I turned from my helper without even

a word, wheeling the pram down the aisle to execute the
hairpin corner at its end, wondering as I performed this
manoeuvre whether he chose his staff or they were chosen
for him, and entering the new aisle to see his back a broad
expanse of dark suit.

He was so tall that his shoulders were higher than my
head. He was alone when I reached him, the person he had
been talking to, lecturing even, having left for a different
aisle perhaps. I found a nobility in his profile: a strong nose
and high forehead; this I saw because he had turned back
to the shelf and was surveying it, the condiments stocked
there a reef of colour, his eyes behind thick-rimmed glasses
moving slowly over them and when a hand rose to manipu-
late one of their number, to turn its face to match that of
all the others, it did so with almost a physical sadness that
I found affecting, and not in the least affected, because I
could identify with this act: the horrifically banal attended
to by the hand of artistry.

Softly I called for his attention. The young child below
us both was silent in the pram. The man heard my voice
and his eye, what I could see of it, widened slightly, and there
was the tiniest movement of his head. He began to turn, a
slow and deliberate revolution, his profile changing to reveal
a slight handsomeness, a boyishness at odds with the power
of his voice, his eyes large and brown, innocent and cow-like
behind their heavy glasses. And once I could see both his
eyes – as soon as he turned to me I could see a vagueness
that seemed to swim lazily from one eye to the other, as if
there was a large and diseased fish labouring across the front
of his brain, an alternating shallow glassiness and depth in
his gaze towards me making it suddenly evident that all was

not well with his mind, that he was in fact insane. In that moment the edifice of my hopes for him fell away to nothing. And through a cluster of bewildering reconsiderations I realised that what he exuded was not the power and grace of leadership, but an unintentional haughtiness stemming from mental impairment.

He stood looking at me and I at him, an uncertainty and slight surprise shared between us. I noticed there was a small amount of congealed spittle or food at the side of his mouth, yellowish in colour, and this I must admit disgusted me; it made me think of the attendant maternity, who would have to dab at this mouth with her own saliva-slickened napkin, who might still have to kiss and coo at this ungainly giant to comfort him from some anxiety or rage. I imagined the pale walls of their flat, dulled by the sadness and hardship contained within. I did not like to think of these things and so almost as an antidote, I asked him plainly where the product I was looking for might be.

He said: 'Yes, it is in the next aisle, next to the dairy section.' This was said in his loud monotone, which coupled with the impassive stillness of his face, was rendered completely devoid of inflection or emotion. 'I cannot show you because I am doing the sauces here,' he continued flatly, 'which I do not enjoy but am made to do by Sudra.'

'I'll find it.'

'Yes, I do not like doing the sauces.'

'Okay,' I said.

'I do not like doing them at all.' His face changed, became altered by a fresh earnestness that was powerful enough that I could not simply disengage by walking away. His eyes, huge and brown in their little glassy tanks, were locked to mine, so that I was impatient but gripped, and also slightly curious: I found that I wanted to sample the demented reasoning which I knew would be shortly forthcoming, of why he did not like stacking sauces.

'Yeah, why?' I said.

'Ravi!' a new voice called. We both looked towards the tills, towards the real power in this diminutive supermarket: a small and fleshy man, his features jovial but now frowning as he leaned past the shoulder of the person he was serving at the middle console, the positioning of which allowed him to look down the aisle to where we stood. 'Don't bother the customer!' he said, as if it were a slogan, a catchphrase.

'I was not bothering him. He asked me a question.'

'I asked him a question!' I called back.

The manager looked at me, his face beaming with a false smile. It was an expression meant to ensure my happiness, to stoke the general customer happiness of the supermarket, and I thought that I might show my contempt for his efforts, and the world in general's efforts to keep me happy by continuing my conversation with Ravi, the idiot they employed – but Ravi had turned away. He had returned his attention to the shelving, his eye again flying over the colourful jars and their labels. He seemed very far away, his beholding of the sauces almost dreamy. I could have spoken, but it would have been futile: wherever he was it was no longer here in the aisle with me, and though there had been no direct rebuff, I understood plainly that we would not speak further. So I took up the weight of the pram, reversed a bit and made my way to the next aisle, without farewell, gesture or even a glance back at him.

Grateful that his directions were correct, however, I acquired the product I was after and left.

And even though I did not go to the supermarket every day, and Ravi did not work there every day, I often encountered him during those dark months still spent pushing a pram. Quickly I gained his trust, and when he saw me coming with the child he would straighten from whatever task was at hand, extend up to his full height, way above everyone and say, 'HELLO, GENTLEMAN!' in his oxen tone: a sound amply filling the three or four short aisles of our local outlet branch.

'I'm sad today,' he would say immediately.

'Yeah, how come?'

'Because I was supposed to unload the dairy cage but there wasn't a dairy delivery today because of a problem at the depot.' His large frame would be perfectly still saying this and his voice flat. The only signs of animation were the opening and closing of his hands, and his eyes flicking slowly from mine to the same point on the floor and back again. 'Dairy is my favourite to unload and because there was a problem at the depot I cannot unload it and that makes me sad.'

This made me wonder exactly how he conceived of The Depot: whether it loomed for him darkly, a distant and unknowable agent of pleasure and disappointment. But then his face would change: it would brighten as something gripped him inside and he would begin spitting out something like, 'Did you know that polar bears never eat penguins . . .' and he would tell me, without brevity, not only the reason for this, but all known associated facts of the Arctic and Antarctic, his eyes aflame with a passion for each morsel he was imparting – and he would indeed spit, the occasional fleck flying from his high mouth so that very soon I learned to park the child's pram a little to the side, to not stand so close myself.

And then his face would change once more and the exposition would suddenly stop: an expression would come that I could never quite understand but was like the arrival of a dark cloud, and one that always preceded him either abruptly turning away from me or walking quickly off, as if we had never been speaking, as if we must not speak.

On other days it was I that turned from him. I would imagine myself to be hurried, or irritated, and hearing his voice would pulse an annoyance into my head that would allow me the temerity to not even look him in the eye as he approached, to say a brief hello full of self-importance, and then declare how much of a hurry I was in. And only when I had explained that I would not be stopping for our usual exchange, a distinct expectancy in the efficacy of what I was doing giving me perhaps the first pleasure of the day – only then would I look away from the shelves, or up from the scrawled list I held in one hand (the pram in the other) to his face, to see the desperate disappointment there.

I would nurse guilt for this. All the way home I would nurse it carefully so that once in the safety of our flat, once the heavy front door was closed behind us, I would frighten the child by bellowing, 'HELLO, GENTLEMAN!'; I would extract him from the pram with my eyes vacantly shifting from his to the wall, telling his startled face how sad I was because The Depot had burned down killing all hands, a terrible tragedy, yes a very sad terrible tragedy – and then while twisting and shaking him out of his fluffy hat and coat I would improvise all known idiot facts about condensation, or similar, before abruptly turning the tap off and shutting the character down.

I confess I would take Ravi home and practise him in this manner frequently, because I aspired to be an actor.

This aspiration, and the long shadow of failure that always stalked it, was perhaps the primary reason the world was my enemy: the dirty street a thing to be hated and feared, the cars crocodiles in a river I must cross and the Polish, and the Indians, and the Muslims, and the disabled, worthy of contempt, because it must have been them holding me down, for some reason. The struggle to get the heavy grocery-laden pram through the door, the memory of all the minor shames just borne and still to face would result in my sudden explosion into character (once the door was closed), as if ranting and spitting to an audience of one no-longer-fearful child would offset the rejection and failure in audition and application, would steel me further to pick up the trade paper once more and start another search, another fruitless quest for work.

Yet one day it did come, the communication I awaited: that I must attend an audition. Mercilessly I prepared, and my wife granted me great liberty from my duties in the evening, and during the day the immortal lines were never far from my mind, were whispered in the shower, their glorious syllables like secret jewels in my mouth; they were said while pushing the pram across the road, waving heartfelt thanks to the drivers on both sides – and they were still shoaling around me when I entered the supermarket, no longer a merchant like them in the scum of normality, but an actor: a player angling for his part, for his very future. There I stood.

I had hardly told anyone that I had a big audition, a really big shot at something very good, preferring to keep it as a delicious secret. My wife knew, and outside of her and my immediate family I think Ravi was the first person I told. He may even have been the first person I spoke to after the fateful telephone call, when the excitement was at its purest, when I still shook with prospect, and was unpolluted by any of the dread that would follow. He had been perplexed by what I had said, instantly making me feel foolish, and I surmised on the way home that while the idea that people acted might be perfectly reasonable to him, the further conceptual leap that people acted in order to get parts as actors, might have blown a gasket. But it did not stop him approaching or engaging me whenever he saw me, and one day near to the big day itself I came across him in the refrigerator aisle, where he was moving packets of something from one crate into another.

'HELLO,' he said.

'They have you on the salads today.'

'Yes.'

I nodded.

'I am sad,' he said.

He was winding up to something, so I stood passively, looking up at him, the child in the pram with an even greater kink in his neck.

'I am sad because my favourite helper at the centre, Sarah – Sarah is going to Australia and I won't be able to email her because they're not allowed to give their email addresses out.' He had not looked at me once while saying this, had only stood with one hand opening and closing, the other rising to scratch at the back of his neck. And this insight into his life was a portal that I had not seen open before. I had not thought of him as existing anywhere other than at home and the supermarket, perhaps picked up by his mum in the car, or sometimes his father (who would be ashamed of him), but never deposited anywhere else, and certainly not at a centre, whatever that was. It loomed for me darkly, outside of my knowledge, as the type of place that stunk on entrance.

'Is Sarah nice?' I risked.

'YES!' he bellowed, as if in pain.

'What is she like?'

'She is from Australia,' he said.

'What does she look like?'

And this made him falter – his eyes rose from the floor and began looking from the fridge to the aisle opposite, down to the packets in the green plastic crate, to me and everywhere as if looking for her, in order to be able to describe her. He turned to me and there was fear in his eyes. 'She . . .' I nodded to encourage him. 'She has brown hair . . .' but he could go no further. I worried that he was becoming upset, had visions of him picking up the green crate and smashing it repeatedly against the refrigerator, scattering the lightweight flimsy packets, making an angry keening noise with each impact.

But this did not happen. Instead he became silent. Behind me I could hear that our local outlet branch manager, Sudra, was in the same aisle. His voice was getting louder; I could not understand what he was saying because it wasn't English (or French), but I did recognise his tone: which was the tone of someone saying something authoritative to someone else while walking away from them. Despite my heightened state I was not immune to the annoyance of this fat little man and I turned to him sneeringly, taking in the dark and shiny skin and porcine eyes, expecting him to say something to me or Ravi – but he just smiled brightly and falsely and walked through us, parting with an alien, idiot clucking noise for the child's amusement.

'Caesar salad is called Caesar salad because it was invented by a man in Mexico called Caesar Cardini in nineteen twenty-four.' I looked down to Ravi's hands, to the packet he was holding; inside it there were croutons. He had not been able to muster the usual passion for this fact, had delivered it almost flatly, as if a part of his normal speech. He was depressed and it was clearly the woman, this Sarah, that was bothering him, and to this I could relate; also I was impressed that he was capable of experiencing heartache. Here was his big love going away from him, and there was nothing he could do about it.

'Why don't you buy Sarah something before she goes away?' I said.

'I don't have any money,' he answered.

'What about the money you get from working here?'

His eyes moved up from the floor to mine. 'Money from here?'

'Yes.'

'I don't get money for working here.' His brow became furrowed. 'They have an agreement with the centre, but I don't get money.'

'You don't get paid?' I was indignant. I felt I had known he was getting stiffed all along and now here was the evidence. 'That's illegal! They have to pay you. They must pay you.'

'Illegal?' he asked, his eyes now wide and frightened.

'Everyone else is getting paid.'

'But at the centre they said it would be interesting. That it would be fun.'

'Yeah, but it's not fun, is it? Apart from when you get to do dairy. And even then it's not that much fun.'

'Dairy is my favourite.'

'What about sauces? You don't like sauces.'

'No I don't like sauces. And Sudra, he makes me . . .'

'What?' I said quietly. I could hear Sudra's voice nearby, chattering away to a customer, spreading the store-wide happiness. 'What does he make you do? Tell me.'

'He . . .'

'Tell me, Ravi.'

But then Ravi folded away from me: his face went blank, his eyes left mine and he returned to the green crate, to pick up the Caesar salads there, to push them onto the back of the shelf in the refrigerator. I remained for a few seconds, considering whether to try to engage him further, watching his huge body bend and unbend to stack this product, knowing it would be futile and feeling a slight anger for his noble emperor's profile: the duplicitous carving of high brow and strong nose and chin, a sight that must sting his mother but more his father when they look and catch him in this thoughtful aspect, and are forced to wonder what might have been if he had not been damaged, if they had not damaged him with whatever it was they had done wrong.

*　　*　　*

I left the supermarket that day resolved to help Ravi in some way, a resolution that was almost completely dissolved by the time I had reached the front door, another wave of nervousness for my audition filling me with trembling to exclude everything else – except perhaps the hungry whimpering and pawing of my child, whom I promptly fed. That was the worst time of it: a period of only a few hours on that day when doubt and uncertainty of preparation were not outweighed by hope, by great feelings of ambition, and when it felt as if there was still time to completely undo all the preparation and rehearsal that had been done already, and substitute it for something of a completely different demeanour. In those few hours I quietly agonised whether a wholesale change of approach was necessary.

But by that afternoon I realised it was already too late to change everything – the course was set and I must simply run down its rails – and once on board this metaphor the days felt not long at all until I was on the Underground, sitting still with a straight spine and focused on my breathing, the mix of people around me bundled with their own worries, but surely none of them holding such a nest of snakes in their chest as I: none of them on the precipice, on the very edge of success or failure, a horrible mixture of hope and fear making the sounds of the train at one moment loud and threatening, the next an enjoyable crescendo. I can remember the stations changing and the passengers mixing further, the tension I held guardedly suddenly disappearing somewhere around Holborn, so that when I stood to alight there was no shake or tremor that I could detect bodily, my voice was steady and low in ordering some tourists to part before me, and when I stepped down onto the platform I knew I was a very fine actor indeed.

Steps up from the station, steps from the station out onto the street, steps into the building, steps up to the appropriate floor: all these ridges of concrete or stone I took calmly and with a rhythm, a pulse that was like breathing, but without its necessity, a thing for pleasure. There was a bright corridor with chairs (all empty) and I sat for perhaps a minute there before I was called into the room, to find the expected battlement of table and three figures seated behind it: this the fortress I must storm, the heads within it faceless but discernible as a mixture of male and female, of different ages, different blurry grades of baldness.

I did not see these things clearly because I was not looking at them but within myself – I had found the character, as if he was lying asleep and I now sat on his chest with my hands around his throat, and when one of them asked me to begin I delivered him so cleanly from this source, gave him the gift first of breath and then of freedom of movement, ushering him out from the great danger that my ownership of him constituted so that when he appeared before them they were spellbound: it was clear they were spellbound, the great wall of their table very quickly merely a flimsy thing on which they rested their hands, no impediment to me reaching into their hardened judgemental hearts, to squeeze and pull at will.

I finished and the last immortal words lingered in the room, the room itself emerging to my senses as the character dissipated in me: a clear and shining place with a distant white ceiling and a polished wooden floor, long windows along one side and the face of a grand stone building opposite peering in.

'Thank you,' said a woman's voice. I turned from the windows to the table. She was seated between the two men: a woman who seemed to me medium in everything except her clothing – which looked excellent. I surmised that she was probably the producer. She would not be the director because I believed him to be sat on her left: the dark T-shirt and tan suit jacket, the unkempt hair and the wire-rim glasses, the slightly sensuous movement from sitting with hands on the table to leaning back in his chair. This man's face was impassive: it was handsome and I guessed it had borne witness to much romping through various casts, but only the female contingent, because the lustre in his eyes that beheld me did not signal the creepy (but flattering) predations of a homosexual, but rather the sterner stuff of ambition: he had seen his lead before him and he was going to have me, and when I risked a long and direct glance to him there was nothing but affirmation for this, no hint of any weakening, perhaps even the merest of smiles from us both – and inside I dared to feel the beginnings of a great elation, except that experience had taught me such feelings were dangerous, despite these clues from the man's face, and from the certainty that I had just delivered the performance of my life.

But it was the third man who spoke next, who sat on the other side of the woman and was very bald, whose bright head I had glanced on entering to make me think they were all hairless to some degree. His nose was sharp and his eyes watched me from its bridge: close-set and intelligent, dark and unblinking, and in them a wildness that I realised with shock was suspicion, so that instantly I knew that he was impressed but unconvinced, and that he might still nurture hope for a different aspirant. He said: 'Tell us about yourself.'

I was responding succinctly, cycling through various minor productions that I knew were listed on the sheets of paper on their table, and looking to all three of them in turn when the man interrupted. 'Improv?' he repeated.

'It was entirely improvised. Ran for eight weeks.' This I said directly to him.

'That must have been difficult,' he said.

'Yes and no.'

'Why yes and no?'

'Mostly it was easy. Sometimes you would find yourself in a corner.'

He watched me for a second, then: 'By what the other actors did? By their lack of inspiration?' Though he had hardly moved, had not straightened or leaned forwards in his chair, I could sense a sudden alertness from this man. He was offering me the knife, tempting me to claim an elevation above those that I had worked with, this perhaps to begin opening the door to the possibility that I was arrogant, that I would need to be controlled, that I might not be pleasant to work with. The director looked like an affable type: one to charm and cajole people to his vision rather than drive them forcibly; perhaps this line of questioning was more for his benefit than mine.

'Some of them,' I said slowly, 'were shit.'

'Good for you!' said the bald man happily.

The woman nodded and she looked at me with renewed courtesy. 'There's no excuse for bad acting,' she said. 'At least there shouldn't be, even in improv.' And thus our little club was formed: a union between these two and I, who had with a brief exchange quickly found common and fundamental ground on the very issue of why we were all there. I had risked much to put the knife in but they had added their own, and at that moment, though nothing had been directly said or promised, it felt like it would take a force of nature to prevent me landing the role. I could feel the sides of my face, the corners of my mouth being pulled upwards when the director, no longer louche and contented, but leaning forwards and with a sudden hungry expression said, 'Improvise something for us now!'

It was a friendly enough request, containing to my ear the warmth of familiarity and indulgence – as if it would merely be an extra pleasure for all of us, for this to happen. But beyond the exuberance of the director the request was cold and dangerous, because it quickly stripped away the assuredness I had garnered myself with, to leave me in that room feeling as if it had suddenly darkened.

'Now?'

'Yes.' There was a trace of hardness in his voice, of will.

'On what theme?' I asked.

'You choose,' and knowing that he had given the hardest possible answer he smiled and became soft again in his chair. Helplessly I watched his head receding slowly as he settled himself, how his hands floated up to meet on his lap.

For the first time since the Underground I was aware of my heartbeat, had to consciously work for control of my breathing. I was not panicked but its approach was palpable; I had heard of strange requests given in auditions, yet this one I faced seemed the cruellest imaginable and I knew I was in big trouble: my mind felt very blank even before I had looked into it, like lifting a weightless box. I had lauded myself boldly to them, now they looked at me and expected proof, and each interminable second that passed (there had been only a few) drew me closer to the ultimate crime of locking up and freezing. It was plain that I must simply begin something – and immediately – taking the risk that whatever was started might be salvaged in-running as it were, and so I drew myself up to my fullest height before them, focused on a point high behind their heads and then allowed my eyes to relax to the point of blurriness – for them to cross even – my arms straight at my sides. Then I tried to picture a gigantic and grotesque fish of the ocean, what it would be like to be such a creature.

'Hello, gentleman,' I began softly. 'Hello, yes, hello.' I said this still softly and with a tapering sadness, but not without hope. It felt like a good start. 'I have a secret.' I looked to the window, turning my head to see the stone on the other side of the street, to feel its hard and ancient texture entering the bone and carriage of my chin and jaw: to make the profile of these things and the nose and forehead above them a solid display of grandeur to the three sat behind their weak table. Then an old trick: a sudden step towards the audience to look again at the point on the wall above their heads.

'TODAY,' I bellowed, 'today at the supermarket Sudra came and told me that I was not to unpack the dairy cage; I had to do meats and fish instead and that made me sad.' I opened and closed my hand, could feel it scrabbling at my thigh. I took a little half step forwards and then back again, dropping my head down so that my arm could rise to scratch at my neck: a scratching that was gentle at first, but became increasingly frantic until it was as if I had remembered something – the instruction of a carer: not to scratch too much, not to scratch in public – and I dropped this hand to resume staring ahead. Vaguely I could see the three faces below, could ascertain much information from this indirect vision, but blocked most of it, solely acknowledging that while I did not have them, nor had I lost them yet.

'I hope it is my mother who picks me up tonight,' I resumed. 'When my father picks me up I am afraid because I have to try and tell what mood he is in, but usually I don't do that because I just start talking about what I have had to do in the day, and if he is not in a good mood . . .' Here I became less loud, allowed fear to creep into parts of my face. 'Sudra is always in a good mood! But he makes me, he makes me . . .' Suddenly I convulsed – not largely but acutely: a tremor that ran from the fist held at my side to end with a ticking flick of my neck. 'Once I tried to tell my father what he makes me do, but he shouted at me.' I paused. 'When my mother asks me why I have dirt on my knees and why I'm not hungry for dinner I get too scared to tell her. Sudra says I am his big dog. He says I will do anything for sweets and there was this one time when he got all the other people there; then he made me beg on my knees.' Slowly I got down onto my knees. 'And everyone took it in turns to throw the sweets into my mouth.'

Then, from this low position, I looked at the three behind the desk. It was clear that the woman in good clothing was suspicious, that her faith was being tested. The bald man at her side was impressively passive: he gave nothing away – but Monsieur le Directeur's head was tilting back, his mouth was slightly agape and behind the small lenses of his glasses his eyes were bright and interested.

'I wanted them to stop but I wanted the sweets more!' I shouted angrily, to make everyone jump.

The director sprung to his feet. 'What are you doing?' he yelled. 'What the hell do you think you're doing?' In anger there was a foreign tint to his voice, a flavour that had not been there before, which augmented the will he had shown earlier into something suddenly blazing and monstrous, and made me think that he might be dangerous, possibly Israeli. I could feel heat at my face: it was the shame of my imminent failure, and I began to struggle up from the pain and hardness of my kneecaps when I saw that the director was moving, had pushed his chair back quickly to make it scrape against the floor and was now rounding the end of the table, his hair a wildness in profile, his face dark and quietly raging as it bore down on me. 'What are you doing? Get up!'

Ashamed and fearful I looked down at the floor, bringing one foot beneath me to begin the process of standing, feeling the man's anger pulsing in the air between us.

'I told you to get off your knees! Have you done what I asked you?' His accent had become increasingly heavy and erratic; in his rage he was blowing about the map I tried to pin him on as if an escaped balloon. I had my hand on the floor and was pushing with it to help me, to steady me and the shaking that wanted to pervade my every part, a disbelief at the sudden change of events, the shock of it emptying my mind and opening my mouth spasmodically so that it opened and shut without noise.

'Stop that, you look like a fish!' the director shouted. 'Now. Did you do what I asked you?'

'I . . .'

'Did you tidy your room?' he interrupted.

At first I thought I had misheard, suspected he had asked me to leave the room, which I had then converted into a more childish terror due to the state of shock and fear I was in, facing as I was the seeming total desolation of all my hopes, which had just seconds ago felt real and large enough to overshadow every previous inconsequence of my life. But then the sentence he had uttered settled more clearly in my mind, and with it the reason for his meandering accent emerged: that he in fact did not have an accent but was attempting to adopt one, because he was playing a part – convincingly enough that I had been fooled – though he had had the advantage of surprise. I took a deep breath – this was the second shock this man had given me – and scrabbled around internally to recapture Ravi, to feel his aspects determine a delicate relaxing of muscles in my face, to change the way I was standing and the prepared flat inflection of my voice.

'No, Father, I haven't,' I told the floor next to the director sadly. Then I looked up and met his gaze and held it, a movement not only of eyes but of my whole body: I put everything into that movement to not only push a force onto him but to drag up the attention of the two still seated, to create a pregnant silence of my own making, and one that no longer felt hostile. 'Father!' I risked, taking a step towards him. 'Father!' I was nearing him, my arms beginning to open, displaying a clear desire to embrace, but a tentativeness in my arms and all other parts of me to reveal a powerful fear of its rejection. 'Please, Father, I'm so sorry!'

'What for?' Father replied. 'What have you done now?'

And I thought of Ravi, of his home with the stains on the walls, of his parents and the embarrassment he must subject them to; the pain of this. Perhaps on some days, when they have entered a new place where they are unknown they can enjoy for a few seconds the illusion that they are a normal unit, that their son is in fact taking them out: he is not a huge parasite stuck to them that looks and sounds normal until a tipping point is reached and this fascia begins to erode, and the fellow diners or shoppers that surround them begin to notice that there is something wrong with the big loud man. His parents must repeatedly witness this realisation passing over the faces of strangers. The stares these strangers give, who do not understand Ravi or could ever love him; and the sniggering ignorance of children must be like the trident grip of a raptor sunk deep into their chests, to grasp at will and cause them a permanent agony.

'I'm sorry for how I am,' I tell Father in a perfectly intense whisper, accompanied by a flashing change in eyes and face: the quick and temporary acumen of the fool.

The director had been leaning back away from me, his brow furrowed and his mouth in a sneer. But these things then relaxed into a smile, and as he straightened I lowered my arms away from his shoulders so that simultaneously, we both emerged from our roles to become normal standing men. 'Very good,' he said.

'Speak for yourself,' I replied.

'Well. Just a bit of fun.' He turned to include the two seated. 'I am decided. Yes? Yes?'

There was a brief pause.

'We cannot say anything definitive now, but . . .' The woman turned to the man seated next to her.

'Yes, not definitive,' he said back to her. Then to me: 'I think you should go home a happy man, however.'

'Definitive! Bah, don't listen to them, they're just being coy.' The director had moved closer to me and was holding out his hand. 'Well done, sir; I shall see you at rehearsals, if not before.'

And he told me his name, which was Horner, and which I recognised vaguely but would only confirm later with research, to discover him a director of some repute beyond what I had dared hope for, and there was I: recently met with him, holding a verbal promise (from his face to my face) that the part was mine, to spawn several days of quiet ecstasy and celebration with my family and those around me.

Except that the promised confirmation, the official contract through the post did not arrive.

In the first couple of days this was to be expected and of no concern, but as the third day passed and became the fourth morning – still without any contact from the company – I started to become doubtful. At best I thought the post was delayed, but at worst I imagined that after I left the audition one of them must have said something perceptive: a small but powerful objection that had worked its way through them all until, to their combined mock regret I was dumped from the production before I had even got home.

Or worse the director, in the same fit of sudden inspiration as he had shown with his own acting, had sprung up in the middle of the night with someone else in mind – someone who would be absolutely perfect – and totally enlivened by this revelation he had telephoned them or their agent immediately, to thus steal happiness from my own home and spark it somewhere else. And at this new house the contracts would arrive the next day, everything would be signed and finalised, with just the unpleasant task of letting down the young actor who had also been quite good – a task easily prevaricated upon.

These were the possibilities I developed, which festered silently in me while carrying out the duties that had become automatic, and which I had become accustomed and resigned to once more. I believed strongly that it was not my role to chase them, to question what Horner had promised, especially as that might make me appear pushy and demanding, and if the decision was somehow still in the balance – as surely it could be, seeing how crucial it was to me and my family's entire future – it was not worth risking everything by phoning. And perhaps it was on the fifth morning of this torture, when I was in the midst of devising a particularly devastating scenario involving an old enemy from college, who had by some cryptic route been gifted the part instead of me, that I pushed the pram into the sterile serenity of the supermarket, to almost immediately be greeted by Ravi near the bakery section.

In those few days I had developed a loathing for the supermarket, barely hiding my hostility for Sudra, who was clearly an abuser, and unable to entirely absolve his victim Ravi either, for it might be the imitation of his form that had caused me to fail in that room, once I had left and objections were free to be raised, probably from the woman.

But it was a mild blame, as this was only the first time that I had seen him since the audition; instantly I decided that I was in no mood for his idiocy.

'HELLO, GENTLEMAN!' he said.

I had wanted to swerve around him with the pram, greet him abruptly as I passed but he had turned into the aisle, almost standing in its centre, a wire bin full of colourful promotional goods near enough that it would require me asking him to move. His hands were large and hanging at his sides, the fingers pointing downwards in an affected ordinariness to give his entire aspect a rigidity I had not seen before. But curiousness could not soften the anger of rejection, which that morning was pulsing just behind my eyes, and I muttered a greeting in response, to stare pointedly at the shelves, as if with sole intent for their contents.

'How are you today,' he stated flatly. 'I have not seen you in a while. Have you been away?'

'I've been busy.'

'I looked for you on Friday but you didn't come into the shop,' he said. 'I looked for you on Saturday as well but not on Sundays as I'm not here then. And I wasn't here on Monday. Were you here on Monday?'

'No. I don't think so.'

'I didn't see you on Tuesday or afterwards and today is Thursday so that's why I thought that you might have gone away.'

I looked up from the shelves to his face. His eyes were enormous behind their glasses, and instead of ranging the floor and the wall beyond, they were fixed to mine: they did not flinch or even blink, even though I must have been frowning at him, and perhaps even more than that – perhaps I was staring at him coldly. 'I did not go away, Ravi.'

'Where were you then?'

'Not here!'

'So you didn't go away?'

'I have to go now,' and thinking that this would end the conversation I was lowering myself to push the pram forwards, to force him to step aside, but he was steadfast.

'I was hoping to see you because I wanted to tell you something.'

'Yeah? What?' I straightened, resigned in this movement to the adsorption of everything he knew concerning bread and baking or whatever, to better brush it off once in the next aisle. I was worried that it would be a long lecture, because Ravi looked focused, more alert and intelligent than I had ever seen him, and I feared that he had found a new favourite to usurp dairy, and with this new passion there might have followed a period of deep research in the grotty library of the centre; he had sat and studied all the books he could find on cakes and pastry, getting the helpers to read the longer words for him (could he read?), had taken the books home and continued to study them until he was bursting to get to the supermarket the next day, hoping to see me, his captive audience, so that he could deliver proudly what he had learned. And of course I had not been there for days – I had been absent while his knowledge grew and grew with no outlet, and if I was ever to get past him and continue with the crap that constituted the rest of my day, I would have to be firm. 'Hurry up, Ravi. What is it you wanted to tell me?'

'I wanted to tell you that Sarah . . .'

'Yes?'

'Sarah is Australian.'

'I know that. Is that what you wanted to say?'

Ravi was beginning to falter: his eyes had left mine and were wandering; I sensed that he was going to close up away from me and so I began to apply pressure on the pram. But with a slight convulsion he gathered himself, and then blinking, with a flashing, strained facial expression he suddenly blurted, 'Sarah is five feet eight inches with brown hair and she wears glasses; she has freckles on her nose and her cheeks and her eyes are green.' His hand began to pump open and closed. 'Her hair is brown and curly and when she is near me helping me sometimes she puts her hand on my shoulder and it feels very warm and light!' This he had started quietly, but had ended at his full bellowing volume. He blinked a few times and then looked at me. 'Once I went to the Butterfly House, have you been there? Yes, I went to the Butterfly House with my parents. The Butterfly House is not there any more because they built a hotel instead, and they had to tear down the Butterfly House to build the hotel, but I don't know why they built a hotel there because it is a luxury hotel, but it is a luxury hotel right underneath the flight path for the airport, and when we went to the Butterfly House I counted fourteen planes before we had even got to the Butterfly House. Have you been there? When you went there did a butterfly land on you? When I went there a butterfly landed on my shoulder and I could feel it through my T-shirt; I was only wearing a T-shirt even though it was winter because I knew it would be hot.' He paused, his eyes left me and seemed to hang on nothing in the air before him.

After a while he said, 'How long do you think it would take to get to Cockfosters?'

But the passion had drained from his face, the aperture of his eyes was reduced and he turned away from me, returning to the loaves of bread that he lifted from the red crate, to continue lining neatly and carefully the shelf he attended.

So he had wanted to describe his big love to me properly, to put right what once went wrong: namely his inability to do this several days ago. Perhaps I should have remained and said something to him – thanked him even – but any empathy was paralysed by the pendulous failure that seemed to slice at me with every spare breath spent in reflection. I had no spare capacity to reflect on the problems of others, thus I could not acknowledge his outpouring and moved on, bought the necessary products, stood blankly in the queue, handed over money with regret, pushed the pram home and through the front door to run over the junk mail strewn in the hallway.

Nestling within these envelopes and leaflets was my contract, and a personally written note from Horner, which was full of anticipation and excitement for the production ahead.

This success led to a more magnanimous mindset generally, and with it a clamouring of guilt for what had happened earlier, as well as a thirst for expensive alcohol – so I decided to return immediately to the supermarket. When I entered with the pram, after a short walk of simple but wide contentedness, it was apparent that Ravi was no longer in the bakery section, but I quickly found him at the end of the aisle, standing with a basket crooked in his arm like a shopper.

He was surveying the contents of the nearest fridge much as a shopper would, except that his body was outsized, and he was bent with his face very close to one of the shelves, while his hand was hovering above a row of thin packets, the fingers walking through them to part them individually. I wondered whether he would inspect each slice of meat with the same meticulousness, lifting them from the plastic packet and turning them over in the unshaded light of their drab kitchen, looking for some quality or checking for flaws, before slapping it into his childish hash of a sandwich.

'Doing some shopping before you go?' I asked brightly.

His hand shot away from the packets and he convulsed with fright, then he straightened and looked at me briefly with wide eyes before turning his head towards the tills, which he would just be able to see from his height, but still had to lift himself up on his toes and weave a bit to do so, his hands now clutched to his chest like paws.

'I didn't mean to frighten you.'

He looked at me blankly, his eyes still wide, the hum of the refrigerator surrounding us and then another noise joined it: a low and unmodulated keening that could only be coming from the back of his throat. The wire basket at his elbow was filled with packets: thin plastic wallets like the ones he had just been leafing through, which must contain sliced meats and other sliced things. It had never been the case before that I should have to direct the conversation with Ravi, but now, with him not turning away from me and still holding my gaze, I was compelled.

I pointed at the basket. 'Sandwiches?'

At the mention of this word his head jerked and his eyes widened further. Also the keening noise he made was no longer limited to living deep in his throat but started to escape through open lips, developing into a low and slightly wavering 'Uhhh' – and I thought that if there was ever going to be a time when he became totally crazed and smashed the place up, this was it. I had the pram gripped tightly and my weight was in my feet, the rubber at their soles feeling reassuringly sticky on the supermarket's floor.

'It's okay, Ravi. I'll leave you to it.'

'Wait!'

I had half-turned.

'This is what Sudra makes me do!' he whispered loudly.

'What?'

'This is what Sudra makes me do!'

'And what are you doing?'

His arms relaxed away from his chest and he moved the basket off the crook of his arm to hold it out. Inside it there were sliced meats and cheeses.

'Are you a vegetarian or a vegan or something?' I said.

'A what?'

'What's so bad about putting some packets of ham in a basket?'

'They're nearly out of date,' Ravi said. 'I have to go round and put things in this that are nearly out of date.' His whisper had vanished and he was speaking loudly again, but his eyes were still wide; the way he hunched over the basket and leaned towards me was laden with unsophisticated conspiracy.

'Why does Sudra make you do this?' I asked carefully.

'Why? I don't know why,' he bellowed. 'But he puts them in a box and takes them out to his car. Sometimes his car has more than one box in it and then I have to help him take the boxes out.'

I nodded.

He leaned closer and whispered, 'I don't think he pays for them, but he still takes them away, which is ILLEGAL.'

'Sounds illegal all right.'

'Do you think so?' he asked.

'Yeah! But you shouldn't worry. You're just following orders, right?'

'Yes.'

And so in this manner it was confirmed to me that Sudra was a crook, and worse, was unashamedly using Ravi as his henchman, who was aware enough to know that something immoral was occurring. Sudra had obviously underestimated Ravi. The nearly out-of-date products packed into boxes and then put into his car: either he was taking them home or he was selling them.

Ravi had said that sometimes there were many boxes, which made me think it was more likely the latter, and this would be more fitting for someone of Sudra's ilk, because I could see his small eyes gleaming greedily as he watched Ravi struggle to lift a heavy box, him thinking happily of all the cost-free profit contained within, a profit made at what for me would be the most frightening and dangerous of all black markets – worse than hand weapons or domestic slaves – the type only the poorest and most desperate knew of: a *food* black market – dark places where ageing meat was studied carefully by old and practised eyes, sniffed at before being bartered for, taken elsewhere, and perhaps sometimes used to make takeaway food, or fed to culturally spoilt grandchildren. Ravi, in his way, must also have sensed some of this, and that is why he did not like to do Sudra's bidding.

Dormant resolutions to become involved in the situation were woken, and from then on I began to enter the supermarket in a state of latent opportunism, continuing to talk with Ravi as usual, but always supplementing our chats with a mention of what we had discussed, to show that I had not forgotten, that I would help. And Sudra I watched with increasing dislike: his smile and laughter, the bright and friendly tone with which he would greet a customer or answer their query; even the purposeful way in which he led them to the product they requested would cause my lips to curl in anger, for it was a walk saturated in hypocrisy, topped by the final, affected flourish of hand to point out exactly where the product was.

One day, during this period, I happened to be accessing cash from the machine opposite the supermarket, pushing the dirty buttons, shading the dingy screen from the sunlight and doing all this while perched on the thin saddle of a bicycle. I had finished and turned, only to find Sudra standing behind me. He smiled and I probably frowned in response, and if it had been anyone else I would have moved off, but the enmity I now held for him caused me to pause and drink in his squat vileness, watching as his short stubby fingers reached grubbily out for the buttons, and then the lucre, and throughout this operation his shiny-shoed foot was tapping on the pavement, and he was humming a little tune to himself (out of time with his foot). I watched all this from my bicycle with growing distaste, hoping that he would turn to me again and witness the unbridled contempt I was projecting from beneath my helmet, but he did not look and instead he walked sprightly to a car parked in the road. And in this car was the clear brown cuboid shape of a very large cardboard box, sitting on the back seat, too big to get in the boot, too stuffed with stolen food.

The sun was shining, it was the weekend, my wife was at home with my son and I had little to do. I had a sudden and powerful urge to gather information, which would lead to the prosecution of Sudra. So when the car pulled away, I eased my bicycle down the kerb and onto the road, a raw and mixed excitement as blindly I felt for the pedals, my eyes unmoving from his car.

It was not a particularly long chase, and buses and traffic lights meant he could not escape. After a half a mile or so of main roads we turned onto a residential street, and I feared that he would stop and unload the box and take the goods into a house, which might be less implicative than a warehouse, when I made the call to the police. Then, on one side of the street the houses ended and a large pale-green facade arose in their stead. It was a building that looked like it would have a large hall for civic use, for hire even, and into its car park Sudra entered with an undiminished swoop of speed. I cycled on past the building, a figure upright and casual, until the houses had resumed and I thought it was safe, whereupon I stopped, dismounted and locked the bike around a lamp post, to then begin creeping back.

The houses there were tattered and the street was treeless; many of the gardens had been paved over and there was a sun-baked tiredness to the place as if the inhabitants did not care, as if they would not care that there was a food black market in the green building among them. I walked towards the building with nervousness and a low excitement, because I intended to look in, perhaps even exchange a few words with a stunned and floundering Sudra, and when I turned to walk from the pavement into the open area of the building's car park I had a sudden and pleasing sense of my own correctness: the feeling that everything I had ever believed might just be true, because in its sixties-dishevelment the place seemed the perfect host for something illegal: a state of disrepair that mirrored the houses around it, that showed that the council, or whatever group it was that ran it, were not interested in its renovation, did not keep an eye on the low behaviour of its users.

The door was glass and wood-framed, and I raised my palm to it, the sun bright enough that I could not see through, but instead could see my own still-helmeted reflection. I pushed it open and stepped inside; instantly the smell of urine assaulted me, strong enough to make me grimace, to quadruple my disgust for the little man Sudra. There was a corridor of sorts and muted noise coming from the end of it: hushed voices full of purpose and avarice. Though the smell was bad enough to sit sourly in my throat and lungs, I stepped ahead to make my way to the double doors at the end of the corridor, motivated in part with the purpose of catching Sudra in the act, but also curious to witness first-hand the underbelly of the city in which I lived.

When I depressed the two bars and swung the doors open, I felt prepared for anything, but the sight that flashed up before me was like the ground at the end of a childish mishap: it smashed into me and there was nothing I could do to stop it, except stare dumbly and await impact. Arrayed before me were tables in orderly rows, and behind them, and in front of them, in fact anywhere you cared to look were dozens of tramps in various states of societal decay.

Some of them were shouting, a few were crying, but all seemed engaged in a terrible struggle for the food that was strewn haphazardly on the tables: packets of everything from ham to biscuits, tins of meat to fresh fruit, and I realised that some of the tramps were selling, while others were trying to buy, and that the currency consisted of little slips of paper that they waved and tried to snatch from each other, and in the middle of it all I spotted Sudra roaming, wearing the same smile and walking the same proprietary walk, not through aisles of products, but aisles of misery and a misery seemingly of his own making: he the king and founder of this hell-market.

This lasted a few very long seconds before the sea of tramps divided momentarily, and then I saw her. She was of average height, had very bright green eyes, long curly dark hair and freckles. The kindness in her round face was the type that pumps outwards silently and constantly. She was nearly on the other side of the hall – but all this was clear at a distance and in the few seconds that I saw her – so that not only was I moved to cross the room, but my whole idea about the room altered. I did not know how and I did not know all, or even any, of the facts for certain, but I knew that this woman had changed things and I must approach her – because it seemed to me impossible that such a kind (and good-looking) woman could be involved in what was happening.

I reached her table to discover it different: it did not have packets of foodstuffs, instead it had plates, and she was not involved in trading, but in the buttering of slices of bread. This was a confusing discovery.

'What would you like? Have you got your ticket?' she

asked me without looking up, a slightly lilting accent in her voice.

'What is this place?' I said.

This made her stop the deft movements of her knife and look upwards. 'This is the Mission,' she said.

'What mission?'

'The Mission: capitalised.'

And when she said this, I thought with sadness that her kindness was merely deceptive: that she was in on Sudra's sick game after all, that my initial impressions of horror had not been wrong. 'Your mission is to recapitalise them?' I said with disgust.

'Who?'

'These guys,' I said, gesturing at the loud and stinking populace around us.

'Recapitalise them? What do you mean?' Her accent was getting stronger: the southern hemisphere rising in her as the facade of kindness started to crack.

'You're making them trade and barter for their hand-out food, with some sort of made-up currency.'

'That's right!' she said happily, and smiled very warmly.

The inputs of the situation before me were confusing and in conflict, I did not know what to either think or say in response to this. I felt on the edge of something I could not understand – something barred to me permanently and beyond my grasp, perhaps due to some defect or flaw in my nature, and a part of me wanted to retreat, to give up on any pursuit of Sudra and leave them to it. I could have turned smartly and left, but I didn't, because there was one route left open to me, which was to act.

'Sudra has chosen you well,' I answered, intending to be

both cryptic and slightly threatening, to display that I was not disarmed.

'Well, I don't know about that,' she said, in a clear Australasian accent. 'But he's a great guy.'

'Where does all this food come from?' I asked her.

'Various places.' She began buttering slices of bread again. Then a man, stinking powerfully, approached the table, the only bright thing about him, which wasn't smeared in dirt and grime, being the slip of paper he held in his hand. He muttered something incoherently and the woman looked up. Her face softened and smiled, the eyes becoming brighter and an even purer green as she very gently prised the paper from his hand, replaced it with a plate that had two thick slices of buttered bread staring up from it. The man muttered something again and shuffled off and I watched him briefly, before turning back to the woman, to catch her discreetly cleaning her hands on a cloth.

There could be no doubting she was sincere; either that or she was a fine actress, which I did doubt. The sound of the hall, the shouting and growling, the smell of urine and alcohol and of lives spent in an obligatory detritivore manner meant I could not think clearly: I was still deeply suspicious that something incorrect, illegal, was occurring – some sort of game with Sudra as its umpire – but at the same time this theory was being battered by the fountain of human kindness in front of me. 'Does Sudra bring food?' I attempted.

'He sure does!' she said, smiling, but still looking down at the knife flying in her hand from tub to bread. 'He's got a great arrangement where he works,' she said. 'They were reluctant at first, but he got them to do it, which is brave, considering he's got to work for them.' She looked up. I was starting to think everything I had ever believed might be wrong. 'You know him?'

'Sarah,' I said.

'Yes?'

'You are Sarah.'

'I am. Who are you?'

'And this place,' I said, gesturing. 'This place is the centre.'

'The Parnaby Centre, yes.'

'But you call it the centre.'

'Yeah,' she said, looking at me quizzically, but not unkindly.

'I'm a friend of Ravi's.'

'Are you? That's great. It's nice to meet you,' and as she said this she truly beamed: her eyes swung to mine as if I were the only person of worth in the entire room, as if beyond it in the dark and threatening world her face would remain proof that there was always the possibility of safe harbour, that no matter how bad things got if you could just get to the point where you saw this face and had it smile at you, all of it would be mitigated, assuaged – and I could understand how a mind that was not on its game, that was even only slightly enfeebled, would be powerless not to fall helplessly in love.

'He's very fond of you.'

'Is he?' Her response was not perfunctory and her eyebrows dropped slightly to furrow her freckled brow.

And seeing this I felt that a door was opened for me, through which I could pass and make good the situation, and help Ravi as I had promised myself I would. First to make sure that he did not need rescuing from Sudra, and then perhaps I could do something for him with this Sarah woman.

'I see him less, now that he has the job at the supermarket,' she said, to interrupt my intent.

'Sudra got him the job,' I replied.

'Yes.'

'But he doesn't get paid,' I remembered, suddenly annoyed at either her ignorance or her complicity.

'No, he wouldn't. He's on the Learning Around scheme.'

'The what?'

'Learning Around. For people like Ravi, it introduces them to work.'

'But he's been there for months, he stacks shelves like the others, he should be getting paid.'

'Listen, I agree, but Sudra did all he could to get him in there in the first place. It takes a while before they progress to getting a full wage.' She said this gently, her face turning and changing to a more intense kindness as another of the tramps appeared with his white stub, to receive a plate of buttered bread. As this man turned to shuffle off she reached down to wipe her hands again on the hidden cloth. 'He'll get paid eventually, I helped him fill out the forms. I can even remember his parents' account number. Ravi made me memorise it in case,' she raised her hands, 'anything went wrong.'

'His parents' account number?'

'Yeah.'

So he would be paid eventually, and just had to be patient, get his Learning Around qualification or whatever it was they called it and then he could start bringing money home to his poor parents, who had suffered for so long in their grim and featureless flat – perhaps for even as long as three decades – what an amount of suffering to repay, but he could certainly begin. And he would have freedom to express a bit of that wealth for himself, and to a limited degree enjoy the undoubted rewards of consumerism, assuming, of course, that his parents did not pocket it all automatically, which was not impossible, especially as they might have beliefs about caste, hierarchy, the natural order of things.

'So he will get paid eventually.'

'Yes.'

She was smiling at me again. At that moment I was mostly satisfied, although I could still not shake the suspicion that I was very deep within a complex and mature scam, and due to some as yet unknown aspect, was somehow being hoodwinked. But then within a breath, suddenly the last remnants of my theories, of my beliefs about Ravi, his parents, about Sudra and his operations at the centre, gave up as if of their own accord: they fell and shattered on the ground, never to be resurrected. I took off my helmet and ran my fingers through my hair, a movement meant primarily for my own comfort and reassurance.

'That's good to know.'

'Yes, it is.'

'I'll be off now.'

'Sure!' she said, and there was that smile again: the source of happiness and affection, the eyes with the mind behind them that could send out a hand to land a butterfly on your shoulder.

'When do you leave?' I asked her.

'The UK? In three weeks,' she answered.

'For good?'

'Likely, yes.'

'Ravi will miss you,' and these words I strove to give a coating of gravitas, holding her gaze intently while speaking, slight movements around my own eyes and an imperceptible lifting of the head at the end of the sentence. My own heart hurt: I had allowed a small part of it to fall in love with the idea of this woman, to try and feel what Ravi must, to be able to affect her more on parting. She did not say anything, the knife in her hand limp and immobile, one green eye higher than the other as she seemed to search me, perhaps for insincerity, or to more accurately assess her own feelings. I turned from her, turning my body to leave, giving her one more flash of sadness before parting with a slight smile, an expression in counterpoint to the light despair the rest of my face conveyed.

Then in the fresh air surrounding the lamp post, I unlocked my bicycle, and reflected happily that a good morning's work had been done.

Weeks passed, the production began, the cast was varied and interesting and the rehearsals went well: Horner was excellent to work with, inspiring, invigorating, occasionally frightening so that you left the studio feeling as if you had been remoulded in a stronger, more powerful human alloy. There I was, the lead of this great play, the greatness of which never lessened and seemed only to grow and strengthen, with me at its forefront, and when we moved from the studio into the theatre, this physical repositioning seemed to make evident what had occurred within: namely that I was no longer bothered by the dull streets around my home, or its inhabitants, because I had a lifeline to the great hunkering nearby city with all its prospect and power, I was no longer struggling just to breathe, just to get out. And in fact get out we did: we moved from there, not so far but far enough that the supermarket was no longer my local supermarket.

Sometimes I would pass through, and pop into the place, but for a long time I did not see Ravi, assumed he had earned his Learning Around licence and gone off to work somewhere, for money. So it came as a shock, long after the production with Horner, to come across him in the supermarket. He was wearing a drab uniform, he had a nametag on his breast that was not printed, but was a white piece of plastic with RAVI scrawled on it in large letters. When he saw me his eyes widened and he stopped what he was doing. I approached, to find he was no longer as tall as I remembered.

'HELLO, GENTLEMAN!'

'Hello,' I said. He looked clean and in good health. 'How are you today?'

'I am depressed.' He turned from me to look at the shelf next to him.

'Oh yeah? Why's that?' The shelf he was next to held misshapen rows of rice, pasta and noodles; perhaps he might be bored by these, it would be difficult to get their slumping forms into perfect alignment.

'I am depressed because my parents' house has become a bad place for me but I cannot afford to move out.'

'Oh.' I was neither moved by this nor surprised by it, that his parents' kindness (if there had been any in the first place) had run out and they, like ugly cuckoo chicks, were trying to push him out of their home. 'That doesn't sound very good at all.'

'NO,' he bellowed.

'Are you getting paid here yet?'

'No, I am still on Learning Around level two.'

'Does level three mean you get paid? You've been working here a long time, surely you should be paid by now.'

'I've only just come back so I haven't got Learning Around level three yet. I was working with the Mohinder family in their shop but they were rude and abusive to me so I had to leave.'

'Oh,' I said again. I could picture what had happened: some emporium on a high street where the signposts are bilingual, Ravi dumped on a family of traders who did not want to take him, but did so under duress or as a favour, and then began to turn on him, mildly at first, but growing in acerbity until they would walk past him and give him a friendly punch on the arm, gently. But when he didn't respond, when he just folded away from them and dropped his eyes to the floor in confusion, when they saw this and began to get sick of his booming voice in their blinkingly lit, dirty little wonky-aisled store, the big man not only telling them how to correctly stack shelves that they had been incorrectly stacking for years, but also informing them of various facts such as how there are five different Lisbons in the world – one each in Canada, USA, Nauru, Pakistan and Portugal – they would hear all this and have to tolerate it until they could tolerate it no longer, whereupon they would see him folding away from them as an invitation to start putting their weight into their punches, an opportunity to smack some sense both into him and into the grey and grim

Western world into which they had debarked, a strange world unalleviated by the colourful signs and lights of the high street, the invitations to purchase and feed like Western pigs always surrounding and above them, but at odds with their lifestyles, their outlooks, so that no wonder every time one of them walked past him, Ravi would have to stop what he was doing and freeze in fear, waiting for the hot pain in the meat of his arm, the flash of teeth from the grin or grimace of his assailant.

It had been months since I had seen him.

'How long do you think it would take to cycle to Neasden?' he asked.

'I don't know,' I said, trying to locate Neasden in my head. 'About half an hour?'

'Half an hour to Neasden!' His eyes widened at this, as if the amount of time was scandalous.

'I'm just guessing. Is that where you want to live?'

'I wanted to live in Cockfosters because it is on the end of the line. How long do you think it would take to cycle to Cockfosters?'

It was my turn to look at the shelving. 'I would say about two hours. It's a long way.'

'Hmm,' he replied.

'I'm sure things will work out for you, Ravi,' I said.

'Yes,' he said to the shelving.

'I hope they do.'

'Yes.'

So I left the supermarket that day and was able to plunge back into the warmer sea of my own life. Yet perhaps because my mind was no longer occluded by thoughts of failure, of struggle, and could instead wallow in the ownership of success and progressiveness, it was able frequently to return to the subject of Ravi, and in particular the image of him standing in the aisle, not as tall as he used to be, but still a tower of despondency as I left him that day, to think alone on his fate. And when he was not working, when he was not earning points for his Learning Around degree, I began to wonder exactly how he existed, especially now as his home situation was malignant; did he see the hours spent at the centre as a relief, or would he be hunched at a craft table, glumly reading a book, while those of stronger strains of impairment dribbled and shouted, threw things – all of this and no Sarah to love, an idol for him to muse upon, to occasionally transport him to a paradise in the brief moments she could spare him her full attention. It was these thoughts that made me look out the window and shake my head and sigh, and watch the world go by, and watch more of it go by and all in my favour, until one day I had picked up the telephone and called the Parnaby Centre, to speak to someone there briefly before informing them that I was going to get a bus, I would shortly be boarding a bus in their direction.

That was one thing I did get right. When I returned to the centre it did not smell as it had previously, there was no Mission that day, but the room that the helper led me to, and in which Ravi was caged, was just as I had imagined it: it was ugly, it had a craft table, it had a very bad smell of its own and it was loud with a bad energy, a frightening movement and noise, of unfortunate people who get lumped with children and collies, when it comes to quantifying intelligence. Ravi was at a table, hunched over a book spread before him, his head resting on one arm as a boy would and when I saw this I had to swallow and blink, I had to pause and take several lungfuls of the fetid sickly air before I felt able to walk over to the table and take a seat opposite him. He continued reading for a few seconds and then looked up, his eyes widened a fraction, and then he said plainly:

'Have you been to Lisbon again?'

Thus, once a week, for a few hours in the morning, I would take Ravi on a day trip of sorts. Often we would end up on the Underground, headed for the museums. It was of endless variety and interest, the looks people would give Ravi. I would enjoy watching them as they watched him, sometimes able to catch the precise moment of their realisation.

'I am a bit sad today,' he would say at full volume, to turn the heads of those not yet acclimated to the carriage.

'Yeah? How come.'

'I was thinking about Sarah this morning.'

I nodded. The movement and noise of the train increased to muffle our conversation, to hide it from the other passengers.

'I was thinking about when she left. We had a party for her at the centre.'

I was tired, had been stifling yawns and not paying attention to what Ravi had been speaking of, but this new topic changed that and I turned to him, to take in his noble profile, which even while seated towered above me.

'You didn't tell me there had been a party.'

'Didn't I?' Ravi bellowed.

'What happened then?'

'I gave her a present.'

'What did you give her?'

'A silver necklace with a pendant,' he said carefully.

'Did she like it?'

The eye that I could see widened behind his glasses. His hands were groping gently at his thighs, which were stretching long out into the passageway between the seats. He did not turn to me, but instead mouthed something to the undulating darkness streaming past in the opposite window. Then he did turn, his head revolving stiffly and his eyes looking out above my head, before he seemed to discover me below him and looked downwards. I was interested: I felt that he was about to say something important to do with the woman Sarah.

Because I could imagine her standing there in that room of horrors with a small blue-felt box open in her hand, her face temporarily hidden as she looked down to its glinting insides, how she would look up to Ravi and smile, how his heart would leap – and then the grace of her that he would feel with disbelief and a dreamlike pleasure as she reached up to place both hands on his shoulders, to take a step towards him to brim his eyes with much of her very close, his nose tubing in long draughts of her various and unimpeachable fragrances.

Then she stands on her toes to bring her face close to his; she is not revolted by the mouth that splatters the world around it in factual dissemination, she is not repulsed by the memory of foodstuff trapped in this mouth's corners, and instead she places a light and unhurried kiss on his lips.

'Thank you, Ravi,' she would say, lowering herself slowly, keeping her hands on his shoulders, borrowing his strength right up until the weight has fully returned to the flat of her foot.

The train was slowing, its noise dissipating so that disjointed words emerged to be heard in the carriage, to form into the quiet flow of other conversations as we came into the station. Ravi was still looking at me and I at him.

'I didn't ask her if she liked it,' he said, his eyes wide and frightened. 'What if she doesn't like it?'

'I'm sure she liked it.'

Then something that I had not witnessed for a long time occurred: his eyes became vague and I realised he was staring straight through me, that he did not even see me, and he turned away with the same slow revolution of his head to stare at the window opposite, no longer dark and liquid but filled with a garish incitement to consume: the legs of a woman long and tapering on a bright blue background, her giant feet in one red high-heeled shoe dangling above the other, as if about to drop on the head of the passenger beneath.